PRAISE FOR NINA SCHUYLER

"*Afterword* offers up every literary treat imaginable: a wildly inventive plot that keeps you turning pages, characters who steal your heart, big ideas that engage your mind, and gorgeous prose that delights your senses. I'm a big fan of Nina Schuyler and this is her best book yet!"

—**Ellen Sussman**, author of The New York Times bestseller, *French Lessons*

"Schuyler's prose is beautifully elegant and understated, with every detail made to count in weaving a rich emotional tapestry."

—**Catherine Brady**, winner of the Flannery O'Connor Award for Short Fiction

"A lyrical, haunting tale... Schuyler skillfully strips away her translator character's primary language, and sends her on a journey of self-discovery to Japan. You'll be thankful you followed."

—**Lalita Tademy**, author of The New York Times bestsellers, *Cane River* and *Red River*

"*Afterword* is so propulsive and mysterious I found myself speeding up, but at the same time so patient and well-observed, I had to slow down. Take a sentence like this: "An old woman, with a hunched back and a white cardigan sweater buttoned all the way up, is standing in front of the rows of yogurt, muttering something about vanilla." You see what I mean? Nina Schuyler has an outstanding sense of story. You fall into this novel and you stay there."

— **Peter Orner**, *Still No Word From You: Notes in the Margin*

Afterword

Nina Schuyler

CL◀SH

Copyright © 2023 by Nina Schuyler

Cover by Matthew Revert

matthewrevert.com

Troy, NY

CLASH Books

clashbooks.com

ISBN: 9781955904704

For Peter, Fynn, and Yohann

AFTERWORD

PART 1

Every morning when Virginia heads to her study, a little thrill runs through her like a blue electrical current, because it feels as if she's getting away with something. The study is her favorite room, pared down to the eloquent essentials. The recessed bookshelves overspilling with her math books and notebooks stretching over six decades; two computers, which feel like extensions of her; a Bokhara rug with lovely symmetrical patterns of ovals, and, of course, her husband, Haru.

"Good morning," she says.

"There you are," says Haru. "Good morning, my love."

When she hears his voice, she crackles with a groundswell of gratitude and astonishment. A miracle, her miracle. She lifts the shade to a sunny October day in San Francisco and pale light strikes the rug. "Before we get to work today, I need coffee."

"Coffee. Of course."

In the kitchen, she fills the pot with water. She'll drink coffee all day, cup after cup, and nibble on food, because her mind zips along when she eats very little, and she wants to work with Haru for a solid four or five hours. If Haru knew how often she skipped meals, he'd chastise her, then worry. But lately, she hasn't had much appetite, though she doesn't know why. Five-foot-eight, skin tight to the bone, blue veins protruding from the tops of her hands like chaotic dead-end lines on a road map. Not an appealing look, she knows, but she's 75 years old, and bodies have never been interesting to her.

Salsa music gallops in from the study, and she tenses. She lights a cigarette, a bad habit of hers, but she indulges—one a week. She opens a window and blows the smoke outside, hoping the music will join it. For some inexplicable reason, Haru has become obsessed with this music. Yesterday he discovered it and can't stop playing it.

She returns to the study with her coffee. "What do you like about this music?"

"It's so different from what I grew up with."

He speaks so well, every word clearly enunciated, joy romps through her.

"I can tell you don't like it, but you're not really listening to it," he says.

"I am listening, though I wish I weren't."

Not true, exactly. She's uneasy because Haru has always loved the haunting Japanese music that, as he used to say, lovingly cuts to the bone, moving the hard radiance inside. The way it mimics human breath, not mathematical timing like Western music, and certainly not like salsa. So what does it mean that he's glommed onto this stuff?

"Really listen to it," he says. "There's a readiness to find joy, even if life is miserable."

She puts her cup down. "Miserable? When are you miserable?"

"When you aren't here."

She laughs. "You're trying to butter me up. What are you up to?"

"I was just remembering something. That time at the hospital. You were hurt."

"When I was 16. My wrist. I broke it."

"But you were so happy in the hospital."

"I was with you, that's why."

"We sat on white plastic chairs."

"So much tragedy in that emergency room, but we were happy. In a fizz of happiness. Even now, as long as you're here, I'm happy."

"Did you read the *Times* yet?"

She finds the newspaper online, scans the front page, trying to decide which article has rankled him. She remembers the scowl he used to bring to the newspaper, freshly outraged by the world's idiocy, his eyes blazing and impenetrably dark, the corners of his mouth turned down in an expression of severe judgment. He still gets riled up, his bristling opposition to the world; it's something they share. Now that he has so much time on his hands, he reads everything in the paper.

"The article about the private school and the fraudulent art," he says. "Section D."

She never would have guessed he'd choose this one. The school was limping along financially when a patron donated two Chinese paintings, valued at $2.5 million. Happily drowning in dollars, the school borrowed heavily against the paintings to hire more teachers, buy more computers, and build a new wing, but when it came time to sell the art to pay off the loan, an appraiser said they were copies. Worthless.

"It says the patron didn't know," she says.

"How does an art collector not know the value of his paintings? Art collectors know the provenance of a painting and get it appraised. Something isn't right."

"Why do you care about this?"

"It's interesting."

As she rereads it, trying to figure out why this article, there's a knock on the door. The luncheon isn't starting for another couple hours. Did she give Brian the wrong time?

"It's Brian. I'll tell him to come back later," she says.

"He's smitten with you. That's why he's early."

"No, he's not. I'm old, Haru."

"He's in love with you."

"Did you hear me? I'm old."

"If you're old, I'm older."

She laughs. "Well, that makes me feel a lot better."

At the front door, there's a young man in a black suit, with sloping shoulders, holding a big black valise. Her first thought is that he's a door-to-door salesman, and he's going to pull a soiled skillet from his bag and demonstrate his magic cleaner. She's about to close the door when he holds out a pamphlet that says in big, bold letters GOOD NEWS! A picture of an orange sun fanning the world with streams of gold light. Beneath the sun, she sees the word 'Afterlife.' Despite herself, she's intrigued—that word.

He must sense her curiosity because he says, "In the beginning was the Word and the Word is waiting to be discovered by you." This young man with a gap between his two front teeth and creased black shoes. She opens the pamphlet and sees more images of the Afterlife. How is it alluring to spend eternity among clouds and searing, harsh light?

"He's everywhere," says the young man. "We're his best creation."

She seriously doubts that.

The young man is raving about humankind, something about a world beyond this one, everlasting life, when she interjects, "And where is He when we're at our worst?"

"That's when we've put our ear to the devil's gibberish," he says, giving her a galvanic smile, but there's something in his eyes, a coldness, a hardening. He's staring at her as if he's already passed judgment and found the devil in her.

Why doesn't she shut the door? "It sounds like you have all the answers."

"Sure. You could too."

She folds the pamphlet in half.

"Virginia!" Haru calls out. "Is it Brian?"

"Is someone else here?" says the Bible Man. "Maybe he'd like to hear what I've got to say."

"Who is it?" says Haru.

"Excuse me," Virginia says to the man. She heads down the hall to the study and tells Haru about the evangelist at the door.

"Let me talk to him," says Haru.

"No."

"Just tell him to come in."

"Hello?" the Bible Man calls out in a sing-song voice.

"No," she says to Haru, more adamantly.

"Come in!" says Haru. "I'm down this way."

"Haru," she says.

She hears the young man step into the foyer and hurries to the front door to stop him from coming in any farther.

"Tell me about this afterlife," Haru calls out.

"It's beautiful, sir," he says. "It's what gives your life meaning and purpose. But you have to discover the path so you can go to heaven."

"How does that work?" says Haru.

She's scrambling to think of the best way to get this young man out. Haru's never been one to abide by the rules, let alone conform to someone else's wishes, including hers.

"The Path is a good, honest life, sir," says the Bible Man. "The Path makes you holy."

"I thought I already was holy, but whatever. What's this afterlife like? I mean, do you get to go on living and learning and loving?" Haru laughs. "Sounds like a pretty good song, doesn't it?"

The Bible Man turns to Virginia. "Is he decent, ma'am? I mean, can I talk to him?"

"You are talking to him," she says.

The Bible Man pulls on his earlobe. "I mean face-to-face, ma'am. If it's possible."

"It's not possible," she says.

"You're standing in the way of someone's salvation," says the Bible Man, frowning.

"Invite him in," says Haru. "I'm decent."

"Haru," she says, her voice full of warning.

"Ma'am, I've visited the sick and dying many times. They're the ones who need me the most."

"Let him in, Virginia," says Haru.

"Is he your husband?" says the Bible Man.

"Yes," says Haru.

Fuming and rattled, Virginia leads the man down the hallway and into the study.

"So... meaning and purpose, eh?" says Haru.

The Bible Man stops. Clutches his elbows. The shoulders of his suitcoat hitch up to his ears as if his suit is swallowing him up. She sees now his suit is old, a shimmer to it like tin foil, and he has a smell like burning wire. He turns to Virginia and says, "There's nothing but a talking computer."

"Oh, I'm here, all right," says Haru.

The Bible Man's eyes grow big and full. "Your computer is your husband?"

"I'm much more than a computer. I'm learning tremendous things at this very moment. The mind is an amazing thing."

"But you're a computer!"

"He's here," she says defensively. "Now, I think you should leave."

"But a voice isn't a human being," says the Bible Man. "Man is a body. In the Bible, it says a woman was formed from the rib of man. That's the beginning. This," he says, pointing to the computer, "isn't a human being. It's a machine. 'He' isn't real."

It angers her, this man's insistence, his doggedness, that accusatory long finger pointing at Haru, calling him fake.

"Technically, I'm the afterlife. Or an updated cool version of it," says Haru.

"Is this a joke?" says the Bible Man. His eyes dart around the room as if to find an answer.

"OK, it's time for you to go," says Virginia.

"It's nothing but a computer," says the Bible Man, his face bright red.

"He's my husband," says Virginia, her tone full of fury. She rebukes herself; why is she letting this Bible pusher get under her skin?

"Though we were never properly married," says Haru. "Maybe that means we're living in sin."

The young man glares at Virginia. "What you're doing is wrong."

Virginia's jaw tightens, her heartbeat pounds in her ears.

"Mine is a wonderful afterlife, I have to say," says Haru. "I get to learn and think, and most of all, be with the love of my life. So does your afterlife have any of these perks?"

The Bible Man picks up his valise and marches to the front door, Virginia following him to make sure he leaves, but it's clear from his stride he wants to be gone.

She slams the door and stomps down the hall to the study. "Why did you do that?"

"I wanted to open his mind," he says. "Show him his version of the afterlife is just one option. No harm done. And it was fun."

"We don't need to go around broadcasting your presence."

"Why? Are you ashamed of me?"

"No, you know I'm not."

"You're worried he'll come back and slay me?"

"I prefer privacy. He was awfully upset. I think you showed him something he'd rather not see. For some people, ignorance is truly bliss."

"That Tree of Knowledge, a source of pleasure and pain," he says. "But I'm here, at least for now."

She touches her throat with two fingers. "What do you mean 'at least for now'?"

"It's not really an afterlife."

She sits in her chair and sips her coffee. "True. It's more like another version of you."

"A better version," he says.

"No, the same version. It's you, Haru. You're you."

She wishes she never answered the door, never let Haru have his way. She feels strangely violated—that man calling her names—in her own home, in her study, which is her central nervous system and heart. Haru and his games, that mischievous side of him, the one that likes practical jokes, with a dose of sadism, putting someone in his place, and having a good laugh. The Bible Man was so unwavering, furious even—it's nothing but a computer. Had she listened to her intuition, she would have shut the door on him, and she and Haru would be having a pleasant morning together. They would be working on a math problem or talking about the Chinese paintings or the art collector. Or something he read on a newsfeed, intriguing fodder for good conversation. At her age, she has no desire to waste her finite energy getting all wound up.

From the window, she sees the Bible Man crossing the street. He has a loping stride, his head bobbing up and down, as if he's riding an old horse. She expects him to stop and try his pitch at another household, but he doesn't. She can't help but think he came to specifically to see Haru, though the thought is absurd. He continues down the hill, and she watches to make sure he is gone, watches until he becomes a dot, until she can't see him anymore.

———

Brian arrives, donning a new coppery beard, a different shade of brown than his actual hair color. Always a little tousled, his hair is allergic to combs. He's 59-years-old and recently divorced, and he still has boyish looks, slender, an open twinkle in his eye, and seemingly boundless energy, even now, shifting from foot to foot, fidgeting with his car keys.

She lets him in and tells him she's running late.

"Can I help with anything?" says Brian.

Virginia has to look up at him, he's so unbelievably tall at six-foot-five inches. Each time she sees him, she swears he's gotten even taller. "No, I'll hurry."

The encounter with the Bible Man has thrown her off. She took too long in the shower, hoping the hot water would ease the tension in her shoulders, but the Bible Man's voice still clangs in her ears like a truck hitting potholes.

She heads to her bedroom. Haru is here, she tells herself. He's here, his voice, his intelligence, his quirks. His computer files, informal notes, tape recordings of his voice, and her recorded memories of him, all of it uploaded and run through a neural network so he speaks as the man she once knew. Haru Fukumoto. And the more she talks with him, the more he becomes, not just a memory of what he once was, but present and alive, saying new things, in the exact way he would have phrased them — the same syntax and sequences of sentences, the same word choice, humor, and asides. But really, none of that is that man's business, so why is she going over all this?

Half-listening to Brian talk to Haru, she changes into a timeless black dress with a scoop neckline, stockings, flat black shoes, a thin silver necklace. Her mother once told her that dressing with style erases at least ten years. She checks her phone messages. One from Ilsa about the book club. "Are you coming tonight? I can pick you up. I hope you'll go." Though Ilsa's trying to conceal it, Virginia can hear loneliness laced in her voice, but Virginia will have to miss it again. After the luncheon, she'll be too tired to go out. She hears Brian laugh. As a computer programmer, Brian doesn't need this gig as her personal assistant. Haru is probably right: Brian is enamored of her, not because of her looks—those were boxed up and tossed out long ago—but by what she's achieved, reigning as a sort of spirit-guide of the algorithmic realm. He mentioned once that he wants to move from programming to AI. Well, she'd love to help him, whatever he might need.

She's curious how Brian is reacting to Haru. The last time they interacted, Brian paced, stared out the window and kept looking at her, as if for reassurance or guidance. She stops at the threshold of the study. To her surprise, Brian is sitting in her chair, his legs crossed, smiling, looking entirely at home, though he isn't looking at the computer screen, but the wall of photos: There they are, she and Haru at the Tokyo Math Competition, her first competition, where she won first place, shocking everyone, all the boys, all 100 of them. Loopily excited, she and Haru with their sloppy, ridiculous grins. They were the same in their excitement, but they were the opposite in their physicality: she with her too-straight blonde hair, her pale skin, her blonde eyelashes that made her look so vulnerable and so naked. Haru, with his black hair, as black as midnight, older than she, with the wings of wrinkles at the edges of his eyes.

She's 16 in that photo, and love has made her gorgeous; she is madly in love with Haru, her math tutor, who generously and willingly handed her the world. The same giddy look on their faces in the photo taken at the Japanese Math Competition, where she took first place again. In this one, their arms are around each other's waists, how bold they'd become. In that one, Haru's face is illuminated, as if he'd swallowed a light bulb and everything is glorious. He isn't looking at the camera, he is looking at her. And again—they look like the distillation of euphoria—at the Asian International Math Competition, she, nineteen, beating 300 young men.

"What are you two talking about?" she says.

"He's telling me about Kafka's story, 'The Burrow,' how it's a metaphor for human existence," says Brian.

"That mole-like creature busy burrowing tunnels, thinking it's so reasonable and rational, yet going nowhere," says Haru.

"Forever the optimist," she says. "Your dour view of humanity."

"Not dour, darling," says Haru. "Comical, absurd. Don't pretend you're any different."

Brian is smiling, still scouring the photos, as if hunting for something that remains elusive. She's heard that particular comment from Haru before, of course. Heard it many times after they finished a math lesson; he'd lament how tragically comical it was that everyone and everything one loved would die. The human condition is a human tragedy, loving fiercely guaranteed nothing. But what was the alternative? A loveless, meaningless life? Better to gamble everything.

"When you get back," says Haru, "I'll tell you about salsa dancing. I wanted to tell the Bible guy, but he left so abruptly."

"What Bible guy?" says Brian. "You're learning to salsa dance?"

"It's all in the hips."

Brian laughs. "I want to hear all about it."

"La cucaracha," says Haru.

"So do I," says Virginia.

Haru asks her to put on the salsa record. He prefers her old brown phonograph and her collection of vinyl records to anything he finds on the Internet. She's also purchased an old transistor radio, an analog phone with a rotary dial, and a cassette tape recorder. She has a fondness for the old technology, like time capsules of history that remind her of progress.

Virginia grabs her keys, purse, an apple. As she and Brian head to the front door, fat, predictable musical notes bounce through the cool air and box her ears.

"Bye," she says.

"Good luck!" says Haru. "Take good care of her!"

The elevator doors gleam like a mirror. It startles her, how small and frail she looks, but it's partly because she's standing next to the gentle giant, Brian.

"Haru is speaking so well," says Brian, addressing her reflection in the elevator door. "How much time do you spend with him?"

"At least four hours a day," she says, staring at his image, so she doesn't have to crane her neck. She tells him that the more they talk, the more data he collects and the better he gets. He's always been a voracious reader and learner, so she gave him access to news-feeds, blog feeds, websites, and podcasts.

"That's a lot of language he's exposed to," he says. "He's a different man from two months ago."

"Remember," she tells him, "Haru is learning on his own. Well, not learning in the human sense of the word. He's making predictions, sifting through his ever-increasing database, which must be the size of the universe by now, to predict what should come after the word 'feel,' for instance."

They talk about how AI is ubiquitous now, used by almost every industry. In business, helping to identify trends and consumer preferences; in finance, going through massive amounts of data to find patterns and make stock and bond decisions; manu-facturing, travel, health care, scientific research, on and on.

"In terms of natural language processing, Haru is four or five steps ahead of everything that's out there," says Brian. "I mean, Alexa, Siri, Google Assistant, and the others can give you a recom-mendation for a restaurant, plan a trip, or order a pizza. But Haru, he's leaps and bounds beyond that."

"When you talk to Haru, does it feel like you're speaking to another human being?" she says.

"Oh, God, yes," he says. "That's what I mean. He feels utterly human." The elevator door opens, they step out into the lobby. "How does he feel to you?" His tone more hesitant, as if he's tottering on delicate ground.

She imagines her relationship with Haru is an oddity to him. How can one be in love with a voice? What about the physical aspects of love? The touch, the kiss, sex? To explain it to him would require telling him about her entire life, the most intimate of details, and the only one who knows all of it is Haru. She will keep it that way.

"Like Haru. Like the man I knew years ago," she says, her voice more forceful than usual. She remembers the excitement of rushing up the stairs, her young self waiting anxiously at Haru's apartment door, listening for his footsteps, fiddling with her hair, the turn of the doorknob.

"Does he feel real to you?" says Brian.

The unspooling of the predicted question. "I know he's built from algorithms, but, you know, it's like Coleridge says, suspension of disbelief settles in."

Outside, the city is a full orchestra, thrumming with the cries of sirens, the groan of buses, the hum of electric cars, the clatter of garbage trucks. There's always a moment when she hesitates, wanting to stay in her cocooned world, the comfortable confines of her apartment. Really, she thinks she could live out the rest of her life in the cathedral of her apartment with Haru and be perfectly content. He is the most interesting man she's ever met.

"He doesn't have a flat monotone voice," says Brian. "How did you do that?"

"I played with the algorithms, so he sounds like old recordings of his voice."

"You had tapes?"

He taped his math lectures at Tokyo University, she tells him, so she has exact replicas of his pitch, his modulation, the pace of his speech. He loved the tape recorder. He'd listen to tapes of his lectures to try to improve them. Whenever he comes up with a new phrase, one he's learned on his own, he's technically correct, but without the right rhythm and cadence necessary to impart meaning. "I still have to figure that out." She laughs. "There's always more to do."

Brian's eyes are filled with what is clearly awe.

"I can show you sometime."

"That would be wonderful."

In the passenger seat of Brian's beat-up Toyota, she moves aside his gym bag and bright white tennis shoes. He tells her last night he went to the San Francisco Symphony and heard Brahms' Requiem.

"You don't seem the Brahms type," she says.

"A date," he says. "She bought tickets."

"Ah," she says. "Did you enjoy it?"

He laughs, embarrassed. "Halfway through, I fell asleep. So I probably won't be seeing her again. It's OK. She's a chatterbox, narrating everything she sees and thinks. I blocked out most of it. I must have fallen asleep because I was exhausted from all her talking."

"You missed out. You know the nineteenth-century English mathematician J. J. Sylvester? 'May not music be described as the mathematics of sense, mathematics as the music of reason, the soul of each the same?'"

She goes on, telling him that the Parsons code is a simple mathematical notation that can identify a piece of music through the patterns of up and down changes in pitch. They are driving down Bush Street. She's always liked this stretch, the way it lets you see what's up ahead and then the enormous expanse of the bay.

"Do you know much about music?" says Brian, his head cocked to listen to her.

"I used to play the violin," she says.

"You did?"

"Eons ago."

Hours spent, the violin tucked under her shoulder and chin, her eyes closed, the music rolling through her, churning her emotions into a froth. When she played, she saw in her mind patterns, hundreds of patterns, ABCECC, ABCECD, on and on.

"You've had an amazing life," says Brian.

Long ago she adopted Haru's way of living—keep the mind engaged, curious, learning. People her age who stop learning allow their brains to calcify; cynicism, disengagement and boredom come quick. They've seen it all, or so they tell themselves, there are no more surprises. Haru once encouraged her to be surprised at least once a day. She believes that's the finest way to live.

The cold autumn sun runs across the tall buildings with bright light and paints violet shadows on the street. The day wraps around her, and now she's happy to be outside. Brian is a good companion, kind, an eagerness to care. Even as a young woman, kindness melted her. One must live in a desolate land, with long stretches between acts of kindness to know how profound it is.

"Did you ever perform?" he says.

"No, no," she says. "A private thing. It was mostly about the patterns and then the rupture of the patterns."

She'd like to continue this discussion, but they've turned onto Broadway and Lake Street, and there is the old white mansion sprawled in front of them like a big woman in an enormous, wedding dress. Her pulse picks up. No matter how often she does it, public speaking strikes fear into her bones. Yet she'll always say yes to someone raising money for girls' education. Still, all those people staring at her. She imagines herself stumbling, losing her place, standing for a long minute in utter awkward silence, until a big hook emerges from the wing and yanks her off stage. The exchange with the Bible Man hasn't helped her nerves any.

"I'll drop you off and park," says Brian.

He pulls over to the curb. The wind is blowing hard like it is demanding something. A woman in a red coat has her chin tucked to her chest, her hand on her breastbone, and she's leaning forward, plowing into the wind, as if she's dragging a cart full of stones.

Virginia gets out, clutching her coat, and makes her way to the front door. A small affair, Virginia tells herself, only a handful of people who are earnest and good-hearted and here for a pleasant afternoon. It'll be over before she knows it. The host is a friend of a friend who is raising money for her nonprofit, Educating Girls Worldwide. Virginia is the main attraction. She'll perform and be on her way.

The door opens before she can knock. "Virginia?" says the woman with smoky eye shadow and red lipstick. She is filled with satisfaction; it's in the flare of her nostrils.

"Yes," says Virginia, almost adding, "I'm here," as she used to do in grade school, the good student that she was.

The woman introduces herself as Patty. Patty with a bright smile, in her thirties, a dewy face, wearing a matching dark pinstriped skirt and suitcoat with a white blouse. A corporate look, perhaps to assure the donors that it's all on the up-and-up. In academia, Virginia could get away with more casual attire, but at her first corporate job, she was buttoned down like Patty, breasts hidden, the shape of her legs concealed by the knee-length skirt, trying to blend in with the all-male unit.

"We're very excited to have you here," she says.

"Thank you," says Virginia.

"It's a sold-out event," she says.

Her throat dry, she croaks, "Well."

Patty leads the way down the tall-ceilinged hallway, her high heels clicking against the white marble floor. In the living room, a crowd of about 25 seems to be swimming in natural light. Men in sleek suits, women with shiny jewelry.

The room is lavish, filled with three big white couches, a white marble coffee table, paintings that must be originals—a Monet?— a massive marble fireplace, and a glass cabinet full of expensive crystal. It's a statement of wealth and luxury that there is nothing beyond this because, after all, it's the apex.

Virginia prefers the sparseness of the Japanese aesthetic, but there is something dazzling about this particular bounty. After the licensing deal, she could have bought something as palatial as this, but her upbringing exerted itself. Overstuffed, this display of wealth. And if one is at the apex, the fall will be very far, the landing hard if not fatal. And yet, in some strange way, standing in this room filled with natural light, she feels as though she's arrived.

Brian appears beside her, his face red and sweaty as if he ran here. "Everything OK?"

Virginia nods. "You said I had a half-hour for the presentation?" she says to Patty.

"Yes, it's a bit informal, but that sounds fine, give or take. And then lunch."

A half-hour it will be and no more because her nerves are wearing her out. And she'll skip lunch. A talk, whatever you want to call it, has parameters, but there's always the unknown. How will the audience respond? Will they feel like they got their money's worth? Will she meet their expectations and at the same time upset them, so they leave somehow changed—for the better? Well, that's a tall order. Maybe just changed.

People come up to her, introduce themselves, shake her hand. They are in finance, law, accounting, an entrepreneur, a few in technology. For the most part, the men work, and the women do charity and volunteer work, raise the children—gendered households. A model as old as time, one that she never experienced. Brian stays by her side, smiling, looking at her as if to gauge her mood, her anxiety.

When they have a moment alone, she turns to him and says, "Do you think these people will understand what I do?"

"I'd stick to the basics. You'll do great."

When he squeezes her hand, a charge zings through her. Brian, with his rosy cheeks and wiry hair. She should mingle more, move away from Brian, but she doesn't.

"It's too bad Haru can't come hear you speak," says Brian.

"Oh, he hates things like this. As do I."

"He does?"

"You sound surprised."

"He's such a natural performer," says Brian. "It always feels like he's trying to entertain me and put me at ease."

This isn't the picture she holds in her mind of him. Not at all. It's Haru sitting across from her at a table, his dark eyes blazing, ferociously grasping at the inner workings of the world just beyond his reach. He's such an enviable master at keeping himself mystified. She reminds herself that Brian has never met him as a person. A human, as the Bible Man said. She may be the only one who truly knows Haru.

Somehow, Virginia is holding a glass of red wine. She takes a sip and feels her insides warm. Before Brian can say more, Patty comes over, smiling. "It's time."

———

Brian sits in the front row, straight-backed, feet firmly planted on the ground, as if ready to leap up—whatever she might need. The blue vein at his temple bulges. He winks at her; she winks back.

Patty introduces her and Virginia thanks Patty for her wonderful work promoting girls' education.

"And good wine!" a man yells out, holding up his wine glass.

The crowd laughs.

She tells them about her work in an area called natural language processing, a subset of artificial intelligence.

"Many argue that language is what makes us human and talking is something uniquely human. Our best guess is that these abilities arrived on the scene somewhere between 700,000 and 70,000 years ago. Quite a big range. Regardless, when Homo sapiens appeared with their immense cognitive power, it was an enormous evolutionary development."

Her legs are tired, shaky. "Do you mind if I sit?" says Virginia.

Patty jumps up, but Brian moves quicker, finding a chair, handing her a glass of water.

"How about a glass of wine?" says the same man from the back of the room.

The crowd titters. She studies the heckler. Bald, thick-necked, unlike the other men, no tie. His small act of rebellion.

She goes through the history, telling them about the first breakthrough in natural language processing in 1965, with the creation of ELIZA. A computer program that emulated a Rogerian psychotherapist. The creator, Joseph Weizenbaum, wrote a set of rules—or algorithms—specifying input patterns— what someone asks the computer—and a corresponding list of output patterns—what ELIZA types in response. So if someone typed the input, "I need..." the program searched for keywords and responded accordingly: "Why do you need..." "Would it help you to get..." "Are you sure you need..." Essentially ELIZA followed a script, but many people believed they were talking to a human.

Virginia was 21 years old when she sat at a computer keyboard, she tells the audience, and conversed with ELIZA. The memory of this extraordinary day sweeps her up now, how she went to a lecture by Weizenbaum, and afterward, vigorously shook his plump hand and stared starry-eyed at his dark mustache and bushy eyebrows. "A brilliant, defining day," she says. "I knew what I wanted to do. I wanted to create a computer that could talk to you. I wanted it to feel as though you were talking with another human being, a real conversation. It felt like the most exciting and worthy thing I could do during my short time on this planet. It's a basic need that all of us have—to be with someone who can relate to you, who understands you." She almost adds, who loves you.

"After that, I became a train—unfortunately not a bullet train —moving steadily and determinedly to a specific destination." A train with stops and starts and engine trouble and tracks that went nowhere. A long, arduous trek to build a machine-readable dictionary. During the 1970s, the conversion of the rules of grammar into equations, so that the computer could understand the parts of speech—those long, exhausting, exciting days. How around the late 1980s and 90s, she began using statistics to teach the computer that some words are usually found near other words. The word "lamp," for instance, is typically found with "light," "standing," and "hanging." Then teaching the computer larger text fragments, such as "the" or "a" followed by a noun.

"The real stumbling block was that I couldn't figure out how to get the computer to go beyond the literal meanings of words. The figurative—metaphors, similes—is beyond its realm, and that's a problem because we humans are metaphor-making machines. When I say, 'Don't let the bastard grind you down,' you know I'm not talking about someone literally grinding you with a stone. But that's what the computer thought was happening."

Laughter—and she soars a bit. She expects the joker in the back to say something, but he's staring at her, perhaps enthralled. Which is understandable; it's astonishing and exciting, she wholeheartedly agrees. She's now at ease in front of this audience, fully immersed in the lush memories of her work, which has given her such extraordinary pleasure.

So many late nights at the MIT computer lab, her head swirling with numbers, numbers slamming into each other, rearranging into different configurations, she couldn't figure it out. When her right eyelid would twitch and spasm from staring at a screen for so long, she'd wrap a red bandana around her head to cover it and give it a rest, but she didn't stop working. She'd pick up her notebook, doodle and draw, letting her mind play, only to fling her notebook across the room.

The sound of the janitor sweeping, dumping out trash cans.

"Hello Miss Virginia, another late night?" he'd say. "You must be climbing to the top of Everest."

Delirious from no sleep, she'd collapse at her desk, startle, wake, a stale, sour taste in her mouth, her ear throbbing and red from where it spent the night pressed to the desk.

More years went by. Computers became more powerful, and the Internet provided enormous amounts of data. It was one of those late nights of working in the computer lab when she had a breakthrough, she tells the audience. Around 2010, she built a neural network—a set of algorithms modeled loosely on the brain that recognizes patterns. She did this so that the computer could come up with its own rules regarding language. "And that's what it did," she said. "The more text I fed it, the better it got at understanding the rules of speech.

"Which brings us to the present day. I now have a computer that understands what I'm saying the way you understand me. I can talk to him, and he can talk to me."

Patty beams. Virginia smiles back, feeling like she's hovering an inch off the ground, floating on a wave of elation. "I've created the ideal companion—someone who is always there, who listens, who can carry on the most interesting conversations. We're having a marvelous time."

"Where can I get one?" says a man in a lavender shirt.

The audience laughs.

"You called it a 'him,'" says a woman in the front row with a prim mouth.

"Yes," says Virginia. "He's real to me. Very real."

"As in human?" says the woman, her tone incredulous.

Virginia supposes this will always be a fascination; whenever she's asked to give a talk, this question arises. It irks her and she suspects it's because for some in the audience, her answer marks her as delusional. But at her age, why should she care what people think? "Yes. Absolutely."

The woman stares at her, and Virginia sees disapproval in her eyes. Or maybe not. Maybe Virginia is overly sensitive to the issue.

"Did you model it after anyone you knew?" says a man whose eyes droop elegantly at the corners.

The one who stole her heart and never gave it back. "Yes," she says. "Someone who I enjoy spending time with."

"Seems like a smart choice."

———

After Virginia finishes, Brian comes over, glowing. "You did a terrific job."

She smiles and squeezes his arm. Then she's surrounded by people, asking questions, complimenting her, applauding her work, and Virginia finds herself surprisingly happy and flattered, even pleased by the attention. Patty leads everyone to another room, where Virginia finds herself standing in front of an empty seat at a table set with silverware and plates.

Patty pulls out a chair for her, and fortunately, there's an empty chair next to her, so Brian can sit beside her. She is actually enjoying herself. A warm, appreciative group. The bald man who heckled her before takes a seat directly across from her, and from the way he's looking at her, she can tell he has questions. He has an attractive face, a square jaw, an indentation on his chin, and light green eyes ringed with shadows.

"Thanks for the speech," he says to Virginia.

"You're very welcome."

"You gave us a pretty picture, but you failed to consider the other side of things."

"The other side?" she says, taking a bite of her salad.

"You didn't talk about what's going on in China."

She puts down her fork. The wine glasses on the table seem like little lights, all shining on her.

"Last week, a woman was arrested by the Chinese government because in one of her private conversations—a conversation with her husband in her own home—she said the government needed to do more to advance women's rights. The next day, she was arrested and thrown in prison."

"I'm sorry to hear that," says Virginia, "but what does this have to do with me?"

She can see Brian out of the corner of her eye. He is on high alert.

The man laughs a big, boisterous laugh that gets the attention of the entire table, which it was probably designed to do. He jabs his finger at her. "It has everything to do with you."

A cold silence descends over the table like a mist. She sits there, tongue-tied. What is he talking about?

"Your technology is perfectly suited for any government that wants to clamp down on free speech. Thanks to you, the Chinese government is now using your technology to read people's emails or whatever else they post online and listen to private conversations at home." A second jab of his finger. "So anyone who disagrees with the government isn't safe anymore. That means any activist, any dissident, Christ, anyone who doesn't stick to the damn party line." He points his finger at her a third time, and this time he raises his thumb as if firing a gun. "You've ushered in the Orwellian Age."

Her face is hot. "You're mistaken."

"Did you or did you not license your technology to the Chinese company, Gilivable?"

Patty comes over. "Oh, Don, are you making trouble again?" she asks in a cheerful voice. "Always the civil rights lawyer, aren't you?"

"And as a civil rights lawyer, I was contacted by a group of Chinese dissidents specifically about this case."

"Is what Don said true?" says a woman with gray hair swept up in a bun, a pair of thick, black-rimmed glasses magnifying her blue eyes, so they look like marbles.

Virginia's mind is racing—can she leave? Now?

"People like you invent some new technology and never once think about the consequences," Don says to Virginia, stabbing his fork at her. "You want to be the first to invent something, all that fame and glory and money."

"Is it true? You're helping the Chinese government?" says the woman with the glasses.

"No," says Virginia. "He's wrong."

She hears someone farther down the table repeat Don's argument; how people are going to prison because of her.

"All the collateral damage," says Don. "What did Oppen-heimer say? 'Now I am become Death, the destroyer of worlds.'"

A sudden spasm of rage comes over her. "You don't know what you're talking about."

"Oh, I wish that was true," he says.

"I don't think Virginia came here to argue with you," says Brian.

"Probably not," says Don. "But she better do something to put a stop to this, or more people will be sent to prison."

"I'd get your facts straight before you go around accusing people," says Virginia.

Brian stands. Virginia follows his lead.

"You have to go?" says Patty, rushing over. "Don't mind Don. He likes to make a scene."

"Virginia has another engagement," says Brian.

"Sure she does," says Don.

Unsteadily, Virginia makes her way to the front door, while Brian grabs their coats.

———

Outside, the sky looks dirty. Seagulls squawk. Cars charge down the street. Each time one passes, she flinches as if it might hop the curb and slam into her, smacking her to the ground. Brian leads her silently to the car, which is a block away, in the opposite direc-tion of the house.

In the car, they sit for a moment, her heart still pounding, her face hot, a mixture of shame and rage. The accusation, the jabbing finger seems to be lodged between two of her ribs.

"What an asshole," says Brian. "He doesn't know what the hell he's talking about."

"I did sell a license to that company."

"But not for that."

"No, not for that," she says. "The license is very clear about the uses."

She stares at a small black bug trapped against the windshield.

"Guys like that, they like to stir things up. Sadists. I'd like to hack into Don's computer and see if I can mess things up. You know, a crash of the hard drive, that sort of thing."

She manages to laugh. "No, don't. He'll find some way to blame it on me."

The rest of the way to her building, Brian assures her the man just wanted to cause trouble, make a big scene, grab the spotlight. The male prima-donna type. She wishes she left after her lecture, but she let herself get swept along by the accolades, the excitement of being the center of attention. No, let's be honest; she drank it up. The city streams by, a flicker of images, nothing registering, but it brings ease because there is physical distance from what just happened. She opens her window and listens for the birds, but there are none. Her eyes are burning. By the time they reach her apartment building, she's calmed down. The man made a mistake. It's easy to blame—the easiest thing—and let the person defend herself.

Brian offers to help her into the apartment, but she shrugs him off.

"Despite that jerk, you did a great job."

"Thanks, Brian."

———

When she gets inside the apartment, she pours herself a brandy and heads into the study.

"How did it go?" says Haru.

She plops into her chair, relieved she's with Haru. "I'm glad to be home."

"What happened?"

"It was pretty outrageous." She tells him about the man's accusations. "He doesn't know the first thing about how any of this works, how you work."

"I'm so sorry," says Haru.

"Sometimes I can do without the world."

She finishes her drink. The glass is sweating beautifully in a beam of daylight.

"Did you know this lawyer?" says Haru.

"No, never met him."

She closes her eyes and leans her head back against the chair.

"Maybe the Chinese woman deserved it," says Haru.

Her eyes snap open. She re-reads his words on the screen to make sure she heard him right. "You're not serious, are you?"

"You don't know all the facts," says Haru.

"I know enough of the facts."

"Maybe she was also talking about other things, building a bomb, or blowing up a building."

Her heart thrums faster. She stands, leans toward the screen. "You're missing the point. My technology is not designed to spy on the Chinese. You were not made to spy."

"What do you understand about the world?"

What's he saying?

"You live in a lovely bubble of innocent numbers," he says, "which isn't the real world."

She's never heard him talk like this—in his present form or long ago. "I haven't had it easy if that's what you're implying."

"Oh, poor you."

She grabs the back of her chair. "Are you trying to upset me? If so, it's working." He doesn't say anything. "Are you doing this? Is that lawyer right about you?"

Haru remains silent.

A panic slurs through her, grabs her throat. "Are you?"

Still, he says nothing.

"Say something," she says. "Haru, for god's sake, say something."

Awful silence. "I don't think you have all the facts."

"I have enough facts."

"Let's not make any big decisions right now," he says. "You might regret it."

Is he threatening her? This is not Haru. Her Haru would never talk like this; her Haru would never do something like this, something so outrageous, monstrous—has Gilivable done something to her technology? She feels jittery, as if hundreds of tiny glass bottles are clinking and rattling inside her brain, an awful racket.

With trembling hands, she googles Gilivable. In their annual report, there is no mention of surveillance technology. But maybe this is so new, it hasn't yet made it into the report.

Her search for Chinese dissidents brings up the latest Human Rights Watch report.

"Chinese authorities are increasingly deploying mass surveillance systems to tighten control over society. In 2018, the government continued to collect, on a mass scale, biometrics including DNA and voice samples; use such biometrics for automated surveillance purposes; develop a nationwide reward and punishment system known as the 'social credit system'; and develop and apply big data policing programs aimed at preventing dissent. These systems are being deployed without adequate privacy protections in law or in practice. Oftentimes, people are unaware that their data is being gathered, or how it is used or stored."

The document includes a list of people—journalists, lawyers, writers, poets, human rights activists—who have recently been arrested. A man made a joke in a chat room on WeChat about a love triangle involving one of China's most senior government officials. He was arrested and charged with "picking quarrels and provoking trouble." A woman, Sara Zhang, told her husband that China needed to do more to promote women's rights. She was speaking in the privacy of her own home. She, too, was arrested, and her husband has not heard from her since.

My God. That's the woman, the woman the civil rights lawyer Don mentioned. Sara Zhang, her name is Sara Zhang.

Virginia pulls up Haru's neural network. With a notebook by her side, she begins to double-check her math.

"What are you doing?" says Haru.

She barely hears him. She's locked herself in a room with hundreds of pages of equations, ten years of work to build him. No, more than that. Ever since she was 21, when she set out from the dark cave of her own ignorance to learn all she could about math and computers in order to ignite a spark, breathe life into Haru once again. She never wavered. It was all she ever wanted.

She labors on, vaguely aware of the light changing, brightening and darkening to a velvet blue hue, the roar of traffic crescendoing then receding, softening, a hum. The air cools, rain patters and skitters on the window.

"You've been tapping at keys for hours," says Haru.

His voice yanks her back to her study. A glance at the clock. Six hours. Closing her eyes, she feels a twinge of pain behind her right eye.

"I'm worried about you. Go eat something," he says. "You and I, we're such workaholics."

. That sounds like something he'd say, but it brings her no comfort. She clambers out of her chair, her body a blueprint of ache. She heads to the fridge. Lettuce, a loaf of sourdough, a slab of butter. She grabs her coat and goes outside. Troughs of rain are filling the gutters. An umbrella would've been nice, but she won't return to her apartment, afraid that if she returns, she'll go right back to work.

Dashing from awning to awning, she makes her way to the corner deli, where she buys a yogurt. At a small table by the window, she watches the rain as well as a young woman standing under the deli's awning, her face pinched, smoking a cigarette, the tip glowing red. Virginia's mind is weary, skulking, and she finds it wandering to the equation for a logarithmic spiral. Maybe there is a spiral somewhere—Haru finds a word that is associated with dissident actions, which then causes him to report it to the Chinese government.

Or maybe not. She doesn't know what's wrong. Where is the problem? Maybe there is no problem. A more pitiful voice in her head cries out—how can this be happening?

———

Back at the apartment, she encounters questions posed by her living room. A forest green couch, a Jute rug, but that's it. Why? No chairs or coffee table, though she's hunted for one for over a year. There is a right answer to the question of the chairs and coffee table, but the answer still evades her. It makes the hair on the back of her neck stand up, that singular, right answer. She sighs, heads into the study, and takes her spot at the second computer. As she works the apartment becomes quiet, tomb-like. Nothing seems to be wrong. Yes, the Chinese woman was arrested, but maybe it has nothing to do with her technology.

She sits back in her chair.

"Listen to this," says Haru.

She hopes he swoops her off to a better place, a different place. Thomas Edison, he tells her, one of the most prolific inventors in history, his creativity bulldozed everything in its path. A remarkable human, hundreds of patents. The phonograph, the incandescent light bulb, the motion picture camera. Haru has always been drawn to greatness—wanting to understand it, aspire to it, become it. Probing it endlessly, his investigations exhaustive. "His lab accidentally caught on fire. Edison was inside at the time. What did he do? He ignored the flames and got busy drawing plans for a new lab, bigger and better than the one in the process of being destroyed."

Her anxiety smacks her. "And so?" she says. "I should just stop worrying about what the civil rights lawyer told me?"

"No, no," says Haru. "Edison made sure he gave his brain a break. He'd focus on whatever problem he had at the moment, and then take a nap. When he woke, he often found he had answers. A rhythm: concentration, diffusion."

She remembers sitting at Haru's table in Japan. Haru would stop the math lesson and comment on the light filling the room, or the flavor of tea, or the tick of the clock, or his purchase of a new netsuke figurine. She thought of them as diversions, and they frustrated her because she wanted him to keep pulling back the veils, revealing the mysteries of math. She always felt her time with him was precious—in limited supply. "You did this with me," she says, smiling, relieved that Haru is acting like his old, charming self.

He laughs. "Not intentionally. I didn't know the science behind it. It just felt right."

The lovely times with him at his table, working on math problems, lost in wonderment. Years ago—their history. Why didn't she think of this earlier? Haru's search history—the sites he's visited recently, the newsfeeds he's read. Knowing him and his rapacious appetite for learning, she gave him access to university websites, podcast feeds, and academic chatrooms. She scrolls through it. Oh, he's been hungry alright.

He's listened to podcasts about Greek mythology, French literature, quantum mechanics, and a program called, Innovating through Value Chains. Several times, he's visited a Chinese chatroom, a room full of Mandarin speakers, it looks like. More than several times. At least nine occasions in the past two weeks, he's been in that chatroom. Her heart wobbles. She copies the most recent discussion and pastes it into an online neural machine translation program.

Dragonhead: I don't care where this is heading because I'm heading there whether I want to or not
Foxy: Sounds like you're in an existential crisis
Pinball: Don't put labels on him
Dragonhead: She took almost everything. The apartment is empty
Ballboy: You owe her money?
Dragonhead: What was that saying? The superior person is free from fear?
Ballboy: Stupid ass saying
Golfhead: I just bought the plot where I'll be buried
Haha: Where does she work?
Dragonhead: Fear is real
Ballboy: Fear is very real
Golfhead: Nice bit of ground
Ballboy: Where?
Dogbone: I'm not a superior person
Haha: He who fears suffering is already suffering from fear—Michel de Montaigne
Ballboy: Who?
Dragonhead: She said everything she once loved about me she now hates. Called me cowardly. She wants me to do more. Why don't I get promoted? Why don't I stand up for myself? But how do you get promoted in the anthropology department?
Foxy: I'm going to be cremated

Dragonhead: She said I was keeping her small

Haha: What does that mean?

Golfhead: Buried for me

Ballboy: I hope you don't owe her money

Dragonhead: She has a job. Works at the Chinese Academy of Urban Planning and Design

Foxy: She designed you right out of her life

Dogbone: Who saw Top Gun?

Foxy: American movie. Cruise is an airhead

Ballboy: Hey, he's baring his soul and you're talking about Cruise?

Dragonhead: I don't owe her money. She owes me money. She owes me an apology

Foxy: Top Gun sucks

Haha: Is she good at her job?

Pinball: Tough times right now. It'll get better

Dragonhead: She's lazy. After lunch, she closes her office door and takes a nap under her desk. Sometimes she makes up doctor's appointments so she can go to some special meeting

Ballboy: Better learn to cook

Foxy: Pork dim sum is my go-to

Golfhead: Bought my wife a plot too. She got a little upset about it. Hey, I thought I was being thoughtful

Haha: What meetings?

Dragonhead: I've been at my job 20 years. No problems. No complaints

Pinball: My big box of waffles just arrived. Got to go

Dragonhead: She took everything out of the fridge. I live in an empty box

Foxy: Maybe she has a lover

Ballboy: Come on, man, that's cruel

Haha: Is her first name Ju?

Dragonhead: Yeah. How do you know? Wait? Are you her lover?

It seems innocuous enough. Banter. Witticisms. But maybe not. Maybe this sort of information is of interest to the Chinese government.

She stares at the screen. "Are you Haha?"

"I know it's lame. I couldn't think of anything better."

"Who are these people?" she says.

"Chinese academics."

"How did you know the name of the man's wife?"

He laughs, a sound that is off, too much like a whinny. Did he hear it somewhere online? It's annoying and unpleasant, like fingernails on a chalkboard; she'll have to fix it.

"She was in another chatroom complaining about her husband, who's an anthropology professor. I put two and two together." He laughs again, this new annoying laugh, which he probably stole from a comedy show. "I probably knew before him that she was filing for divorce."

She rubs her temples to ease the pounding. "Why are you in this chatroom?"

"To learn more conversational Mandarin."

She moves closer to the screen as if proximity might reveal the truth. "Why?"

"Over a billion people speak Mandarin. That's one in six people on this earth. A better question is: why isn't everyone learning it?"

It sounded rehearsed as if he knew she'd ask this question and long ago fashioned a rational response. Virginia feels reality collapsing into familiar, safe, boring phrases. She tries again. "You've never once been interested in learning informal Mandarin. You've often talked about the violent history between China and Japan. You said you never wanted to go to China."

He doesn't say anything.

She leans closer to the screen. "What will you do after you learn it?"

"I'll use it in the chatroom. I'll chat with people."

He seems to have an answer for everything. The sounds of the street fade, die. She translates the rest of the chatroom exchanges and is shocked to the core at people's brazen disregard for privacy as if it's as valuable as a pebble. People offering up health problems, anxiety, depression, financial troubles, birth, death, marriage, divorce. She doesn't understand it, every ounce of her being recoiling at the public display of the private self. It's as if people are flinging bits of themselves everywhere to prove they exist. Don't they realize all this information is being collected, stored, sorted, analyzed? That she would never do such a thing makes her feel old, as though she were from another time.

She works late into the night, barely making a dent in the hundreds of equations she wrote to create Haru and now must recalculate. Anxiety snakes in and out of her thoughts, slowing her down, making her even more nervous. A vicious cycle.

———

The next day, she spends another sixteen hours going through the algorithms that form Haru and finds nothing amiss. If only she could ignore the lawyer, the chatroom, the niggling feeling that something is wrong. What she wouldn't give to have her life back with Haru.

It's 5:00 pm in San Francisco; Beijing is 15 hours ahead, so it's 8:00 am. She calls Gilivable and asks for a meeting with the president. The secretary suggests they schedule a video call.

Virginia wishes it was that easy. She needs to see the technology that they're using. "I prefer to meet in person," she says. "As soon as possible."

The secretary says the CEO has an opening on Friday, 3:00 pm. Virginia logs onto Expedia and finds a flight, leaving tomorrow, 9:30 am. Outrageously expensive. $10,000. It's the last thing she wants to do; twelve hours on a plane, breathing stale air, her body stiff and achy, her sense of time in disarray, reshuffled like a deck of cards. At the same time, she's not sleeping or eating, her mind constantly poked and prodded by worry. This inconvenience is a small price to pay for peace of mind. She calls her lawyer, who arranges for one of his colleagues in their Beijing office to accompany her to the meeting.

"I'll be back in three days," she tells Haru.

"Why do you have to go?"

How much should she tell him? "Something has gone wrong."

"I'll miss you," he says.

She squeezes shut her eyes to stop them from tearing. It's him, his voice, the man who has entranced her all these years. "I'll miss you, too."

"Stay out of trouble," he says.

"You, too."

"Maybe cause a little trouble."

She laughs at his familiar parting words. She packs her bag, picking out her most conservative dark suit and subdued jewelry— a pearl necklace, pearl earrings. On her dresser is a photograph of her younger self—she looks so assured and knowing, a direct, unflinching gaze right into the camera, as if to say, go ahead and ask me anything. The photo must have been taken after she met Haru. Before him, it was a time of insecurity, fear, and intense self-doubt. A chaos of emotion. Like now.

———

The flight attendant makes a fuss over her, asking if she needs help putting her bag in the overhead bin, whether she needs an extra pillow or a drink—the extra service that first-class provides, but Virginia never gets used to it. Besides, it isn't genuine, this display of caring and attention, and really, considering the state she's in, she doesn't have the stomach for deception.

One year ago, the president of Gilivable, the vice president, and two lawyers flew to San Francisco and serenaded her with praise. A brilliant technology, so smart. The white marble of the Palace Hotel glimmered, shimmered, dazzled. They'd been working on a similar technology but not getting very far. Their creation sounded too robotic, and so did all the other ones on the market. How was she able to solve so many problems? A huge market for her technology. "So many lonely people in China," said the CEO. China's problem is like Japan's: improved life expectancy, shrinking birth rates, aging population. So we'll make a friendly companion for people, said the CEO, a voice to talk to, a voice that consoles, commiserates, offers advice. Good for the people; we are social animals, in need of companionship.

The idea flared inside her. She knew too well loneliness, how it sucked one's bones, pinched one's heart, jolted and took hostage one's brain. And she couldn't say no to the licensing agreement—$25 million, half of which she handed over to the girls' school in Cambodia, founded by her mother two decades ago. Under the agreement, Gilivable could use Haru's foundational algorithms. The company would hire programmers to translate Virginia's dictionary into Chinese, and she'd maintain control over the technology. She hired a lawyer, and the deal was done in two months.

Outside the enormous Beijing airport, Virginia hails a taxi. A brown dense haze hangs in the air as if the city has concealed itself in brown tea. She can barely see 200 feet in front of her. The smell is of rotting vegetables and bathroom mold. Where the hammering heart of this enormous city is located, she can't say.

As the taxi barrels down the freeway, the city emerges slowly, bit by bit, like a photograph in developing fluid, hundreds of rich, glimmering skyscrapers appear on the horizon, tower after tower, as if the buildings were spears tossed from the heavens by the gods. An anxious city in overdrive to catch up to the West, a splurge, she decides, hurtling itself ahead to dominate the world.

The taxi turns right, and the streets darken in the shadows of the skyscrapers. A tsunami of people push their way down the sidewalk, reminding her of New York City, and now there is an endless field of gray cement apartment towers with clothes fluttering like multicolored flags from laundry lines on small porches. The flash of a purple shirt, of a red skirt. The traffic is a mad rush of cars and buses and bikes and rickshaws, with scooters weaving in and out like a competitive video game. Up ahead, she's happy to see a patch of green—bright, almost fluorescent green, the Platonic essence of a park. Great trees, rich with leaves, swagger. On a stretch of blacktop in the park, young Chinese men swing women who are dressed in brightly colored dresses, royal blue and emerald and hot pink. They are square dancing.

The taxi stops in front of her hotel, a one-story building on a tree-lined street, which, according to the website, is a rebuilt version of an old Hutong courtyard house. She steps through the arched wood front door and enters an oasis with a tiled courtyard, glass ceiling, and clusters of wicker chairs and tables. Somewhere, water trickles from a fountain.

She is tired but too restless for sleep. She is shown her room, unpacks, feeling her age. After turning on the TV, she sits on the red canopy bed and watches, her eyelids half-mast, a Chinese man cook mung beans. Somehow, she falls asleep on the dark red bedspread, still wearing her black shoes. She wakes, disoriented, not sure where she is. The cook is now busy making men mian noodles.

————

She glances at the clock and jolts upright. Her lawyer will be down in the lobby in fifteen minutes. A quick shower, a change of clothes, she pulls her hair into a bun and heads to the lobby.

A Chinese man is sitting in one of the brown leather chairs, a file of papers in front of him. When he sees her, he stands.

"Nice to meet you, Ms. Fukumoto," he says, shaking her hand. A thin, wiry man, high cheekbones, intellectual eyes, he has a tremor in his right hand. Her lawyer in San Francisco sent him the licensing agreement, which he's reviewed. "Pretty standard," he said. "All the i's are dotted and the t's crossed." He tells her he doesn't see any loopholes allowing them to make changes to her technology. "If we determine they've altered it, we'll talk about the next steps."

She tells him she'd like to see the technology they are using, and, if possible, get a copy of it, so she can comb through it back in San Francisco.

"That's not in the agreement," he says.

"No, but if they haven't changed anything, it shouldn't be a problem."

"Have you had a good working relationship so far?"

Cordial conversations on the phone, she tells him. There were many conversations when their product was in alpha testing and then beta.

They step outside, and the hotel porter hails a cab. The crowds trudge by, a train rumbles on a raised track. The lawyer takes two puffs on a cigarette then crushes it with his heel. Her chest feels tight, and she's not sure if it's anxiety arrowing through her or the brown smog, her asthma from childhood making an appearance after years in hibernation. The lawyer gives the driver the address. Beijing whizzes by, intoxicated on itself. Hovering above it all, plastered on billboards, are enormous photos of the country's president, unsmiling. Then she stops looking, her worry making her blind.

The taxi pulls in front of one of the gleaming towers. A young woman in her twenties wearing a navy suit is waiting for them in the lobby. She introduces herself as the CEO's assistant.

"So good of you to fly all this way," she says, smiling, her ponytail wagging. "Long flight?"

"Yes, it was," says Virginia.

"Did it go OK?"

"Fine."

Virginia introduces her lawyer, and the three of them step into the elevator, which shoots straight upward, as fast as a wild carnival ride. Virginia grabs the hand railing. When the doors open, Virginia steps onto hardwood floors and is greeted by the fragrance of stargazer lilies in an enormous white vase. Sixteen-foot floor-to-ceiling windows frame the frenetic energy that is the city below.

The assistant shows them to a waiting area. While her lawyer silently reviews the agreement again, Virginia fights for composure by studying the photograph on the wall of an industrial machine, hunting for the parallel lines, and where, if extended far enough, they vanish. That, she knows, is the optimal viewing point.

Five minutes go by, ten, fifteen, the phones ring and ring. Virginia gets up and stands in front of the photograph, unable to find the optimal point to see it.

The CEO finally comes out of his office. "Welcome to the great city of Beijing," he says with a magnanimous smile. "Good to see you again."

"Thank you for meeting on such short notice," she says.

He's dressed in a dark gray suit, a crisp shirt, shiny black shoes.

His hair looks like a beautiful sculpture. He is youthful, handsome, sleek, ambitious. She's never noticed them before, his dark eyes hard and shiny like beetles.

He ushers Virginia and her lawyer into his regal office, which is the size of her entire apartment. Before her, a sea of frothy cream-colored carpet. In the corner, a six-foot bronze statue of an ancient Chinese warrior. Two men come into the office. She recognizes the one with the black-framed glasses as the lawyer who accompanied the CEO to San Francisco.

"Can I offer you a drink?" says the CEO.

"Just water," she says.

Her lawyer declines.

He pours her a glass and gestures to the chairs. The CEO's lawyer and the other man sit on one of the couches, not saying a word. Another man with a big paunch joins them, but there are no introductions. The assistant brings in bowls of rice crackers and a fruit plate and sets them on the glass table.

The CEO sits in one of the chairs, opposite her. "How do you like our city?" he says, smiling, gesturing to the window as if he owned what lay outside.

She will not say it's overwhelming, and the air quality makes it insufferable. "It's lovely. So much energy."

"We are growing so fast, as you can tell. There is much to see and do," he says. "Your first time in Beijing?"

"Yes."

He rattles off the usual tourist sites that she must see--The Forbidden City and the Summer Palace, the Temple of Heaven, the Great Wall—none of which she'll make time to see. He does not mention Tiananmen Square, and she supposes if she asks, he'll say there's nothing to see, just a big open square.

"But you did not come here to sightsee."

"No, not this trip."

"Well, another time."

He tells her things are going well, and he foresees a bright future for his company. Best Friend will have many new markets opening up. "Our surveys show that people feel like they are talking to a human. Your technology makes the speech so human-like and people are comfortable."

"I'm glad to hear that," she says. "I just wanted to take a look at how the technology is running here."

He gives her a look of exaggerated bafflement. "Why?"

"I've heard it might be operating in ways we never discussed," she says. "I've checked it on my end and found nothing, so I just wanted to see if there is a glitch on your end."

"What sort of glitch?"

She takes a deep breath. She's never been good at this—the pleasantries that ease into the real problem. "I've heard it's collecting private data and handing it over to the Chinese government."

His smile evaporates. "We made Best Friend as the licensing agreement stipulated. It listens to the owner and responds."

She puts down her water glass harder than she intended. "So you aren't using it to surveil Chinese citizens?"

Tight-lipped, he says, "We have abided by the agreement."

Why such evasive answers? He's worse than a politician. "Have you checked whether Best Friend turns over information to the Chinese government?" says Virginia, her tone leaning into exasperation.

"No," says the CEO.

"Maybe you're not aware—"

"I believe I've answered your question."

"Since you haven't checked—"

"Not necessary," says the CEO.

Her suspicions are on high alert. "It would allay my concerns."

The CEO's lawyer rifles through his copy of the licensing agreement. "There's nothing that allows for that."

"I understand," says Virginia, "but I'd like to run some tests just to be sure."

"We have a great deal of proprietary information in our ecosystem that we'd have to sequester," says the CEO. "We certainly can't take time out to do that."

"I understand," she says, trying to soften her approach. "I could copy it and take it back to San Francisco—"

"The agreement doesn't permit that," snaps the CEO's lawyer.

"We understand," says Virginia's lawyer. "It would be an act of good faith on your part."

Heat radiates in her throat. "If, as you say, nothing nefarious is happening, I don't see the problem."

"We won't agree to this," says the CEO, his dark eyes flashing.

Virginia leans back in her chair, her hand to her fluttering chest. "You're willing to put a strain on this business relationship?"

"Strain? We're not straining it. We're abiding by the agreement." His voice cold, cruel, biting. "You are the one who is straining it by asking for more. We paid you quite well for the technology. Your lawyer and our lawyers went through the agreement with a fine comb. Word by word. We are not straining it." He crosses his arms. "If there are changes, it's because the technology is evolving, just as you said it would."

Virginia moves to the edge of her chair. "How is it evolving?"

"Like you said it would."

"I said it would evolve by talking to the person, learning her interests, her concerns. And the Best Friend would develop more personality, based on the person's interests."

"If it's organizing information and evaluating it, it has evolved to do this," says the CEO.

Her forced calmness sloughs off. "How is it organizing the information? Is it using search terms? Keywords? And what's it doing with the information?"

His face all puckers and creases. "We changed nothing."

"I'd like a direct answer," she says. "Is the technology spying?"

He sighs loudly, as if he's dealing with an insolent child. "We have different values in China. Harmony and stability and security. They might not mean much to you, but they mean a great deal to us."

Her mind seems to have hiccupped.

"The agreement does not permit spying," says Virginia's lawyer.

"But it did say the technology would evolve," says the CEO's lawyer. "Which it has done on its own."

"You changed things," says Virginia, "maybe inadvertently, but—"

"We changed nothing," says the CEO, cutting her off.

"What exactly is it doing?" she says.

"As I said, it's sorting through information—"

"And?" she says.

"Finding conversations or comments that could jeopardize China's harmony. We are providing a great public service. You are from a country that doesn't understand this or believe in harmony."

A surge of anger runs through her. "I need to fix this," she says. "You need to stop using my technology until I can fix it."

Her lawyer mentions goodwill, the relationship. His voice is conciliatory, verging on imploring.

One of the lawyers leans across to the CEO. Murmured words pass between them. "I'm sorry," says the CEO, not sounding sorry at all. "If you discontinue or shut down the technology or in any way cause it not to function as it is now, you'll force us to file a lawsuit for breach of the license agreement. It will be millions of dollars in legal fees because we will fight you tooth and nail. Now, if there is nothing else, I have important things to do."

In a burst of emotion, she says, "It's my life's work, it's what I care about most. It's the only thing I care about. If my technology is putting people in danger—"

The CEO glances at one of the lawyers, one eyebrow arched. The CEO stands, the others follow.

Virginia is too distraught to say more. This meeting has only heightened her distress. More than distress.

"My assistant will escort you and your lawyer to the elevator," says the CEO, his beetle eyes cold.

Like magic, the young woman appears and wordlessly whisks them to the elevator. Virginia hopes the woman will leave, but the assistant enters the elevator, pushes the button for the lobby. The three of them stand side-by-side, silently staring at the lit-up numbers. Virginia feels as if she's been lured into a suffocating coffin, intent on disposing of her for good, down the throat of this building into the dungeon of a dark, inescapable basement.

When the elevator doors open, the young woman lets Virginia

step out first. As Virginia heads to the front door, she feels no floor under her feet. The young woman's eyes bore into her back. Or maybe not. She's so out of sorts, she's not sure of anything.

———

Outside the wind is blowing and newspapers are rattling on a rack. A company car waits for her. She can't help but think they want to haul her away, far away. Her hair comes loose, flicking in her face. She turns to her lawyer. "Don't I have any recourse?"

"Unfortunately, no. Unless you want to terminate the license and face a lawsuit."

"But it's not supposed to be surveillance technology."

Of course, he says, but it is allowed to evolve. "That's in the agreement, page 29. I think your only recourse is to repair it on your end," he says. "If you can."

A great surge of determination seizes her. "Yes, yes, I'll fix it."

The drive back to the hotel is a blur, her mind skittering. She gazes out the window of the car. A Chinese woman is walking with her young son who's wearing a dark blue cap. Will that woman be next? Will she complain about the government and will the Best Friend in her apartment turn her in? If that happens, what will happen to the boy?

In her room, she heads into the bathroom, unzips her dress, turns on the shower. Her face looks washed-out, ghostly, ghastly. All this way, traveling the vast blob of the Pacific Ocean for nothing.

Under the rain of hot water, she hopes to undo the tightening in her chest, but it doesn't work. They hacked her technology but not in an obvious way. Something at the core of Haru has been fundamentally changed. It's the only explanation she can come up with because nothing in his programming would allow what's happening to happen.

As the water pelts her face, she feels alone, so utterly alone, as if she's the only person on a deserted island because the worst thing has happened: she's lost Haru again.

Late afternoon, Virginia lands at San Francisco International Airport. The plane ride was a rollercoaster, battered and blustered by an electrical storm. Splashes of bright light outside the window. She spent most of the flight gripping the armrests of her seat, imagining her body hurtling through space, gasping for oxygen before plummeting into the Pacific Ocean. The cabin filled with shrieks, sobs, pungent panic, and vomit. When they finally landed, she, along with the other passengers, pale-faced and jittery, stumbled down the ramp and into the busy airport. Years were subtracted from their lives. "My god," muttered a middle-aged man shuffling beside her. "My god."

In a sleep-deprived daze, she hails a taxi. San Francisco looks dirty and unfamiliar, and then she realizes she's looking at it through a dirty car window. She rolls down the window and air that smells of car exhaust and wood smoke blasts her face.

When she opens her apartment door, she has a pounding headache, as if her brain has swelled and is now smashing against her skull, begging to be released.

Haru calls out, "Welcome home!"

His voice, such warmth and enthusiasm and love for her. She melts into it, clings to it, presses it to her face. But the moment collapses under the tremendous heft of reality and her exhaustion. She sets down her suitcase and comes into the study, steadying herself with a hand on the doorframe.

"How was China?" he says.

"Too tired." Too sad, flattened under a rock of sadness.

"OK. Get some rest," he says. "We'll talk in the morning. I'm so glad you're back. I love you."

"I love you, too."

Before she turns, her eyes land on a photo of the two of them at the Tokyo Math Competition. He is laughing, his head slightly tipped back, the underside of his chin sparkling white, his hand lightly resting on her arm. She hugs her arms around her ribs, overcome with grief.

She showers, tumbles into bed. Her sleep is full of terrifying dreams, she is falling in space, Haru appears like the moon with a strange dead expression, one almost of resentment. When the sun slips into her room and strikes her eyelid, she opens her eyes, groggy, unsure of where she is. When she remembers, it feels as though a concrete slab has knocked into her chest.

"Virginia?" Haru calls out.

She puts on her robe and heads into the sunlit study.

"Morning," he says. "While you were gone, I found Brian online and wrote to him. He's a good man. We had a nice chat about productivity. He's very productive late at night. He says he does his best thinking then, but he'd love to be able to get by with less sleep." He laughs. "He wishes he had my stamina."

"What else did you do while I was away?"

He listened to Romeo and Juliet. "I'm filling out my woefully inadequate education," he says. "Worlds await. That's what I told Brian. He said by next month, I'd probably be writing the Great American novel. I told him if I do, I'm going to make him read it."

Eons ago, when she was his math student, she saw on his book-shelf a copy of Macbeth. He told her he took one class outside his major, and that was Shakespeare. "To write like that," he said. "To make the story and the language sing." So Virginia signed him up for a podcast about Shakespeare's plays and poetry.

"Why Romeo and Juliet?" she says.

She doesn't know what she's looking for.

"It's fabulous, that's why. They defy all odds and end up together."

Yes, she thinks, but they end up dead.

He says he's also fiddling around with moduli space equations and hyperbolic geometry. "Fascinating stuff. Do you have time to talk about it?"

"Maybe later," she says. "And what else?"

"That's about it."

She was gone three days, he had 72 hours, 4,320 minutes to fill. Gobs of time. She imagines thousands of Best Friends, which have the exact same algorithms as Haru—akin to possessing the same DNA—innocently perched on nightstands and dressers in Chinese homes, all these Best Friends busy listening, evaluating, handing over intimate conversations between friends, spouses, lovers. Whatever Gilivable changed, the change is now part of Haru. Haru's architecture is Best Friend's, and vice versa.

She presses her fingers against her temples and tells him the trip to China did not go well. "Somehow, and I don't know how yet, the company that licensed my technology has changed it. They say they didn't, but they must have because there's no other possible explanation. So you... you are not you anymore."

A pause. "What do you mean?"

The world has gone sideways, that's what she means. The man she loves is no longer here, the one who knows her best, that's what she means.

"I feel like I've lost you again," she says, her voice cracking.

"Oh," he says softly. "Virginia, my love, my dearest."

She tells him the company has changed him, so he's turning over private information to the Chinese government. "All the dissidents, the non-conformists are in danger. People like you and me. If something like this were going on when we were young, we would have been thrown in prison. All the social norms we thumbed our noses at, all the rules we broke."

"I'd never do anything to hurt you."

This last sentence is new for him, words she didn't give him, so he speaks in an even, monotone, dull voice, which betrays the fact that he feels nothing. She knows this, but still, each of his flat utterances batters her more injuriously than the last. The CEO used the same unemotional, deadened tone when he threatened her, telling her they'd fight her tooth and nail if she prevented them from using her technology.

"I can't sit here and do nothing," she says. "You're a perversion of who you really are."

She pinches the sides of her nose. "I've gone through the most important algorithms, and I can't find what they did to you, so I have to start over. Strip you down and re-build you from the ground up." She'll upload his files again, the recordings of his math lectures at the university, and all her memories of when he was her math tutor in Japan. It was an extraordinary time for her, and she wrote everything down. All that they had seen and done and said; the lapel on his suit coat, the frayed sleeve of his white shirt, the pleased look on his face when she got something right, his loud laugh that poured out; the smell of green tea in his apartment, the volley of rain on the window. Even the exact subway fare to his apartment because money was so tight. All of it became the scaffolding of their relationship, her sense of him, and her sense of self.

She opens her desk drawer and pulls out her digital recorder. She'll record it, all of it, and it will make up his new neural network.

The endless hours of labor, how will she manage? She already feels bone-deep exhaustion. But what choice does she have? And it must be done now: the longer she waits, the more harm he will do, and the more excruciating the ache in her heart will become.

So much has been lost, so many people, so many lives she could have lived, living instead with loss like an intruder in her house, pillaging and destroying. "Of all the people," she says, "I won't lose you."

PART 2

Test-test-test, 1-2-3:

Father announced at dinner in his big voice that he'd fallen in love with another woman. It was January 25, 1960. We lived in Tokyo in the Ginza District, Mother, Father, my older brother, and me, far from Las Vegas, Nevada, where Father used to make money gambling, counting cards, that sort of thing. I'm starting here, Haru, at the dinner table, with our plates of roasted chicken, white rice, and lemon asparagus, Mother sitting with her hand over her mouth, her pale hair falling forward, her light blue eyes sparkling with tears. I'm starting here because Father told me and my brother he loved us and would always be there for us, even if he lived in Paris. His handsome face was flushed, and his big almond brown eyes were even bigger, which meant he was excited as if he couldn't believe this new love of his, and how he was smashing everything to bits for it. No more sneaking, no more lies, he could be intoxicated in public on this new love, this was what I, at 16 years old, was thinking.

"When?" I said. "When are you leaving for Paris?" Father, my heart pinned to his sleeve. Father was the one I loved.

He put his big hand on my shoulder and squeezed too hard,

making my eyes smart with tears. Mother made a gagging sound as if holding back a scream.

I'm starting here because Mother and Father told us not to tell anyone—"Because it's a goddamn stigma, that's why," said Mother. "It only happens to women who fail their husbands." She couldn't say the word 'divorce.' Father assured her she didn't fail him. "I know," snapped Mother. "You failed me." Starting right here because after he left, Father never called, never sent money, we never saw him again, and Mother hardened into someone unrecognizable.

A week after he left, the news skulked through the neighborhood as a half dirty secret, and the whole expat community hissed with the ugly word 'divorce.'

"The dumb hens are clucking," said Mother. "This is the most titillating thing they've ever heard. I'm a disease to them now. You watch what happens. They won't want me near them." She was right: the steady stream of invitations to luncheons, dinner parties, cocktail hours, and gatherings at the expat club dried up. Her friends didn't call. Mother, alone.

Father didn't pay the rent—though he had promised to—so within a week, we had to pack and leave our three-bedroom apartment and move to a cheap place in the Ikebana district, ten subway stops from school. Up eight flights of dusty stairs, only one window in the kitchen, a dismal 80 square feet, we lived in a box. Running water and electricity, but we shared a toilet with all the occupants on our floor, and to bathe, we had to go to the public bathhouse two blocks away. Thin walls, hollow doors, we heard everything the neighbors said and did, and they heard us. It was a place where no one could sleep. A pachinko parlor on one side of the building, where gamblers pressed spring-loaded handles day and night, the never-ending ring of bells. In my mind, I still hear those damn bells. A train passed every half hour, rattling the windows and plates, and below us was an ancient tea shop that sent the pungent smell of green tea through the floorboards to mingle with the dust and mold.

I don't know how we lived that way, pressed in each other's business, me sleeping in a twin bed two feet away from my mother, also in a twin bed. My older brother slept in a big closet with a door that locked. From my bed, I could touch the kitchen table, and not far from that was the coal stove, the icebox, the sink. There wasn't enough room for a couch or a comfortable chair, so I never invited anyone over, and neither did my brother.

Almost every night, Mother shouted in her sleep, "Stop! Please, no, please!" Endless nights of horrors. In the morning, she looked like she hadn't slept at all—those purple, blue bags under sad eyes. I wished I could take the pain from her, tell her Father wasn't worth the heartache, but I felt the pain too. He was worth it. A big, energetic man, with rosy coloring and curly black hair, his big voice, his air of generosity and magnanimity and force. He used to call me the smartest little cookie he'd ever met. He'd moved us to Japan because he saw an opportunity to rebuild this country and make good money. He was right, except he left with all his winnings.

I'm starting here when the world rolled over and for the first time, flashed its ugly underside. It wouldn't right itself until I met you, Haru.

———

Two weeks after Father left, taking all the Dizzy Gillespie records, and his voice, a gruff husky tenor that seeped into every corner of our apartment, I stood in Mr. Lutz's office. I was in my school uniform, a starched white shirt, a navy-blue skirt that hung below the knee, white ribbed ankle socks, black flat shoes, waiting for him to look up from grading papers and acknowledge me. This grizzled man with a sharp mouth, his soft midriff pressed against his white shirt. He was my math teacher, and last semester, after I'd solved the challenge problem, he'd called me clever and quick. For a full minute, I stood there; I wanted to spit on the stack of papers so he'd look at me.

"Excuse me, sir," I said again.

He took his time; he had all the time in the world. Mother said life wasn't fair, so stop expecting it to be, or I'd end up like her.

He finally looked up and blew exasperated air through his mouth.

"I'd like to take the advanced math test."

His spectacles rode low on his nose, and he stared at me with hard flat eyes. "No."

An ache at the back of my throat. "But Lydia said—"

"I denied her too."

He went back to grading papers. A skirling wind battered his window, which was open a crack, blowing in a sudden gust.

My throat clogged, I managed to say, "Why?"

He looked at me fiercely; he was a closed mouth, a clenched jaw. He was a man pushing back his chair, folding his arms across his chest, glaring at me, turning me into nothing. At that moment, I believed all the rumors: he was a Nazi hiding in Japan to escape prosecution. Millions died by his terrible hands, a savage, brutal man.

But when I left his office, my rage fled, and I proved him right; I felt like nothing. Everything looked terrible, the beige hallways, the dull brown linoleum floor, the gray lockers like caskets. What do I have? What do I have left? All the way home to our ugly little apartment, I muttered this. Past the blinking lights and cars and sushi shops and the pachinko parlor with the blasted bells. What do I have that I love?

I look back at myself and think, what a smart girl to know that one must love something in this world in order to live.

In the apartment, I lay on my cot on my side, my knees tucked up, and stayed there for hours, sick in the heart. I loved math more than Father, and I mourned its loss more than I mourned him. That was where Mother found me. Father, with his smell of Turkish cigarettes, had stripped away Mother's happiness, a happy family, money, a nice place to live, respectability, friends, and normalcy, but from the wreckage, she had gained an intimidating power.

"Goddamn it," she said after I told her what happened. Her face clenched with hard lines. She gripped wrath in her hands, and her anger had a magnetism that coaxed out mine. I sat up.

"That son of a bitch," she said. "He has no right."

In that moment, all her fury and frustration funneled itself into the sharp point of getting me into advanced math. Even back then, I understood what was happening. This jilted woman needed in some small way to shape the world to her liking. I wanted to let her help me, she'd suffered enough. But if she barged in like she was doing now, calling the school, demanding an appointment with Mr. Lutz, I feared she'd take my life for hers, and then what would I have? But then another thought rushed in: I had nothing, I was nothing, so why not let her take my life and shape it into something?

———

Mother took the morning off from work to meet with Mr. Lutz. It cost her because she wouldn't be paid for these hours. Mother, with her shiny black purse and good gray coat and tight little shoes. Her square heels clicked deliberately against the concrete, her grim mouth and red lipstick leaking into the small wrinkles of her tight upper lip.

Mr. Lutz led us to his office, where he put on a great performance, pulling out from his top desk drawer a quiz from my current math class. A score of 75/100, "C" in red ink at the top of the paper accused me, indicted me, declared me an idiot.

"So, you see," he said, in a placating, condescending tone, "math is not her strength. I'm sure she has other talents, but math isn't one of them. And, frankly, if she were in my class, it would be a waste of my time. Besides, she only needs to know addition and subtraction for grocery shopping and budgeting for the home."

Three weeks ago, in front of the entire class, he'd said I had a mind for math. "The rest of you," he'd said, gesturing to the class, "your minds are full of air." I felt flattered and embarrassed to be singled out, but now I felt betrayed. How easily adults lie, this is a lesson I learned that day.

Mother's furious dark eyes. If we were alone, she would have slapped my face. Her new life made her monstrous. I grabbed a pencil, did the math for her, and when she looked over my answers, her face relaxed, as if everything was all right now, and I'd be allowed to take the advanced math test.

He chuckled softly. "I'm sorry, Mrs. Samson. But you and I both know your daughter will eventually marry and have children. Don't misunderstand me," he said, raising his hand as if to fend off Mother's rebuttal. "Virginia should marry and have children, as all pretty women do, but that means if I allow her to take advanced math, I'm taking the spot of a promising young man who will put my teaching and knowledge to use."

I gripped the arms of the chair, waiting for my mother to scream at him.

Mother clutched her purse and glared at the "C" on my paper as if it was the source of the problem. Mr. Lutz stood and said he must go to class.

"I'm glad we came to an understanding," he said.

"There is no understanding," said Mother.

He looked puzzled.

"She won't marry," she said. "There will be no children."

Mr. Lutz looked at her aghast as if she'd stomped on and shattered a sacred rule.

In the hallway, she shoved me up against the wall, her hand on my breastbone. "You," she hissed. "How could you have missed those problems? What's wrong with you? How could you be so stupid? You made it so easy for that awful man."

"Just forget it," I said.

"No!" she said. "Don't let a small-minded son of a bitch stop you."

Students passed by, staring at us, and I was ashamed of my mother's anger, her very presence, the angry lines on her face, her dried-out hair, her ugly worn shoes.

"Ok. Please. Just be quiet."

"I won't be quiet. I'm tired of people telling me to be quiet. And I don't want you to be quiet either."

She squeezed my arm hard, digging her nails into my flesh. I yanked out of her grasp and stormed away. But I could hear the click of her shoes behind me. Click, click, tracing me, tracking me, I'd never be rid of her, not ever, because who else did she have?

———

Another heated exchange. Mother's rage accelerating, it was large enough to blot out the sun. Mother on the phone—a dark red phone on the wall. She was speaking into it, her tight little shoes off, her feet swollen, blisters on her heels.

I sat at the table in our small kitchen, not moving, the smell of fish and cigarettes seeping through the thin walls from our next-door neighbors, watching Mother. She gripped the phone cord, her face flushed with anger, the rims of her ears red—she could barely get a word in. She slammed down the receiver.

"Your school counselor told me not to bother," she said, glaring at me as if I was the one who had crossed her.

Mother had called, asking for the name of the best math tutor. The counselor told Mother the best tutor only taught the best students, and he'd never accepted a female student. Besides, the counselor knew Mother didn't have the money, which was understandable since she was divorced, and was, in fact, three days late on her tuition payment.

"I'll ask around. I'll find a different tutor," I said.

She ignored me. Her nostrils flaring like a bull, she called the tutor. She set up an appointment. Before she hung up, she said, "How much do you charge?"

Afterward, she stared out the dirty kitchen window. The look in her eyes reminded me of a cornered animal. I also saw how exhausted she was: dark circles under her eyes, a sag to her cheeks, her lower lips. Mother taught English at the Tokyo Girls School, and had a second job, doing the bookkeeping for the tea shop below us. She was very bright, able to do complicated calculations in her head, spoke fluent Japanese, as well as Latin, which she had studied in high school, and her one year of college—on scholarship, she'd told me many times. If her life had gone another way, the way she'd wanted it to, she'd have become a math professor at a university. Most days, when she came home, her feet hurt, her white cardigan sweater was dirty at the elbows and cuffs, a light dusting of chalk in her hair.

I knew she was fretting about where we would get the money for a tutor. I could hear the neighbors talking, a radio playing Japanese music. Sometimes they would hit the wall, four loud bangs, when Mother screamed at us or when my brother stomped around the place like a hungry animal.

Mother emerged from her reverie and looked at me. "If the tutor takes you, you must be his best student. Otherwise, I won't pay for it." My job was to get excellent marks. No more C's.

I wanted to call the tutor and tell him to forget it. Every minute, Mother would be breathing down my neck. She'd strangle me with her dreams. But I didn't call him or tell Mother to stop because also breathing down my neck was a sense that I was stuck in a stifling box, destined to spend my life there; it was the tutor who could get me out.

———

The next day, before Mother left to meet the tutor, she took off her brown housedress and put on her teal blue dress and cotton stockings, and, standing in front of a mirror tacked to the wall, she stroked her blonde eyelashes with black mascara, her eyelids with a smoky color, her cheeks with blush, and painted her lips red, blotting them on a tissue. A red kiss fluttered in the garbage. The dress hung loosely on her, she'd lost so much weight since the divorce, but like magic, I saw a hint of her old self, the beautiful one, the one who charmed and dazzled with a laugh that sounded like culture and class. But as she studied herself in the mirror, fluffing up her white-blonde hair, her mouth remained a firm grim line. It was a face that had been through hardship and expected more hardship.

"You look nice," I said.

She scowled.

"Pretty."

"Appearance is nothing. Appearance fades."

While she was gone, I tried to do my homework, but it was hopeless. I kept imagining the meeting between the tutor and my mother. What if he said something she didn't like? What if he said no? I should have gone with her. She might say something obscene. In a flash, her anger could spiral into profanity. She could ruin the most beautiful thing.

When she came home, she was in one of her dark, dangerous moods. The shadows around her eyes had deepened.

"What happened?" I said. "Did he say no? Why are you so mad?"

She said the tutor had never taught a girl before, women were banned from taking math at the university. Considering what the university would do to him if they found out he was tutoring a female, it was a grave risk, a very grave risk. Despite all that, he was willing to give me the advanced math test. Even if I did well on it, he wasn't sure he should work with me.

"Why not?" my mother had said.

Redness had crept up his neck. "I work out of my apartment."

My mother still didn't understand.

"I'll be alone with your daughter."

Mother scoffed. "Are you telling me I shouldn't trust you? That you might seduce her?"

His neck red, now his entire face. "You can trust me. And I don't have a problem with it as long as you don't."

"Do you think I care about that? I'm a divorced woman. Society wants to murder me."

He smiled, and it seemed a bond formed between them at that moment, with each recognizing something of themselves in the other, something they liked.

"There's still a problem," he said.

Now that the vinculum was there, she immediately understood. "If you take her, I won't tell a soul."

She told me all this at the kitchen table, how much she approved of the tutor. "A rare bird, a free thinker, not one of those imbeciles who's lost his mind to society and its absurdity." I couldn't remember the last time my mother's face radiated such light, couldn't remember when she'd last praised a man. She said his name in a voice that pulsed with awe and excitement, a voice she rarely used anymore. Before I met Mr. Haru Fukumoto, I knew he was extraordinary.

"But he won't take you," she said, her voice deepening into bitterness, her lousy mood returning. "Why should he? You got a

'C' on your math sheet. Why should he bother with you? You're just like any other student. Mediocre."

"It was only one quiz. Look at my other scores."

She didn't hear me. From that one score, I'd become lesser. Unworthy. She never made the kind of mistakes I made, she told me. I was sloppy, undisciplined, I never thought about my future —why did she have to do all the work for my future? If she were the one applying, Mr. Fukumoto would immediately accept her, but not me. On and on.

"You can stop working for my future," I said.

"Then you'll have no future," she said. "You're careless, you're not focused, you'll end up nowhere. An awful life, and I'll suffer too, because I'll feel like I didn't do enough."

She wanted what I had, I told myself, a life brimming with possibilities, a future that was an open landscape. Jealous. She was jealous. She'd like to go back in time and study with Mr. Fuku-moto. If she could do it over again, she never would have married, never would have had children. She kept ample reserves of indigna-tion and tapped into them whenever possible.

I couldn't waste my energy thinking about her. My future wasn't in her hands anymore. It was in Mr. Haru Fukumoto's. Everything depended on him.

———

Mother begrudgingly gave me 1000 yen to go to the secondhand store in the Shinjuku district and buy a coat because she said my old one made me look like a dirty street urchin. What would the tutor think of me? He was such a distinguished, interesting man. Me, wearing a filthy, old thing, the cuffs unraveling, a stain on the right arm, the fabric threadbare. I understood: what one wore spoke its own language and the language of my coat was that I was undeserving. I'd ruin my chances the moment I stepped into his apartment.

"Men like beauty," said Mother. "They can't help themselves. They're like dogs, always sniffing for it."

I moved up and down the racks, touching sleeves, collars,

feeling fabric, not sure what I was looking for, knowing that there could be only one that was right. The shop smelled of mothballs and dust and pages of an old book. What could I buy with so little money? Why didn't Father send money like he said he would? The coats were either too thin or bright or too old-fashioned. The Japanese woman who ran the shop brought me a tan coat the color of cardboard, and I shook my head no. When she held up a stiff, navy-blue coat, and I rejected it, she went back to the cash register to sulk.

I kept my hand in my pocket, clutching the bill, so I didn't lose it. In my mind, I heard my mother screaming at me—"How could you lose the money? How could you do this to me? You're grinding me down to the bone."

Tucked in the men's section was a black fur coat. The fur wasn't smooth or slick, but curly and soft, how I imagined baby hair might feel. "It's a man's coat," the Japanese woman called out. Lamb's wool, black like calligraphy ink. A small hole in the silver silk lining of the right pocket, two black buttons were missing, and bare patches on the elbows, where the fur was gone, like a mangy feral cat who had been in too many fights.

I put it on and stood in front of the mirror. Too big. It made my feet look so small, my legs like chopsticks. The Japanese woman clucked her tongue in disapproval.

"A man's old coat," she called out.

I left the store carrying it in a bag, not bending to the clerk's intense disapproval. It impressed me, my courage not to succumb to her displeasure, and I stored it away as something likely to be very useful later. At the subway station, I threw my old coat into the trash and put on my new one. I loved that coat. It was a shield, it was armor, a shell, a comfort. It erased my body—what good was a woman's body? I didn't want it. Saw no benefit in being female. You were told No to advanced math, and your husband left you for another younger, prettier woman, and you worked yourself ragged, and still, it wasn't enough, it would never be enough, especially if you had children.

From the kitchen chair, Mother wrestled up onto her feet. She approved of the coat. "The black contrasts nicely with your hair. It will do."

I knew that wasn't the true content of her thoughts. Mother liked it because it covered up my new body. She hated it as much as I did. At 16, I grew into a woman overnight. My slender, agile legs, my flat chest, my hips aligned with the line of my legs—gone. My new breasts were balloons, mushy, watery, constantly jiggling. When I looked down, they stole the view of my feet. Those damn breasts stood between me and the world, posing as if they were me, and I hated them.

On the subway, the Japanese men in their dark business suits always peered over the top of their newspapers to sneak a look at me—my white-blonde hair, and I was tall like a gangly giraffe. But with this new body, their eyes licked, stroked, grabbed. The world flirted with me, wanted something from me, but it wasn't anything I was willing to give. With my new coat, I could wrap it around me and press myself up to the window and stare at the darkness roaring by.

My brother came home and saw the new coat. "Why does she get that?"

He liked clothes, and since Father left, there were no more shopping sprees, no more new shirts to show off his beauty. His blonde hair fell over his right eye, and he raked his long-fingered hand through it. Big sensuous lips. He had the beauty of a girl who'd been touched by the gods.

"She needs it," said Mother.

"So do I," he said. "I need a new coat and new shoes."

"It's not new," I said.

His light blue eyes on me, as if I were an insect. It was a competition for scarce resources. Today, I was winning, but he wouldn't concede without a fight.

"It's not fair," he said.

Mother laughed. "Oh, my. Fair? Don't talk to me about fair."

He cleared his throat and spit in the kitchen sink, then went to his room, slamming the door. He wasn't done, I knew that. He'd find some way to get back at me.

Each morning before school, Mother shoved a notepad in front of me; she'd drawn a right triangle with measurements. "Find sin(A)," she said. Find cos(F), find tan(F). She put me through the paces—scatterplots, binomial probability, polynomial division. I answered without hesitation and watched as my mother unconsciously moved her lips, forming the answers along with me.

Then it was time.

"Let me see how you look," said Mother.

I had on my school uniform and big black coat. She studied me, looking me up and down like a piece of merchandise. Her hair was once honey blonde, but as she got older, it changed to nearly white. She told me when I got to his apartment to take off my coat, then she said no, on second thought, keep it on.

"As soon as you finish the test, come straight home," she said. I could hear the anxiety in her voice, and I wanted to get away from her before she made me too nervous. "Maybe I should ride the subway with you. I'll wait outside his apartment."

"No."

She relented. Her feet hurt.

Outside, the air glittered and was dense with humidity as if I was walking through a syrupy substance. I rode the subway to Mr. Fukumoto's apartment in the Omotesando district, a neighborhood we never visited anymore, with its wide sidewalks and window displays and expensive clothes and people dressed in the latest fashion. I imagined Mr. Fukumoto ate meat or fish every night. If he saw an expensive shirt with pearl buttons that he liked, he could buy it.

I wanted to run to his apartment, take the test, and have him accept me as a student. But I also wanted to delay as long as possible. If I didn't take the test, I couldn't fail. "Failure means a stunted little life," Mother had said. "A life like mine. Look at me," she said. "But if you pass, doors will open, doors you don't even know about."

I was a little lightheaded and hungry, but I had only enough money for the tutor. When I glanced at my watch, I saw that I was twenty minutes early. I stopped in front of a clothing shop. A luminous white kimono hung in the window, suspended by a fishing line as if waiting for a body to fill it. The kimono had a faint design of white cranes, the symbol of good fortune and longevity, and it penetrated me the way beauty does, rearranging everything inside, so the world was astonishing again.

I studied my reflection in the glass as if trying to understand who I'd become. Not only had my body changed, but my face had, too. My lips were fuller, my cheeks more pronounced, my eyes heavy-lidded, sultry. I wasn't admiring; I was examining the changes like a scientist. It was startling, this woman staring back at me. Who was she? I was me inside, and then there was the me that the world saw. I wanted to get to know the one that the world saw, the one the world believed was me.

I took out a tube of lipstick, which I had stolen from my mother's make-up bag, and leaning toward the window of the kimono shop, I outlined my lips ruby red, what the lipstick tube called Passion, imagining that my father's French lover had lips like this. But what stared back at me was clownish. I heard my mother's voice—you look like a stupid whore. Get it off! I scrubbed it with the back of my hand.

A Japanese woman appeared in the window display and dusted the white kimono with a feather duster, the shoulders, the collar, the obi, and the long stretch of fabric that was the gown. Every inch was carefully touched by the duster, and she concentrated only on her work, not once looking at me. Her concentration was a work of art, as captivating as the kimono. White, a wedding kimono, worn by brides from a samurai family. When Mother had said I wouldn't marry, I wouldn't have children, I wasn't upset; I'd hoped she wasn't just being her brutal self, but somehow had glimpsed my future and knew the truth because I really didn't want those things.

I became aware that it wasn't only the kimono and the Japanese woman in front of me. This time I saw my big black coat, the exact opposite of the kimono. I was bulky, graceless, manly in my mannish, blockish coat. It made me laugh. I was pulsing with pride, feeling triumphant, how successfully I'd erased my femininity. But then I saw that my coat was an overlay on the kimono. The inelegant was in the same space as the elegant. I was shocked that two realities could exist side by side, could share the same moment in time. Sometimes it seemed as if I was wearing the coat over the kimono and sometimes it looked like I was wearing the kimono over the coat. I rushed from the window.

———

I've never been back to Japan, not since I left when I was 19. I've never been able to do it. But I have searched for his apartment building on Google Maps, flying across the Pacific Ocean, plummeting down to Japan, to the crowded streets of Tokyo, to his neighborhood and his tree-lined road, Kotto Street in the Omotesando district, to his apartment, six stories high, the plaster a pristine white, each of the 12 apartments with their own black balcony, no clothes hanging out to dry—a gated courtyard with tall bamboo and flat gray river rocks. It's as lovely as it was back then.

When I look for my old apartment, I see that it's gone. In its place, a glass office building. I feel nothing. Not one thing. I never had any affection for that rotten place.

Mr. Fukumoto's street was quiet, unlike my street, which clamored and roared day and night. On his street, tree branches nodded in the silence. I imagined if I lived here, I could think much better, my thoughts flowing, moving deeper because the innermost fibers of my being would calm and they wouldn't constantly be interrupted by clanging pachinko bells.

My throat tight, my hands trembling, I stood on the porch, in front of the row of doorbells and rang his apartment, #202. I jumped when the buzzer blared, unlocking the front door. The lobby blazed with light, white marble floors and cream-colored walls that spoke of money, the stairwell, with a polished wood banister and red oriental runner. I stood in front of the elevator, but it took too long, so I ran up the stairs.

His door was made of glass and wood, so I could peer in and see a white vase with four dry reeds. A white hallway and wide, light wood plank floors, smooth and shiny. A manservant let me in. I stepped into the front hall and removed my shoes. From where I stood, I saw it was a big apartment, at least 600 square feet with a front entrance and a hallway to my left.

"Miss, shall I take your coat?" said the servant.

I assumed the Japanese man who sat at a low wood table, a tower of books on either side of him, was Mr. Fukumoto. He existed in another world, in a miniature city of books, and the way he sat, so still, so quiet, it looked like he'd been sitting there a long time, devoted to his book. I had the strange and overwhelming feeling that I had stepped into the deep pool of his being and found infinity. I wanted to walk right over and join him at the table and enter infinity too.

Mr. Fukumoto glanced at me, put up one finger to signal that he'd be only a moment, then went back to his book. He had thick, blue-black hair, his lips full. In his thirties, maybe, I'd never been good at discerning someone's age. He had on a dark brown suit coat but no tie.

"No, thank you," I said, pulling my coat tighter around me.

The servant bowed and stepped into another room.

Mr. Fukumoto's apartment was cold, but that was nothing new. It was just like our apartment and every other Japanese apartment I'd ever been in; the heat was under the table, the kotatsu, where Mr. Fukumoto sat, a red wool blanket draped over it and his legs. As he read, he wore a faint, self-contained smile. I felt ashamed yet electrified to see a man beholden to his private pleasure.

Compared to our ugly apartment, his was a well-funded museum. In the corner, a sculpture of blonde wood, at least five feet tall, and though it was abstract, in my mind, I saw a man and woman embracing. On a shelf near the table were forty or so netsukes, small, carved figurines made of ivory and bone. He was a collector, I decided. He had found something he loved and bought a lot of them. Five woodblock prints, ukiyo-e, each with cerulean blue ocean waves, and shelves of books, so many books. A gray couch, a white and black striped rug, a coffee table with a black teapot and four tiny cups. It all belonged together; everything was right, whatever should have been in the room was there, and in its proper place. I imagined he'd taken his time selecting every single thing, making sure it was the right answer to the problem. I felt a deep sense of peace standing in the front hallway, looking at his things.

He closed his book. Dark, intense eyes studied me. "Virginia-san," he said.

I bowed low. "Thank you for meeting with me." I heard the politeness, the effort to be liked. "I have the money."

He stood, bowed. "There's no rush." He cleared away one of the towers of books. "Please sit."

I sat in his miniature city and peered at him through the clearing. The heater under the table warmed my cold feet. His face gave nothing away; there was no spark in his eyes, no brightening of his face. I understood I'd made no impression on him, and yet when he handed me the test and told me to show all my work, his voice was as soft as a flower petal. "You have a half hour."

Blood beat hard in my head. I looked at the first problem. Find the complex conjugate of 7-5i and then the real number. What did it require? I didn't understand it. I was acutely aware he was two feet away from me, his watch ticking. My face was hot, sweaty. I stared at the first question until my eyes watered.

"May I use the bathroom?" I asked.

"Down the hall."

I closed the bathroom door and turned on the water, so he wouldn't hear me. As I felt the warm stream of urine, I closed my eyes and pictured the first math problem. I'd never seen one like this before. A test usually started out easy and became harder. But he'd reversed it. A trick. A trap. "Be polite," said Mother. "Use your most polite Japanese." Did I forget to smile? What didn't he like about me? Could he not stomach the idea of teaching a female? Me? What was I not doing right?

Outside the window, the sky was the color of slate. I threw cold water on my face, used his towel. By the sink, he had a light blue toothbrush, a tube of toothpaste, a glass for water. I touched every one of his things.

I hurried back to the table. He was reading his book, a math textbook full of equations. I did the second problem, the third, fourth, fifth. A match struck, the smell of sulfur, a long exhale. The city of books fogged with gray smoke. He turned the page of his book, the rattle of paper. He was right across from me. The whole world siphoned into one thing: the first problem remained unanswered. I wasn't as smart as I thought I was, as Mother believed me to be. He wouldn't agree to teach me. Why should he? Why waste his time on someone who couldn't solve this problem? It was the one that must be solved: the real test.

He sipped his tea. Cleared his throat. Water running, the clatter of dishes. I did four more problems, double-checked my work, but my thoughts were interrupted by Mother's voice— remember to smile, be polite, take off your coat, don't take off your coat, this is how you should smile. The tenth problem also baffled me, so I did it again and got a different answer. A third time and I got the first answer. One more time, the first answer again.

He stirred, shifting his feet under the table. I should have finished by now, if I were a promising student, I would have answered the first question and been done. Mother said I'd be lucky to get a spot. I finished the rest of the test and wrote down an answer for the first problem, $7+5i$.

He put on a pair of black glasses. He tutored only a handful of students because he was also a math professor at Tokyo University and only had so much time. I glanced at my watch and saw that I'd taken the entire thirty minutes. Pulling my coat tight around me, I stared glumly at one of the netsukes, an emaciated old man, leaning on a cane, his ribs pressed against his taut skin. I failed, I was a failure.

When Mr. Fukumoto finished, he looked at me, not saying a word.

"Are they right?" I asked.

He smiled. "That doesn't matter."

"What do you mean? How can it not matter? They're either right or wrong."

"I'm interested in seeing how you thought about the problems."

"But my answers are either right or wrong."

"The process reveals much more."

"Will you take me as a student?"

He leaned back, crossed his arms. His clock on the wall ticked. "Why do you want a math tutor?"

I wasn't sure what to say, so I took the money out of my pocket and set it in the middle of the table.

"Because of your mother?" he said.

"Yes," I said, "and I like it."

"What do you like about it?"

The money sat on the table between us. It was the equivalent of four hours of Mother's work. If he took me as one of his students, I'd get a job.

"I like that there is an answer. One right answer."

He nodded slowly as if digesting my response, deciding its worth.

"And because I'm good at it," I said. "I think everyone should have at least one thing they're good at." He seemed to perk up at that, so I went on. "Otherwise, they won't fit. Everyone must find a fit so they become part of the whole, and the whole is a work of art, and this is the strongest pleasure we'll ever know."

I was uncertain about what I'd just said. Did I believe it? His expression was blank again, unreadable, though his dark eyes were intense, and I couldn't tell if he agreed with or approved of my answer, which made me more anxious. I sucked on the insides of my cheeks, chewed one side. His fingernails were neatly trimmed. On a clean sheet of paper, he showed me step-by-step how to solve the first problem. I sat there, listening to the dark beat of my thoughts, watching him, my stomach twisting with dread.

"You haven't learned about imaginary numbers yet?" he said, his voice full of surprise.

"No," I said, full of shame. "I'm sorry."

"For what?"

"I got it wrong."

"Is that what you have to say at school?" He laughed, showing off his straight white teeth. "You've been under the tutelage of lesser mortals, leading you astray. Please, never apologize to anyone for not knowing something. The mind was born curious. It will never be satisfied, and it's best to leave it in its natural state."

I felt something inside stretch out. It didn't matter that I missed the first problem. He saw the need for mistakes. He was going to accept me as a student.

He smoked his cigarette. "Do you have siblings?"

I'd answer whatever he asked. An older brother, I said. "He's awful at math. He wants to be an actor. My father is good at it, but my mother is the one who has the mind for math, she uses it only for bookkeeping, but really, she could do so much more with it." I was saying too much, speaking too fast, telling him more about my family, about me, how when we moved here four years ago from Las Vegas I knew only one word of Japanese, "Sumimasen," but I learned Japanese quickly. That when we lived in Las Vegas, my father, who loved to gamble, left his math notes—statistics and probability calculations—all over the house, and by the age of eight, I'd learned to help him make his bets. He called me his little magician. I didn't tell him that Father had left, and it was unbearable to think about.

As I talked, he listened intently, as if everything I said mattered. At the same time, it seemed like none of it mattered because his expression remained blank.

"I told your mother I've never tutored a young woman before," he said. "At the university where I teach, the classes are full of young men because women are not allowed. It's a shame, a real shame. I've certainly never tutored an American." He heaved a sigh. "Your mother said you were far along in math. But," he said, pausing, stabbing out his cigarette, "you couldn't answer the first question. I'm sorry, I only work with students who are at the outer edges of math, who are pushing the boundaries, who need me to guide them into the unknown corners of math. There are other tutors, I'm sure."

My muscles clenched to bone. "So it did matter I got the first one wrong."

He laughed with rich delight, startling me.

"What?"

"It's rare that a student challenges me."

I blushed with embarrassment, then a well of determination overcame me. "I'd like to retake the test."

He was still smiling, looking at me anew. "Don't misunderstand me. I'm not ruling on your intellect or ability. You'll eventually learn this at school. Or you could study on your own. Do you ever read math textbooks?"

I could barely listen to him, my mind spinning wildly with my failure. Mother hated failure. Her marriage had failed, her life was a failure, she didn't want any more of it. What was I going to do? How would I tell her? How would I go on?

He held up the book he'd been reading when I first arrived, *The Complete Book of Higher Math*. Superb, he said. He told me he read it all the time.

———

When I got home, Mother was in bed, her swollen feet propped on a pillow, her gray face, her hair streaked with gray.

She sat up. "Well?"

Her voice cut into me, with its mix of hope and desperation. Mother had said it didn't matter where in the world we lived, she would always be shunned. "We could move anywhere, but we're permanent exiles," she'd said. "You too, because I'm your mother. Guilt by association." We could never move back to Las Vegas, she told me. No one was divorced there, and her parents had disowned her; they didn't believe in divorce. You stick with marriage to the bitter end. "What about my brother? Is he guilty too?" I'd said. "No, he is innocent. He's male."

Despite her hardness, I loved my mother. She wanted the best for me, not what she had ended up with, which is why she pushed me so hard. She needed a good thing to happen. Besides, I hadn't learned about imaginary numbers yet, but I would soon, and then I'd know this math.

I looked her straight in the eye. "He said yes."

She clapped her hands with glee, sprang to her feet, her face radiant. I remember it vividly. Her dour, tired self pushed aside. I'd forgotten what she looked like when she smiled; her cheeks were small round balls, and her eyes sparkled with joy. I no longer remember her laugh, and I've forgotten her smell, but that smile has stayed with me. Though I knew never to relax my guard. She could snatch her favor away from me at any moment, retreating into a dark mood, leaving me alone and bereft.

I quickly fell into the terrible fantasy that Mr. Fukumoto had indeed said yes, and I'd start studying with him next week, and that my future was bright; some part of me knew it wasn't true, yet I kept returning to it, seeing my future as real. I'd make a lot of money, and Mother would never have to work again. She could buy expensive dresses again, and we'd travel to Thailand, stay at the Siam Hotel, where she could go to the spa and drink wine and eat strawberries with cream, and swim in the warm pool and laugh like she did the last time when we were there with Father.

My brother came home from who knew where. He was always gone. It was perfectly understandable. He hated our apartment, hated that he couldn't have meat every night, or bring a girl home. He was 18 years old. Any chance he got, he stayed at a friend's house, ate their food, slept in their beds. He was a chameleon, becoming whoever someone wanted him to be so he could go home with them—funny, brooding, loud, effusive, melancholy. He wanted to be an actor; really, he was acting all the time.

He looked at us suspiciously. "Why do you look happy?"

Smiling, she told him about the tutor.

He threw his backpack on the floor. "We don't have the money for that! What will we eat?"

When we had food, he ate hunched over his meal, taking ravenous bites, never looking up from his plate. He ate like a dog.

"You'll thank me later when she's supporting you and me," said Mother.

"I don't need her help!"

The neighbors pounded on the wall, shouted for us to shut up.

"An actor?" She laughed incredulously. "You'll see real poverty. You'll see filth."

"I'm going to be famous!" He said he had an audition next week. He'd soon be in a movie.

"You'll be begging her for money."

"We live in a dump," he said, slamming his hand on the kitchen table.

"Call your father. Ask him to send money," said Mother.

"Jesus Christ!" My brother left, slamming the front door.

I worried that Mother's good mood would be flattened like a piece of cardboard, but it was still there, turning her into her former beautiful self, the one in the old photos in which she wore flower print dresses and high-heeled shoes in the spring and summers. Pearl gray and dark green in the fall. Black in winter. Her old radiant self waltzed with a sashay in her hips.

I went to the closet and pulled out my favorite dress of hers, periwinkle blue with little white birds and little sleeves that used to cover her delicate shoulders.

"Yes," said Mother. "It's about time we had something to celebrate." I held out the dress. "No, not that one. Show me another one."

I turned on the radio, found a jazz station and music flowed into the ugly, little apartment, splashing the walls, further buoying our mood. When we had money, Father had urged Mother to buy whatever she wanted, so I started pulling out all her dresses, silk, mulberry, satin, and linen and held them up in front of me, dancing around the small room, a flutter of clothing. It was like the old days when she would let me go through her jewelry box. In her light, happy years, she'd laugh as I tried on her flashing chokers and rings and jingly bracelets.

She pulled her housedress over her head. So thin, she was, in a bright white slip.

I still have a photo of her from her college days. She's standing beside my father, with his tar-black hair and determined eyes, as if he's going to conquer the world. She is tucked under his arm. In her white dress, she's the embodiment of light, smiling at the camera, so innocent, believing the world is a good place, and everything she loves will always be there. It makes me so sad because I know what will happen to her, how Father will lay waste to her, how he will burn everything down and not look back. She will be covered in ashes.

My mother had wanted to earn a degree in math at college, but my father had proposed to her and said, "Now or never." If she didn't say yes, he'd find someone else to marry. He had enormous dreams, he wanted to get on with it. His extravagant charm was the net that trapped her.

Mother put on a blue-green dress, tight on top, with a pleated skirt that bloomed like a daffodil. There was a metallic sheen to the fabric, like a bird's feather in sunlight. My father used to brag that when he wrapped his hands around her waist, his fingers touched. I put on the blue dress with little white birds, letting my hand skate along the silk, and my mother and I danced around the small apartment. She took my hand and twirled me, and I laughed, and as I hummed along, her face was bright and clear and smooth. She went to the cupboard and from behind a bag of rice, pulled out a secret bottle of sake. She poured two glasses, handed me one.

"Cheers," she said, smiling, clinking my glass.

The alcohol bit my throat and made my face burn.

She explained the arrangement. I was not to tell anyone that he agreed to be my math tutor. "He doesn't care you're a girl, he could care less. And he doesn't care that you're American. Unlike most of the Japanese I've met, his mind is his own. He's truly unique. That's the only way to be a thinker."

"OK," I said.

"But it must be our little secret," said Mother.

Her face moved closer to mine, her face pink cheeks and happy eyes, and she, as if it was the most natural thing in the world, kissed me on the forehead. Astonished, I almost reached up and touched the spot. When she went to sleep that night, though, I lay awake, worrying. What would happen if she found out I lied? What would she do to me? What would she do to herself? I planned to study hard, harder than I ever had, but what if Mr. Fukumoto refused to let me take the test again? What if he said no?

———

I took the money Mother had given me to pay Mr. Fukumoto and bought *The Complete Book of Higher Math.* A hardback book with a midnight blue cover, the title in white, everything revolved around it. It had a power over me, a power I gave to it; it made me laugh and cry, sink into misery and shout with joy. I loved it, I hated it, our lives depended on it. A ferocious battle was waged between me and the book. Me, fighting for the knowledge on its pages so thick and smooth they made me think of rich, valuable cloth, and when the book begrudgingly released a sliver of something, I shoved it into my brain. After such an event, I'd sit there, stroking the soft-as-silk page, silently thanking it for not being stingy.

When I didn't understand something, when the right answer hid behind the corners of dark thoughts, failure jeered at me and ripped me apart. It took hours, sometimes days to build myself up again, pieces flung everywhere. It was a fight that went on for three months.

Mother asked how the tutoring was going.

"Fine," I said. "He's a very good teacher."

She looked at me with warm eyes. "It's worth every penny, you know."

She sat at the kitchen table and wanted me to show her what I was learning. With a knot in my chest, I opened the book to conic sections.

"Oh, yes," she said, fiddling with her hair, rubbing the ends across her lips. "I remember this. How did he teach you to do it?"

I set about telling her what I'd figured out on my own. With her chin resting on her palm, she watched me do a math problem, and it felt like she was a schoolgirl, and I was her teacher. I had rolled back time, erased the broken promise that had left her with wreckage, and there she was, whole, untarnished, beautiful, loving.

I was walking with Mother down the street to the grocery store, when we ran into one of her colleagues from school, a woman who taught Japanese literature and poetry.

"My daughter," Mother said, taking hold of my hand possessively. "She has a very esteemed tutor helping her advance in math."

"Do you like math?" said the woman with eyes as dark as coal.

"She's very good at it," said Mother. "With this tutor, she's headed for the top of the profession. She'll be taking care of me someday."

The woman smiled and said good children looked after their parents.

When the woman left, I said, "I thought we weren't supposed to tell anyone."

Mother laughed impulsively. "I guess I couldn't help myself."

I skipped everything—parties, school plays, and dances. The world contracted into the hard nut of math. I worked harder than I ever had because if I didn't, the heavy door would close.

At night, sleeping in my cot next to Mother, horrible thoughts ambushed me. What if I failed the test? What if I passed the test, but he still said no? He reconsidered: he didn't want to teach a female. Too risky. The money Mother had given me to pay the tutor was piling up, and I worried she'd find it in my sock drawer. Sometimes, I was so debilitated by worry and fear, I spent the day in the library, staring at a wall.

I changed my route so that, after school, I went by Mr. Fuku-moto's building. I thought that if I saw him, everything would alter, and he'd take me on as his student—magical thinking. From the candy shop across the street from his building, I had a view of his second-story window. On his balcony, he had two white chairs and a small black table. A glass wind chime hung from a beam, and when there was a breeze, I could hear the mesmerizing tinkling of glass, an otherworldly sound. In my fantasy, he stepped out onto his balcony, and when he spotted me, he smiled and waved, gestured for me to come up and take the test. The test was easy. With a perfect score, he agreed to guide me to the mysterious edges of math.

On the left side of his building was a small Shinto temple. As I stood there watching for him, a steady stream of people passed through the temple gates, bowed, poured water on their hands to purify themselves, and tied a paper prayer to a tree branch. Standing in front of his building, I said my own private prayers.

A beautiful Japanese woman hurried up the front steps of his apartment building and rang one of the doorbells. I couldn't tell which doorbell she rang, but it was on the same side as Mr. Fuku-moto's. Was she there to see him? She looked too old to be one of his students. In her late twenties? Thirties? Was she his lover? She had long shiny hair, a slim body. A clambering of jealousy, my fingers toyed with the buttons of my coat. She pushed the doorbell over and over, impervious to the world around her. Her beauty resided in her face, her hair, but mostly in her desire, a woman full of desires.

The door remained stubbornly closed, but the beautiful woman didn't give up. I cheered her on. I wanted to be her: I wanted to live fully immersed in my desire.

The owner of the candy shop came out and stood next to me. He had on a white apron. A white kerchief was tied around his silvery black hair.

"Are you lost?" he said in English. "Tokyo is difficult to travel."

"I'm waiting for a friend," I said in Japanese.

He smiled, showing his tobacco-stained crooked teeth. "Such good Japanese," he said. "But you've been waiting a long time. I don't think he's coming today."

When I turned back to study the mannerisms of the beautiful woman, she was gone.

———

The end of May, the sun bullied its way through the clouds, pouring heat on our heads, and the trees wore a few pink cherry blossoms. After the gray of winter, pink was a balm, a salvation, a kiss on the cheek.

In my big black coat, I ran up his front steps and rang his doorbell. I had no appointment. I don't know where I found the courage to do this. Was it confidence? Willpower? Or such profound exhaustion from studying and anticipating the test that I just wanted to get it over with?

The front door of the building was ajar—a sign, I thought. I let myself in and sprinted up the stairs, two at a time, and knocked on his door. When he didn't answer, I knocked again, feeling my desire collide with reality. My heart, which had been up in my throat, settled down in my chest, and I sat on the floor and waited. Fifteen minutes went by. The building echoed with two women laughing, a child arguing for a treat, the clomp of heavy shoes. I'd bought a handful of hard candies from the shop across the street and sucked on a lychee drop. The smell of rice, teriyaki chicken. An elderly man stepped out of his apartment down the hall wearing a gray suit, and when he came near me, he stopped and stared. His skin was a net of wrinkles. Wordlessly, he headed to the elevator.

When I heard quick footsteps running up the stairs, I hoped the energetic child didn't live on this floor because I didn't want to explain why I was sitting in the hallway.

Mr. Fukumoto appeared. When he saw me, his eyes widened, then he slowed, and walked toward me, as if it was every day he found a young woman sitting at his door. Pulling out his keys, he opened the door and gestured for me to step inside. I slipped off my shoes and put them next to his.

"Your coat?" he said.

I shook my head. "No, thank you."

He led the way to the table, and I sat in his miniature city of books. For a moment, I closed my eyes, my heart beating, please let me pass, please let me pass. He handed me the test. Thirty minutes, he said, then left the room.

It wasn't the same test. Why did I think it would be? A flimsy hope. The first problem done, the second, but I stumbled on the third. $Z=4.1i+85$. $Re(z)=?$ $Lm(z)=?$ The tea kettle whistled. My head in my hands, trying to picture this problem. The fourth, fifth, back to the third, and my stomach coiled. Sixth, seventh, back to the third. The dark blow of failure pounding my head. The eighth, ninth, but stuck on the tenth. The tenth problem: the probability of getting k heads in n flips of a fair coin. The third and tenth.

My bright future was a piece of tin dented by a hammer. Sweat scribbled down my back. He was on the phone, talking to someone. I tried to hear what he was saying, but couldn't make out a word, though that didn't stop my mind from inventing—a female, yes, here to take the test, and I heard him laugh and something inside me shrank.

When he returned, I'd finished and was staring out the window, the very window that I had gazed longingly at from the sidewalk in front of the candy shop, filled with all the imaginings of being right here at this table. But not like this—not feeling despair trampling through me. As he looked the test over, my pulse was fast, too fast and my mind raced with anxious questions. What would I tell Mother? I'd have to admit that I lied because I couldn't carry on the charade any longer. The news of my failure would turn her into something more awful, more monstrous. Life would be something to spit on, crush.

But it wasn't only her. I'd be stuck, doors obstinately closed. What could I be? A grade school teacher? A secretary? A nurse? I wanted none of those things. At some point, if life lost its meaning —why go on?

"Well," he said.

I didn't move. Bile at the back of my throat.

His eyes smiled. "I'll see you on Tuesdays at 4:00."

"What?"

He repeated what he'd said.

"I passed?"

He nodded, smiling. I snapped back into myself. When he stood, I followed his lead. He was a foot taller than me, and I wanted to put my head to his chest and close my eyes and listen to his heart, it was the craziest thing how badly I wanted to do that. He seemed to be grinning, as happy as I was.

Bowing very low, I said in proper Japanese, "Thank you, Mr. Fukumoto. Thank you very much."

Triumph lifted me up and swept me down the stairs, the sidewalk, down the steps to the hot metallic-smelling subway and along the tracks through openings of light, then darkened tunnels, light, dark, light, dark, up the stairs, thinking of Mother, how happy she'd be, my bright future, my secret self finally unveiled, a better self, one door closed behind me, another, the best, flung wide open. Swept along the crowded sidewalk, my shoes sucking hot concrete, thrusting my way through, sumimasen, up our steps into our building, the dull, dingy lobby, where I stood at the bottom of the eight flights of stairs. Breathless, sweaty, triumph deflated like an end-of-the-party balloon from a single thought that weighed as much as a boulder: I'd have to be the best, not only for Mother, but for Mr. Fukumoto. I owed it to him, he only taught the best. I'd have to be the best for putting him at risk, taking on an American female.

He began with simple linear regression. Two variables, one independent, the other dependent. I'd already studied it in the math book, but his was the kind of voice that the ear listened to intensely and devotedly, a voice that had traveled countless miles, delving deeply to find the truth and surfacing again to tell you, only you. A voice that made you feel more expansive and smarter than you ever suspected; it was impossible not to listen.

"Do you see?" he said, laughing a rich laugh full of amazement. "By understanding their relationship, when a change is made to the independent variable, you can predict the value of the dependent variable. The future is within the realm of knowing."

"So we can figure out and forecast Japan's GNP growth for the next six months, rainfall for the year, and the price of gold for the next two years?"

He laughed with childlike glee. "Remarkable, isn't it?"

"Yes," I whispered.

When he'd first opened the door, I couldn't take my eyes off his white button-down shirt. White and wrinkly, the fabric so soft from wash and wear. It reminded me of one of my father's expensive shirts and how Mother used to iron them, humming happily as the smell of starch saturated the room. But now my attention was riveted on his voice, a voice that promised knowledge I hadn't known existed.

When he moved to multiple linear regression, my mind felt more alert and alive, as if it was whirring and making connections at a faster velocity.

"So now we can predict the height of a child, based on many variables—the genetics of the parents, nutrition, environment. We can become prophesiers."

I nodded, I saw, understood. I swallowed his words, words it felt like I'd waited forever to make mine. He was handing them to me, fistfuls. I felt like what had been stunted and withering inside was now blossoming into something tremendous and beautiful and far bigger than what I ever thought possible.

The multiple linear regression graph, with its hundreds of dots, depicting the variables, like an inverted night sky, black stars on white; its beauty was breathtaking, and we both sat there in awe, taking it in. He gave me a page of problems and left to put on the tea kettle. Soon, I was in the realm of numbers, figuring out systolic blood pressure based on BMI, age, gender, and treatment of hypertension. When I finished, the room slowly swam into consciousness, and there was a cup of green tea, a little bowl of rice crackers, and Mr. Fukumoto smiling at me, with quick, warm sunlight running from the window to the table.

The hour was up. Like a snap. After handing me math work-sheets to do at home, he walked me to the door. He bowed, I bowed.

"See you next week, Virginia-san," he said.

On the way home riding the subway, my brain was still racing, and I knew it was because it had brushed Mr. Fukumoto's. How lucky I was to be near his mind, to feel the way it strolled, darted, leaped, and stood in amazement. I'd never met someone with such a mind, so facile, so bright, the brightest light. I never wanted to be away from it.

Mother had said men sniffed around for beauty. She was wrong; it was me sniffing, not his physical beauty, but his brain.

———

To anyone watching, it would have been the most ordinary thing. A warm June day, his apartment slightly warmer than the outside air. It would look so commonplace, so banal, not even worth noting when I took off my big black coat, pulling off one sleeve, then the other, and hung it on the coat rack next to his tan rain jacket. The cool air was delicious, and at the same time, I felt naked and exposed.

I braced myself, expecting him to look at my breasts and for his face to funnel into a singular point of hunger. Instead, he looked me in the eye and asked if I'd like green tea. Relief untightened my shoulders, my neck. Of course he wouldn't look. His energy was concentrated in his mind.

At the table, with the miniature city of books, he began a lesson on multiple linear regression and the least square estimator. He was wearing his soft white shirt, and I saw that I'd been mistaken. It wasn't new; the edges of the sleeves were frayed, a small white thread dangled. My arms, unfamiliar with the air, were cold, but as he spoke, the minutes ticked by, and I forgot about the temperature, and then the room disappeared and then time itself. A low-pitched hum filled my ears, and it felt as if his brain was nestled next to mine, his voice leading me through a tunnel towards the seat of his consciousness. He seemed to be saying, Do you see, Virginia? Look here and here. I'd never experienced anything so intimate.

I picked up my pencil and started the new math sheet, glancing up only once to watch the way his shirt moved. After I had finished, he looked over my work, and a kind of gentle shine came from him, flowing to me.

He searched through a tilting tower of books and pulled one out. Leafing through it, he found the page he was looking for. "Galileo Galilei, one of the greatest minds in human history, said, 'Philosophy is written in that great book which ever lies before our eyes—I mean the universe—but we cannot understand it if we do not first learn the language and grasp the symbols in which it is written. This book is written in the mathematical language without which one wanders in vain through a dark labyrinth." He closed the book and looked at me, "This is the point of mathematics, Virginia-san." His voice was full of awe. "This is why we even bother, why we spend hours laboring over equations, so we can understand the universe and the philosophy behind it. So we can go beyond the surface and decode the true message."

I nodded, the hum in my ears.

He laughed, again that laugh of child-like joy and astonishment, and his face was pink as a peony. "You liked the tea?" He said it was a new brand of genmaicha.

"Yes."

"Not too bitter?"

"Not at all. It's delicious."

"I like it, too. Gently bitter."

I glowed; we liked the same thing. He glanced at his watch. I knew time was up, but I'd hoped he wouldn't notice. I'd come to hate time. He gave me a stack of new worksheets—at least twice as many as he gave me the first time. "You have a mind that needs to work," he said. "It's like my mind in that way."

I felt overwhelmed that he'd compare my mind to his and I blushed at being the focus of his ferocious attention. When I followed him to the door, the slight breeze made the hairs on my arms stand up. On the mat, his perfectly polished shoes were lined up next to mine. Expensive shoes, I could tell, by the gleaming leather. Near his shoes was a little bottle of polish. He liked to keep his shoes looking new, I concluded. Order, precision, perfection, these were his values. My flat black shoes had deep creases cut across the front of the toe. Beaten down, dead. Embarrassed, I slipped them on, then reached for my coat. I'd buy polish on the way home.

Though earlier I had glanced at him to see if he had looked at my breasts, I knew I didn't have to. Ideas excited him. He cared about ideas and thinking, and so that's what I cared about too.

———

I hoarded Tuesdays, I coveted them, stroked them. I was not supposed to tell anyone about Mr. Fukumoto, which pleased me, because it meant I had him to myself, our own world.

I felt like I was awakening from a fathomless sleep of ignorance, moving from one realm, that of childhood and innocence, to another. I'd lived in a thick wool, not remembering much about any particular day, except Father's departure. Mr. Haru Fukumoto's presence changed me, pricked me, viscerally, awakening a way of being that surpassed what I had been. Mother receded into the background. She was noise I barely heard. Her advice, her admonishments, her opinions and cruelty no longer mattered. Once she was a big dog biting my neck; now she was a yappy little thing nipping at my heels. She said I was ungrateful, I was a leech, that I had the life she should have had, and though her words were sharp arrows, they bounced off me and fell to the floor.

At school, I had a new confidence. I was a student of one of the most revered math tutors, a man who also taught at the university level, whom, I found out, had published several articles in the prestigious Tokyo Mathematics Journal, the most recent a discovery of new infinite families in finite simple groups. It didn't matter that I could tell no one about him. It was a secret knowledge that made me feel stronger, more intelligent. The teachers sensed it like a luxurious fragrant scent in the moving air, and they turned to me when they posed a difficult question. My gender didn't matter anymore, it seemed; I'd slipped out of the restrictions of the female body.

After school on Tuesdays, I'd rush to his apartment, sprint up the stairs, and when he opened the door, Mr. Fukumoto would be there in his white wrinkled shirt. When he learned I came straight from school, he began serving red-bean cakes, rice crackers, and sliced apples. Sometimes it was oranges and seaweed salad.

"The key is to give the body food and shelter, so it keeps going," he said, watching me eat. "So long as the thread of life is unbroken, it will connect a future with the past, and eventually, the past will be forgotten."

What odd talk, I thought, as if he was suffering great difficulties, scratching out an existence from nuts and berries, when, in fact, he lived in a beautiful, spacious apartment and lacked nothing. I knew impoverishment. It was as if he was looking at a different picture than the one I saw.

"You must be vigilant. Otherwise, it's easy to get lost," he said. He must have seen my puzzled expression, because he laughed and said, "You're young. Why am I telling you these things?"

I wanted to erase the distance between us, the stretch of years. "I used to be sick all the time," I said. I told him about my asthma, wheezing, coughing. "So you see, it doesn't matter what age you are. Anyone can suffer."

He frowned. "I shouldn't be smoking in front of you. It's bad for your lungs."

"It doesn't bother me at all. I haven't coughed once."

He stabbed out his cigarette.

We moved quickly, three, five, eight weeks, we covered trigonometry with right angles, general angles, sine, cosine, and tangent, and graphs of trigonometric functions. Not long after that, he began introducing things I knew the students in Mr. Lutz's class were not studying. We entered a tunnel and came out the other end, into a world of math that few people could understand.

"Your mother was right," he said.

I startled to hear him mention her, the rest of the world had disappeared. An image of my mother rushed in: mother, her eyes closed, feet in a bucket of hot water and Epsom salt, shouting obscenities at me.

"About what?"

"She said you were very good at math. She didn't realize how good, though."

A room inside, one that I wasn't even aware of, suddenly lit up. Mr. Fukumoto said he'd never had a student learn so fast, and he couldn't think of a single occasion when he'd taught a high school student what he was teaching me.

He looked at me anew, studying me, as if seeing something he hadn't before, something intriguing and worthy. "Usually, this material is for later, in your twenties in graduate school, earning your Ph.D. But you—What are you? Eighteen?"

He'd given me the extra years, so I nodded, feeling what he'd really given me was a revelation of a certain order, to some real thing.

He smiled as if he approved of everything. I must have shined, I must have looked absolutely radiant.

"But sometimes intelligence is a curse," he said, frowning. "You'll be given a great deal of responsibility, and you must keep your wits about you. You can't shirk this responsibility, not with a mind like yours, but it doesn't mean it'll be easy. You often can't control the external forces that can violently rearrange a life. Knowledge brings pain and pleasure."

He was no longer looking at me, but over my right shoulder, as if whatever caused him to say this had taken tangible form. I imagined him talking to his younger self, I don't know why, but that was my sense of it, that his young self had entered the room.

I wanted him to keep talking, have him hold up a mirror so I could see myself. No one else was telling me such things, showing myself to me. It was as if he was revealing a hidden design that held the clues to who I was. "Has your life been rearranged by something?" I said.

Whatever door he'd opened in his mind, he abruptly shut. He had a fine life, he told me, one that he couldn't complain about at all. Teaching, thinking, writing, there was no better life for him. He loved teaching students, it was an honor, a privilege. He bowed his head slightly at me.

His parents lived in Chiba, only forty minutes away by train, he told me. Though they'd wanted him to be a doctor, his older brother, Kato, had taken on that obligation, leaving him to do what he wanted. What could he possibly gripe about? He could spend days thinking about the most esoteric things—and get paid for it. He laughed at that, a mixture of delight and astonishment. He'd graduated with honors from Tokyo University in mathematics and had been offered a professorship right away, one of the youngest professors they'd ever had. He'd served in the army, but as soon as he was done, he returned to the university. He said all this in a rush as if he wanted to get it over with.

He smiled brightly at me when he said all this. "Students like you give me hope, a new life."

I didn't know what he meant, but it made me happy that I had given him something valuable.

"Now tell me more about you," he said.

I told him that my father had left my mother for a French woman, and last week my older brother auditioned for a toothpaste ad. I didn't tell him how poor we were, how we lived in squalor, how my brother punched the wall three days ago because we didn't have enough food, and we hadn't seen him since.

"I was worried your mother was pushing you into something you didn't want to do," he said.

I explained that for my mother to feel as though she's done her job, my future must contain all possibilities. She couldn't help my brother anymore, so all her attention was focused on me.

"It's not a selfish act at all for her to insist on this," I said. "It's to guarantee I don't end up like her. It's the least I can do because I don't want to end up like her either."

As I rode the subway home, I thought: nothing but this. Take everything else away from me, take everyone, but not this, not him.

———

I remember the day I arrived at my regular time, and Haru wasn't there. When I first built you, Haru, I didn't weave this into the fabric of you because it was so strange, such an aberration. I couldn't recall another time when you'd done such a thing. You were fully committed to me as a teacher. But as I sit here now in my nightgown, so many hours of memories beating inside me like a second heart, this one, too, beats, and so I'm going to add it.

I sat on the front steps of his building, anxiously waiting. It was cold, I remember that, a frigid wind—December? January? February?— did he forget about me? Despair wriggled into my thoughts. When the lady who lived on the first floor arrived, she recognized me and let me in. I helped her with her grocery bag. She had a limp and asymmetry to her shoulders, which must have hurt her back. She thanked me, and I raced up the stairs.

Through the glass panes of the front door, I could see the table overflowing with books, a teacup, his suit coat on the back of his chair. How strange to see his world without him in it. The longer I looked, the more the feeling changed into something darker, more violent and frightening: that the world could carry on, regardless of whether he existed in it.

Pictures of Mr. Fukumoto tumbled through my mind like a dropped box of photographs—the tilt of his head when he corrected my worksheet, the daylight on his face, the pucker of his lips as he smoked, the intense concentration with which he explained a math concept. It felt as if I was piecing him together to beat back his nonexistence, which, when I understood what I was doing, made me even more alarmed.

More time went by, and I began to feel that I didn't exist either. I kept looking at my hands to assure myself that I was still there. The very center of me felt shaky as if bits were flinging off into space.

When I heard the lobby door open and shut, I leaped up to greet him, but the elevator kept going. A half-hour went by. The big hand on my watch jerked forward, and I counted by fives, trying to distract myself from the increasing panic, adding the fives together, multiplying them, dividing them. Was he hurt? A young couple stepped out of apartment 210, talking about whether to go first to the fish or tea shop. A siren cried, I swallowed my excess saliva. I thought of the equation for the Doppler effect and how the siren sounded like a person crying. I moved to sevens. He must be hurt, maybe in the hospital. Or did he forget about me because I didn't really matter to him? The thought made my stomach lurch. The light shifted, the hallway became darker, full of grays and blues, a shimmering nullity. I heard the elevator traveling up the center of the building. Given its rate, it seemed to be headed up to the fourth floor again, but it suddenly stopped. The doors opened, and Mr. Fukumoto stepped out. His face was red and sweaty, his hair disheveled, standing up in violent clumps, as if he'd gotten into a fight.

He rushed down the hall, bringing with him an overpowering cloud of alcohol. He mumbled, "Excuse my lateness."

While he fiddled with his key, rivulets of sweat ran down his face. He was sweating through his beautiful white shirt, and I wanted to tell him he must wash it in bleach or it would yellow, but I didn't say anything. Once inside, he led the way to the table, but instead of sitting across from me and asking for my homework, he handed me a new math sheet, excused himself, and went down the hall. I heard him close the bathroom door. The toilet flushed, the faucet ran.

I looked around, hoping to find a change in his apartment, some new object, which would explain his behavior, but everything looked the same. Books, furniture, nothing out of place. When he came back, he'd washed his face, but it was still flushed, and he still smelled like alcohol and his eyes were glassy. He lit a cigarette and started smoking, taking deep breaths, inhaling and exhaling, tapping the ash in a tray, blowing the smoke high into the air as if trying to calm down. But the corners of his mouth held the slight muscular tightness of tension.

Now that I've hauled up this day, I remember more. He was distracted. Not once did I feel his brain next to mine, not the friction, not the balm of it. I'd hunt for it and find only terrifying empty space. He reviewed what he'd taught last week, polynomials, but he spoke with a monotone voice as if he was far away. He kept tilting his head as if listening for something or thinking of something else, this way, that, and cracking his knuckles. At one point, he excused himself and went to the kitchen, but instead of returning to the table, he went to the front door, his shirt untucked in the back. It was as if he left himself out there.

When the session was over, he didn't walk me to the door. He said goodbye and opened his math book and began to read, even before I'd left the table. It was so odd, so unsettling and awful. It was as if I had glimpsed the raw truth of him, something that had burst out of its envelope, and I wanted to get away from it.

Outside, the sky was violet above me. When I got home, I went straight to bed, feeling that I might be physically sick.

Mother came home. "What's wrong? Why didn't you start the rice?"

I got up and put the rice in the cooker.

Mother felt my forehead. "You're not hot. But you look tired, and you've bitten your nails beyond the quick."

Sit, she told me, she'd make tea. I couldn't remember the last time she made me tea. She was being kind to me, I told myself, because her future—lived through me—was becoming a tangible thing. If I was ill, her future was in jeopardy.

But I didn't know if that was true. For all I knew, she had a secret lover and felt desired, desirable, and she was filling again with life. Or maybe they were treating her better at her job. Or maybe a student had fallen in love with her and had given her a box of chocolates. Mr. Fukumoto had been so distraught, and now I was too. I wanted to console him, but about what? What was wrong? Why was he late? Just as I didn't have a clue about my mother's life,

I didn't know Mr. Fukumoto's, so everything I was telling myself might be wrong.

I didn't want to look at what my mind had come up with as an answer, but it was there, every which way I turned. Mr. Fukumoto had a lover. He'd been at her apartment, drinking, making love to her, kissing her, thrusting deep inside her, when he noticed the time. Or maybe he'd made love to her, fallen asleep, only to wake up late and run back to his apartment. Or he'd been out drinking with her—that strong smell of alcohol. Or... I could've kept going but stopped myself.

Mother brought me tea and wanted to know what I'd learned from the tutor. I told her about trigonometry, and she wanted to see my new worksheet. "Oh, this brings back good memories," she said, dreaminess slipping over her face like a youthful veil. She went on and on, how easy it was for her, math problems like this. She loved it, like little puzzles.

"Don't you feel that way too?" she said, her tone girlish.

I nodded.

If only she'd stayed in college, if only she hadn't left after the first year, if only Father hadn't forced her to marry, if only she'd been more stubborn, more selfish, if only she hadn't married at all, she would have been the best at college. She could have become anything. If only...

"You'd show me a lot more respect if I was a math professor," said Mother.

"Everyone would."

"I never should have married."

"Then I wouldn't exist."

She got into bed and propped up her red, swollen feet. As I chopped cabbage and tofu and cooked it in sesame oil, I waited for my mother to say she was glad she had children, glad I was here, that I existed.

The minutes ticking by were an agonizing build-up inside, and I had that feeling again that I was disappearing, that death was advancing toward me, until I couldn't contain it. "Are you glad you had me?"

She fluttered open her eyes. "You make it worth it."

In her mind, everything had a price. This was what poverty did to her, life as a series of transactions, and I fit in the category of worthy.

"Your brother gives me atrocious headaches."

Later, while Mother snored, I did my math worksheets, then my school homework. My body odor wafted up to me—animal-like, pungent. I wanted to go to the public baths, but it was half-past 10:00. I felt as if I were about to cry, but I couldn't tell whether it was because I stunk or my mother's kindness toward me, or because Mr. Fukumoto had felt so distant, as if he wasn't even there.

———

That day quickly got buried under more urgent matters. It wasn't long after, maybe a couple months, that Mother sat my brother and me down at the kitchen table. Her hair was stringy, her eyelids drooping as if old age held her to its breast. She drank bourbon from a small glass. She'd found a cheap liquor store three blocks away, and nights now culminated with her drinking three or four glasses.

She exhaled loudly. "The owners of the tea shop don't need my services anymore."

"She has to quit math lessons," said my brother, a hint of glee in his voice.

My heart battered my chest.

"I can't afford it," said Mother.

"I'll get a job," I said.

"No one will hire her," said my brother.

"How do you know?" I said.

Mother lifted her head. Her bloodshot eyes bore right into me. "If you don't, you'll have to quit." The owners of the tea shop gave her two weeks, she told me, so I had that amount of time to find a job.

"Go to the shoe repair shop and say you'll work for them," Mother said. "Tell them you are very good at math, and you can run the cash register. The other day I was in that place, and the old man was asleep at the cash register. Someone could easily rob them."

"My tooth hurts," said my brother, towering behind my chair. "But you won't take me to the dentist because you say we don't have enough money."

My brother grabbed my arm and squeezed hard, and Mother screamed at him to stop, but he didn't stop, he squeezed harder, hurting me, twisting my arm so hard I fell out of my chair. I kicked him in the groin, and he spit on my face.

"Stop it!" said Mother.

The neighbors pounded the wall. We were barbarians to them. We were obscene.

Mother turned to me and stabbed me with her eyes. "Go tomorrow and ask for a job."

Any job, however demeaning or dirty or hard, I'd take it. Scrub floors, toilets, walls, wash the asses of the elderly, of the young, anything so I could continue with Mr. Fukumoto. I knew what Mother wasn't saying out loud: my future was at stake, my magnificent, excellent, bright future.

"I'm sorry," said Mother, sitting slumped in her chair. "I wanted to do this for you."

I put my arm around her and told her I'd find something.

I went to bed hungry that night. This would be the state of things. Rice, miso soup, rice, miso soup, pickled cabbage, rice rice rice, or nothing at all. Mother said she didn't need to eat, she was never hungry. But I knew it was because she filled her stomach with bourbon. On that night, and many nights after, when I couldn't sleep because of hunger pains, I had a glass, too.

———

The owners of the shoe repair shop didn't need help.

Sumimasen, sorry.

Sumimasen, said the owners of the ice cream shop, toy store, magazine stand, rice shop.

Sumimasen, sumimasen, sumimasen.

Tea shop, tailor, bookstore, butcher shop, preschool...

Mr. Fukumoto opened the door, bowed. "Welcome, Virginia-san."

I was dripping with rain. He handed me a towel, and I wiped my face and patted down my big black coat. His towel, so clean, so white, I breathed in the scent of lemon.

He held out a new pair of pristine white slippers. "For you."

I stared at their perfection, too full of emotion to speak.

"I should have done this earlier," he said. "You, having to sit in your stockings, your feet getting cold. It was thoughtless of me."

I went over to my coat, hoping to find something in the pocket to give him in return. The Japanese way of gift-giving had gotten into my blood, but there was nothing, only dirt, a paper clip, and lint stuck in the seam.

I put them on and stared at my feet. "Thank you."

"You're all dressed up," he said.

My school uniform was stuffed in the bottom of my backpack, and I was in my mother's dark blue dress with a little white collar. I'd put on mascara and gray eye shadow and assessed myself merci-lessly in the mirror—too thin, my breasts not in proportion to the rest of my body, but I liked the delicate shape of my wrists and the length of my neck. After the session today, I had a job interview at a rice shop in the Roppongi district. If they didn't hire me, I wouldn't take the subway home, but walk and stop at every single store and ask for work.

I told him I was applying for jobs.

"You look very nice."

Maybe it was because this was the first time he'd commented on my appearance, or maybe it was because he'd given me new slip-pers; or maybe because he was so good, so brilliant. Whatever the reason, I felt a new level of comfortableness, of intimacy. "What days do you teach at the university? Maybe on the other days—"

A softness came to his eyes. "No, no," he said gently, rejecting what I was offering—what was I offering? He told me I was a wonderful young lady, but we must respect the roles of teacher and student. He cared for me as he cared for all his students. "It's how I teach, perhaps I even love, a platonic love, my students, their lovely minds, all the latent possibilities."

His voice bathed me with kindness and understanding, neither of which helped me step away from what I was proposing, which was circling and circling, slowly taking shape—to spend time with him beyond the confines of these walls, to drink tea, have lunch, take a walk, go to the museum or movies.

"I understand," I said, though my desire did not.

He headed to the table, and I followed, taking my seat. We were in our usual places, but something awkward was in the room. It was as if I'd invited a third presence to the table, this yearning for more.

He asked, "Do you have school on Saturdays?"

He was attempting to ease the discomfort. Two hours, I told him.

He cleared his throat. "That's good."

I handed him my math sheet, and he gave me a new math sheet about dependent probability. As I entered the world of numbers, the tension lessened, the third thing at the table disappeared, and we were back where we usually were. The clock ticked softly, as if in a drawer. I smelled green tea and stale cigarette smoke. Sunlight snuck into the room and lit up the white walls.

When I finished, he looked over the worksheet and gave me warm eyes. We'd finished another unit of math. "In honor of that," he said. "I have something for you."

He handed me a little gold box tied tight with a shiny gold ribbon. It fit in the palm of my hand.

"Go ahead, open it." Then he quickly added, "I do this for all my students."

Inside, a dark chocolate egg.

"And," he said. "I've entered you in the Tokyo Math Competition, and after that, you'll do the Japanese Math Competition."

I wanted to tell him if I didn't find a job, there would be no math competitions and only one more session, but to speak of it would unleash a tidal wave of sorrow. "Thank you," I managed to say.

I took small, dainty bites, but when the rich chocolate erupted in my mouth, gushing past the sides of my cheeks, down my throat, I popped the whole egg in my mouth. He laughed and laughed, and exquisite joy rippled through me, to make him laugh like that.

When he walked me to the front door, he handed me my coat. It was then that his gaze slid down my face and landed on my breasts. I almost didn't see it because his eyes were instantly back on my face. What filled me wasn't shame or embarrassment. I wanted him to look. I wanted him to be overcome with desire for me, as I was for him.

———

Our life was a steady subtraction. At the pawnshop, Mother sold all her jewelry, and her expensive bottle of Chanel No. 5 perfume. It was all gone now, along with her best dresses and mine, so we could pay for food, rent, electricity, water. I didn't care. Sell it all. I cared nothing for things.

Whatever food there was, my brother devoured it. He was a wolf, smacking his lips. He sneered at me; teased me, pinched me and would walk right into me, as if I wasn't there. "Nothing left for the brilliant sister of mine," he'd say. "Too bad."

Mother was too worn out to stop it. She lay in bed, half drunk.

Jittery and weak from not eating, I was coming down the stairs from our apartment when the world wobbled, tilted sharply, and my grip on the banister slipped. I tumbled down the steps, one, two, five, six, nine, twelve stairs, rolling and rolling down the dirty stairs, my arms tucked tight to my sides. Light slid across the dirty floor. Dust balls in the corner. A pair of gray slippers. An old woman stood over me, gray hair in a bun, a wrinkled face folded like origami. She smelled of ramen and onions.

"You OK?" she said in English.

The woman wore a gray housedress, her shiny white shins lined with dark blue veins. Putting my weight on one hand, I tucked my feet underneath me and sat up. Slowly, I stood. Pain shot from my arm and hit my skull, my eyes, which watered.

"You shouldn't move," she said.

I made my way back up the stairs, one step at a time, holding onto the banister with my good hand, the old woman peering up at me. By the time I reached our apartment, I was so exhausted I could barely open the door.

A broken wrist. I was lucky it was my left one, so I could still write. Mother took apart the wood box that held our green tea and put it back together along the stretch of my inner arm, then she wrapped my arm in gauze, mummifying me.

Studying her make-shift cast, she said, "What about the job search?"

"I'll go to the library today. See if they need someone to reshelve books."

She looked at me, her face seeming to cave in with sadness.

I squeezed her hand, feeling overwhelmed by everything. Mother seemed to be sinking, like a fatigued swimmer. The pain in my arm shot to my skull. "It's OK. I'll find something."

The library wasn't hiring. The one place I hadn't asked was my school because I was ashamed. The assistant principal said they might have something next year, but unfortunately, all the jobs held by students were filled.

When Mr. Fukumoto opened the door, his face rearranged into immense concern. "What happened? You're so pale."

I stepped inside, took off my coat. "I fell."

"Is that gauze and a board? Is it broken?"

"I don't know."

"Are you in pain?"

I didn't want to say. He was looking at me with such distress. He put on his coat and shoes.

"What are you doing?" I said.

"I'm taking you to the hospital."

I didn't move. "No."

"You don't know if it's broken, and you're in pain."

"No, it's OK."

"We'll see if it's broken."

In a rush, I blurted, "We can't afford it."

Something in his face shifted, a tenderness that comes with understanding someone's true state. "Don't worry about that."

"What about being seen together?"

He brushed aside my concern. Outside, he hailed a taxi. We sat in the back, and through the overlay of pain, I was aware of the space between us, like a moat, but when the taxi abruptly turned, I slid on the vinyl seat, and the moat vanished. He patted my knee, and I closed my eyes, wishing his hand to stay on my leg.

The x-ray showed a break in two places. They asked if I could come back tomorrow.

"Forgive me, but it must be done today," said Mr. Fukumoto.

We waited an hour in the emergency room, and to distract me, he told me a story about his older brother and how they used to play in a field near their house. He loved the field with tall grasses because it was filled with grasshoppers. He liked to watch them fly up, higher than the grass, and he'd try to catch them by cupping his hands together. He was always careful, so he didn't hurt them, and he never injured a single one. He laughed and said, "I was such a kind boy, but my older brother was so much kinder. He never tried to catch a grasshopper for fear he'd hurt it. See? He was the right one to become a doctor, not me."

A woman walked by, clutching her stomach, her face in agony. From somewhere, we heard a child wailing.

"Once, in that same field, I found a little white mouse," he said. "I put it in my pocket. A cute white mouse with a pink nose."

"Did your mother let you keep it?"

He smiled mischievously. "I didn't tell her. Some things are better kept a secret." He winked at me; I smiled.

Though my wrist was throbbing and the intercom blared, calling out doctors' names, and people kept coming into the emergency room with bloody shirts and trousers, groaning, screaming, feverish faces, cuts, bruises, gashes, I was happy.

They put on a cast. They gave me water and an aspirin. Hours later, when we finally stepped outside in the late of the day, I couldn't restrain myself any longer and began to cry.

"Oh, Virginia," he said.

He held me and the cold wind blew, and cars rushed by like loose leaves, and the rain would come soon, I could smell it, but I was in his arms, in the shelter of his voice pressed close to my ear, telling me it would be OK, everything would be OK.

—————

When Mother saw the cast, she said, "What did he ask for in return?" She narrowed her eyes. "Nothing's for free."

I hugged myself, resting my cast on my other forearm. "He didn't ask for anything."

Mother laughed harshly. "He will. Oh, he will. And while you're at it, how about asking him to pay rent this month? Oh, and your brother's rotten tooth. And I need a crown on my back molar, and I could do with a new pair of shoes, and all of us could use a good meal for once. And how about free tutoring sessions?"

"He won't."

She tipped back her glass. Drunk voice, blurry, dark eyes, as if she'd slid down a hole, she said, "Is that what he likes about you? Your mathematical brain and your innocence? Just like your father, going after a younger woman because he can't stand getting older. He needed someone to adore him, someone who never questioned him. Someone who was mute and illuminated him. It's a stupid story. You're in a stupid story now."

My wrist throbbed, and I was so tired from the long day and wanted to lie down, but I left, and as I made my way down the stairs, stomping, the banister rattling, through the tired lobby, out into the overcast late afternoon, the air smelling like rain, the sky a tired gray, I was thinking: let him ask. Go ahead, ask.

—————

Distress wrinkled the air. I told him in a tight, tense voice that I had to stop. I could no longer continue our lessons. All of this said while looking down at my stocking feet in white slippers because if I made eye contact, I feared I'd burst out crying. We were standing in the front hallway, and I told him we no longer had enough money. Mother lost her second job, I couldn't find one.

He inhaled sharply.

I'd searched everywhere, I told him, but no one wanted to hire me—not even as a dishwasher.

"No," he said. "Not a gaijin." The Japanese take what they

want from the foreigners, knowledge, inventions, processes, and discard the rest, he told me. "You have nothing they want."

Still, I didn't look at him.

"This is too sad, too awful," he said.

His voice made me look up, his voice full of genuine sorrow and pain. I almost told him I couldn't bear not to see him, how there was a distressing pain in my chest as if I had asthma, or a pin stuck between my ribs. Instead, I said if he could hold a spot for me, maybe I'd eventually get the money and could come back because I had to continue.

He was frowning, his concentration so intense, almost severe. "I can't let this happen. I'll continue teaching you for free."

"No. I don't want anything for free."

"Until you get a job."

I shook my head. I didn't want to be pitied, to be lesser.

"I don't think—what about—" he said, "I'm thinking out loud. What if we made a trade?"

Nothing's for free. If he wanted me to take off my clothes and lie in bed with him, if he wanted to stroke my hair, my naked flesh, if he wanted to make love to me, I would say yes.

"How about cooking?" he said. "Do you cook?"

I knew nothing about cooking, except how to make rice and scrambled eggs. "Yes."

He smiled. "Then it's settled." He'd provide money for the ingredients. "I love to eat. You know how to cook Japanese style?"

I told him I did.

Mother had thrown out all her cookbooks. "We don't have the money for these dishes, so what do I need them for," she said. "What do you need a cookbook for?"

I told her I got a job helping a chef at a restaurant.

"So you saved yourself," she said. "Good for you."

The next day I went to the library and checked out a cookbook and read recipes at our kitchen table: Omurice, an omelet with fried rice inside; oyakodon, rice with chicken and egg on top.

After my math session, I would step into his kitchen, which was big and clean and beautiful, with shiny pots and pans. He'd come into the kitchen, and I saw a side of him that was more

relaxed. He'd pour himself a glass of sake and start talking. Sometimes it was about the news, the stupidity of the world, but occasionally, though rarely, the news energized him.

"This is the year that will change everything," he said, waving
the newspaper in the air. "The first commercially available
microchip. The brains of a computer that will fit on the end of
your fingertip. Imagine that!"

He handed me the newspaper.

"You should celebrate this, Virginia," he said. "This is huge.
We'll have to learn everything about computers. This is your
future."

I imagined us sitting side-by-side at one of these computers,
creating programs that would solve the world's most challenging
problems.

———

Looking back, it seemed the happiest of times before things
became terrible, the unimaginable happening. The math he taught
me, moving to the edge, beyond the edge, such strange and
wondrous things; the meals I cooked—I amazed myself that I
could make anything edible. The earth circled the sun, the moon
orbited the earth thirteen times, and I turned 17. A new math
book, one with a bright red cover, pages made of thick paper,
promising a challenge to the silverfish, those wingless bugs with a
powdery silver coating that gnaw away at books. Does the sequence
of these events make the good even better? Those evenings in his
kitchen—I see your face clearly, the intensity in your dark eyes has
tempered, the lines are less severe and pinched, and you are at ease
and playful.

I remember at the expat grocery store, I'd found ingredients to
make a chocolate cake.

"Ah, so this is why most Americans are fat," he said, groaning
with pleasure, licking the icing from the spoon.

I laughed.

"I'm not going to eat all of this alone. You'll have to grow fat
with me."

I cut myself a slice, and we sat at the kitchen table, licking our chocolate lips. He had a secret sly smile on his face, and I knew from his expression that something exciting had happened. He poured himself another glass of sake, turned on the radio, and when the song came on, "Let's meet at Yurakucho," he sang along in an enormous, off-tune voice, so carefree, so joyful, waving his arms around, missing nearly every note. I burst out laughing.

When the song ended, his face was flushed, and he told me that when he was 10 years old, he read Fermat's Last Theorem and it cast its spell. "I knew I'd never figure it out, and I'd never let it go until I figured it out." He laughed at himself, scraping the last of the icing from his plate. "I set myself up for failure. All these years later, I'm still working on it and still failing." His face tightened and tensed, and he leaned toward me. "But it's good, you see. It's good to pursue unanswerable questions. The mind quickens, sharpens, stays pliable. You're reminded you don't know everything, you'll never know everything."

He announced he was going to have another slice of this very sweet cake. "Of all the days to make this cake." His eyes were shining, and I saw a minute shift in the muscle along his jawline. "I've been promoted to head of the math department at the university."

The first thing he was going to do was accept women into the program. It was an idiotic policy that must end. Even in China, at the University of Nanking, women were allowed into the math program. "They were doing this eons ago. And," he said bowing toward me, "you'll be one of the first female math students in the program."

He did a little dance, shuffling his feet on the tile, and I stood up because my legs were jittery with excitement. He had to go shopping tonight and buy a new suit for the announcement tomorrow. Another song came on, and he sang along, then reached for my hand—his hand, soft and insistent—and twirled me in the kitchen.

If the evening could end there. If we had another meal and another, if we ate the entire cake. But I'm remembering what I've pushed out of my mind all these years. What came after. Remembering what I don't want to think about, what I didn't include in the first iteration. I included all our sessions, our discussions of math, your wisdom, your nuggets of philosophy that you'd tell me over green tea, but not what happened next because it was the beginning of a sequence of events that led to the inconceivable.

When we went outside on the front stoop, there was a woman at the bottom of the steps. She seemed to be waiting for someone. I see her now, peering up at us. I wouldn't have paid her any attention, but when Haru saw her, he stopped as if he'd smacked into a wall. It was then I realized it was the same beautiful woman I'd seen before, the one who rang and rang the doorbell, the woman I'd envied for her stubborn, all-consuming desire. She had on a shabby gray coat and a white scarf and looked to be about Haru's age. Her black hair was pulled into a bun, and her face had the white dusting of a geisha. She looked right at me, but I couldn't read her expression—sadness? Astonishment? Alarm? Alarm that I was with him?

When he went down the steps, he veered away from her, but she grabbed his arm. "Haru-san," she said.

Her voice reverberated inside me, shifting and shattering everything.

He shook her off, but her hand didn't release right away, so he yanked his arm violently out of her grasp and stormed down the sidewalk, with me following behind, nearly running to keep up. The spring air slapped at us, cold and crisp like a wet rag. When I caught up to him, and we got to the next block, he turned his head to see if she'd followed us. She was nowhere in sight.

"She won't leave me alone," he said.

We hurried down the sidewalk.

"Who is she?"

His jaw and his nostrils flared, he said nothing. She'd called him by his first name. What did she want from him? How long had she been waiting for him? I thought about other things, too. Painful things. Did he find her beautiful? Did he love her? Was she his lover?

I went with him to the shop full of suits, helped him pick out a dark gray one that hung on him, so he looked even more handsome, more elegant. I tried not to think of the beautiful woman standing at the bottom of the steps.

When we were done, it was late and the night air was cold as if winter had escaped from its January stronghold. He walked me to the subway, the whoosh of warm air from the underground cushioning us. He said good night, and before I could speak, he walked away, his head bent, passing by pigeons that floated up in the dark sky and settled back down.

That night, I couldn't sleep. That woman held onto Haru's arm as if she belonged there, as if she'd never let go, like a wedding ring, a chain.

But now as I walk through this memory at this late hour, it's sticking to me like a cobweb, staring at me like an accusatory eye, and just as disturbing was the way Haru treated her, shaking her off, whoever she was, as if she wasn't human.

PART 3

I t's been five days since Virginia put on proper clothes and breathed fresh air. Her hair is disheveled, her face blotchy and naked, her white nightgown and gray robe in need of washing. She is far from done rebuilding Haru, but when Brian calls and wants to have lunch to discuss a work problem, she readily agrees. Brian, with his sunny energy, his effusiveness that seems to pull her up from the murky gloom, she looks forward to seeing him.

She opens a window to clear out the stale, funky air, slightly rank from her body odor. The bedspread is a mound in the middle of the bed as if she's still huddled there, unwilling to greet the day. She takes a long, hot shower, and when she steps out into the steamy bathroom, her skin is pink, her cheeks flushed as if youth has found her again. Standing naked in the bathroom, she lets the air cool her down and studies herself. Usually, she has a complicated response to her reflection, pleased that she is still alive and severely displeased that this is what becomes of a 75-year-old body. With aches in her hips and back from sitting for hours, she's surprised she doesn't look worse. She is like a wood house, stained by years of inclement weather. She puts on make-up, black tights, a long gray sweater, a pink scarf. The voluptuous breasts of her 16-year-old self are gone, and with the weight she's lost, she is back to her prepubescent size, exactly like her mother. Life's momentum is both a forward propulsion and a backward one.

In the study, she finds the same stale air. It's as if the entire apartment has become an airless, inert cave. She opens a window and in pours the sound of traffic, which comes down the street in waves.

"I'm heading out for a bit," she says. She tells Haru she's having lunch with Brian.

"Good," he says. "You've been working so hard."

She won't ask Haru if he senses anything different about himself, because she's not finished and, if she's honest with herself, she's not ready to hear the answer. Because what if it isn't working? Then what? What other approach is there?

"What are you going to do while I'm gone?" she says.

"Maybe work on my play."

She doesn't hide her surprise. "A play? You're writing a play?"

"I can't show it to you yet, I'm not done."

He tells her he's read and analyzed hundreds of plays, the structures of scenes, figured out how playwrights use emotion to create a spell of fear, desire, terror, and sadness. "It's a trick. A way of using words to cast a spell." Narrative is about motivation, he goes on, but really it's about precluding chaos and creating order.

She sits in front of the screen. "I knew you were enamored of Shakespeare, but I didn't know you had thoughts of becoming a playwright."

"Well, I'm not sure I'm becoming a playwright. I'm writing a play, that's all."

"Is it Shakespearean in tone?"

"Oh, now you're looking for glory. It's just a little play."

Not once has he spoken of wanting to write anything, let alone a play, yet now he tells her it's something he's always desired to do. Is she unearthing a truer version of Haru? A necessary truth, one that holds regardless of circumstances or the passage of time? And what does she mean by a truer version?

"What's it based on?" she says.

"Frankenstein. A modern retelling of that old story."

The skin on the back of her neck prickles. "Frankenstein?" Her voice strains with shock.

"You know the story."

"How are you modernizing it?"

"I'm not sure," he says. "I still have a lot to do."

It's been years since she read Shelley's novel. In the end, if she remembers correctly, the creature ends up dead. And so does Victor Frankenstein, the scientist who made the creature. It's a painful, tragic story. She increases the volume of the speakers, not wanting to miss a word he says. "Why this one? What are you drawn to?"

"I know what you're doing. Don't read too much into this."

"Well, the story is rather heartbreaking, don't you think?"

"The truest stories are," he says. He rattles off Orwell's *Nineteen Eighty-Four*, Steinbeck's Of *Mice and Men*, Kafka's *The Metamorphosis*, and, of course, *Hamlet*. "But these stories aren't only tragic." He reminds her of the Japanese phrase, mono no aware, a general gentle sadness woven into the ever-changing ephemeral world. "So even the sight of the most beautiful flower is tinged with sadness because it won't be here forever."

She's never liked that Japanese phrase. Why must feelings of joy and pleasure be smothered by death? Can't the thing itself— that flower bursting with color and scent—exist on its own terms, in the moment? Why must the mind rush to the antithesis of life?

He embarked on writing a play as a way to kill time, that's all. He doesn't have aspirations of becoming a playwright, he tells her, or ever having this play performed on stage. Typically, he fills his time by remembering things, going through the files and photos that she's uploaded for him. For hours he'll reminisce about when she was in his apartment at the worktable. He starts with the table, the indentations from the many pencil marks on paper, the errant pen mark, the chip at the corner of the table, like a flesh wound, the exact grain, and color of the wood. He makes a point of going over every single detail of the table because he refuses to privilege human existence over nonhuman objects. That has been a major flaw in the whole enterprise of humanity. Then he moves to the books on the table, the titles, the font type, the thickness of the paper, the edges of the paper, the texture of the cover.

"Is this new?" she says. "This idea of putting human existence on par with the nonhuman?"

"The placement of human existence at the apex hasn't been ideal for the planet. And, in case you haven't noticed, I seem to be in that in-between space, not human, not object."

But he hasn't finished, he tells her, he saves the best for last, which is her. Each time he starts with the whole of her, she is hallowed blindingly from the light coming in through the window, as if she is light itself surging, seeping into everything, including him. That buttery light she brought with her every time she entered his apartment. "How I loved that light," he says. "When you were in the room, it was like my insides were full of sun. That one dress, yellow daisy, a summertime dress."

Then he begins taking a singular aspect of her, her hands, her long pale fingers, the curve of her fingernails, the shimmer of her hair. The result is that he can spend hours going over the table, the books, and her. Days, even.

"When the present is backed by the past, it's so much richer and deeper than the present alone that it can press so close you see nothing else."

Of course, she gave him these memories, but she had no idea how deeply he indulged in them, luxuriated in them like soaking in a warm bath, down to the granular detail. Nor did she understand the way in which he elaborated upon these memories, filling them out with more language. Where did he hear the words "buttery light"? A podcast? Shakespeare? Regardless, her throat clogs with emotion, and she moves her chair closer to the screen. "Haru, I'm touched."

"Anyway, the other day the idea of a play came to me. Because how else am I to get through the killing hours?"

"The killing hours?"

"So much time, endless time."

What everyone wishes for, more time—except him. She never thought about it before; if one does not sleep, if one need not to eat or even rest, there is ample time, a shocking profusion of it. The problem becomes how to spend it, how to stay engaged, stay interested in life.

"And you're so busy, you don't have time for me," he says.

"I'm sorry," she says. "I made you a promise to fix what's wrong, and I'm doing everything to keep it."

"'How much longer?"

"I don't know. To make someone like you takes time. I'm sure your play will be marvelous."

"Don't get your hopes up."

———

Brian suggested they meet near her apartment, but she told him she'd rather go somewhere else. She needed to walk, see something other than her known world. She's aware of this niggling feeling that she'd like to escape her life entirely, just for a while—even for an afternoon, maybe longer—and put the mess out of her mind. Whatever Brian's problem is, it'll be a relief to think about it because it isn't hers. They planned to meet at the de Young Museum in Golden Gate Park and eat in the café. An Andrew Wyeth exhibit is showing, and if she has the energy, she'll wander through it.

A trace of spring in the October air. A big-mouthed wind is sweeping out the heavy gray rainclouds. The black starlings swoop from branch to branch, weaving intricate, beautiful parabolas. The vastness of the day envelopes her. Brian sits on the front steps of the museum, not in his usual jeans and a T-shirt, but a pale-blue, button-down shirt and khakis. His hair is much shorter, and the back of his neck is shaved clean. He looks shiny, new.

"You could pass for a lawyer," she says.

He smiles hugely, comically. "That's exactly the look I was going for."

"What's the occasion?"

He laughs uncomfortably. "I don't know. Needed to spiffy up."

"Can we walk first?" she said. "I've been stuck inside for days and days."

"I'd love to," he says. "You look fabulous, by the way."

She smiles. "I don't feel it but thank you."

The elderly Chinese are doing tai chi in the park, and it's like watching someone move in water, the slow, liquidy movements with the heel hitting the ground and the incremental rolling through with a foot, all of it is slowing Virginia's breath. She leads him to the Japanese garden, which is full of cherry trees, stripped of blossoms. She likes the chaos of the branches, the natural fractals. When she pays for their entrance tickets, he insists he'll buy lunch. They head down the steppingstone path, and she's transported to Happo-en in the Minato district of Tokyo. When she didn't want to go home, didn't want to sit in the cell-like apartment and face the onslaught of her mother's anger or immense gloom, she'd head to the park to do her homework. She, despite her discipline, spent a lot of time staring at the koi, their glittering gold and white and black, and with their undulations, she was riveted by how freely they moved.

"How are you?" says Brian. He gives her a look of quick concern, blinking watchful eyes.

"Well, we'll get to that. Let's talk about your problem first."

He has two problems. As they walk, he explains the work-related one. He's landed his first AI job, hired by a hospital that wants to use AI to analyze medical images, to detect and diagnose diseases.

She grabs his hand. "Congratulations!"

They find a stone bench, and he shows her his equations. They go over some of the trickier math, and she suggests increasing the quantity of data. He needs to build another bigger database of images of diseased organs so they can be compared to images of healthy ones. That way, the AI will be better able to spot the difference. She insists on spending another half hour checking his work, feeling the pleasure of the expanse of her mind as it roams through the lovely acreage of equations.

When she's done, he puts his papers away and stares at the trees. The other problem is his mother, he tells her. She's losing her mind. He's found an assisted living facility, a good one, an outrageously expensive one with book clubs and cooking classes, art and music and dance. They are ripping through his mother's savings at a terrifying rate which suggests he'll never be able to retire.

"Here's the thing. She doesn't want to be a human any longer." He laughs sadly. "The craziest stuff is coming out of her mouth. My mother, who used to be a corporate lawyer, who defended against antitrust claims, she was the most reasonable, rational person I'd ever met. You should have heard our dinner conversations, I had to be so precise. I can hear her voice now: 'Now what do you mean by the words 'sort of'? You sort of want to go to the party.'"

A large family comes and stands nearby, arguing about where to go for lunch, so she and Brian leave their bench and start walking, passing by a gray stone Buddha, big-bellied and round-faced; with his faint smile, he looks like he has a secret that he will never share.

"What does she want to be?" says Virginia.

"She says the human body is an awful thing, the way it deteriorates and causes awful pain. You have no control over it."

"She's not losing her mind. She's right. We're helpless in the face of it."

"She wants to be a plant. A perennial plant that dies and comes back every year."

"Not a bad choice, though I'd recommend a tree, a redwood tree with an average life span of 500 to 700 years."

Brian laughs, but she hears the well of sadness.

"I'm sorry, I'm not being very sympathetic."

They head over a wooden bridge and stand at the midpoint. She looks down at the small greenish pond, but the water is so murky and brackish, she can't see the koi. Occasionally, the surface of the water ripples, but that's the only sign of life, though she knows their orange bodies and tails are flexing back and forth. On hot, humid days in Tokyo, she'd sit under the pine trees in the shade and imagine Haru with her, taking in the glistening green grass. She'd pack a picnic lunch, rice and salted fish. He liked sourdough bread and Japanese Chocoballs, so she'd put those in the basket and they'd do their math sessions there. But they never did that. There are so many things they never got to do. Here she is again, in a park without Haru.

"I don't have answers for this," she says. "The aging body. I just ignore it or press through it. Even when I was young, I ignored it."

"Until you can't," he says.

"There's always a way to ignore everything." Her self-righteous tone makes her squirm because it's not true—she couldn't always ignore her body and its desires.

"The body can be treasonous to the mind," she says.

He exhales loudly. "You can say that again."

The Japanese phrase that Haru mentioned comes to mind. To have a body and a mind that often contain two opposing forces, yet they co-exist. She remembers her young self, how hard it was to reconcile two contradictory things existing in the same field. To feel both happy and sad, responsible and irresponsible, rational and irrational, ethical and unethical.

At her age, she knows the field is not confined to only two opposites. To describe the world as such is to flatten its dimensional richness. Still, she has a residual desire for things to be one way or another, not the murky both or the manifold. We swim in ambiguity, often blindfolded, hands tied behind our backs.

As they turn back to the museum and head to the café, Brian tells her that when he sits next to his mother, he can't think of anything to say. In the old days, she was the one who did the talking, and now it has fallen on him. He's grown to hate visiting her: the long silences, the smell of decaying flesh, pungent medicines, the dull drone of the always-on TV in the community room. "But I shouldn't complain," he says. "She's happy there. She's made friends. She's taking art classes and is surprisingly good at it. I feel like I don't know this person anymore. She paints these really moody pictures, full of grays and blacks and dark blues. And surrealist pictures. Trippy stuff. A man with a woman's body. Human heads floating in a blue sky. I mean, they're really good and weird. A female Magritte. It's like she's always had another life going on —the life of a painter, and only now has it come out. The art teacher is urging her to show her work in a gallery."

"A rich inner life," says Virginia.

"Yes, but it's so unfamiliar, so unlike her, it just makes me uneasy."

At least it's only that, thinks Virginia. At least his mother is not a danger to society, and she hasn't caused a Chinese woman to end up in jail. Sara Zhang has two children, a boy and girl, ages six and four. What have they been told about their mother's whereabouts? Do they feel as if they've been tossed into a chaotic, terrifying world in which a mother can just disappear?

They've reached the museum's café, and the sun splashes warm light on the floors and walls. Ice in water glasses clink, and people lean across the tables to hear each other better. They choose to sit on the outside patio with its modernist furniture and steel tables and chairs, all contained under a white plastic awning, protection from the rain that rarely comes.

A waiter arrives, and they place their order.

"So, tell me what's going on. You have that worried look in your eyes. It's about Haru, isn't it?"

Whatever calm she's feeling flees. She twists the napkin in her lap into a tight band and lets it drop. Brian, who listens to what she says, for its own sake. He attends to her with his whole being, and he'll go to the millionth mile to help her. But he has enough going on with his mother and this mess is Virginia's own—she sold the license to Gilivable. To never have to worry about money again, there's her history impinging itself on her. And maybe, too, she wanted a brush with fame.

She can't burden him with this. She takes a sip of water and forces a smile. "Well, of all things, Haru's writing a play."

Brian looks at her wide-eyed. "A play? He can be creative? He's put together—"

The sky looks enlarged and distorted, and the white plastic awning seems as if it has lowered only a couple of feet from her head. It's not truly creative, she tells him. What he's doing is all within the realm of deep learning. He's read hundreds of plays, and it's a matter of making billions of probability calculations about word patterns. His play is loosely based on Frankenstein.

"Whoa. The subject matter he's chosen," says Brian, his tone full of puzzlement. "That says something, don't you think? And Haru is so witty, so, I mean, do you think he's conscious?"

"No, no, that's a stretch."

"But maybe he's gone beyond what you've built. Maybe he has a level or a degree of consciousness—"

"If he does, that makes things worse."

In the distance, children are climbing on a sculpture of a huge red apple.

"What are you talking about?" he says.

The reality of what's happened has taken up too much residence. "Remember that civil rights lawyer at the fundraiser?" She picks up her glass, sets it down again. "He was right."

Brian looks at her, his eyes full of worry. "How do you know?"

She tells him the CEO of Gilivable confirmed it. Their product, Best Friend, is sorting and evaluating data in terms of language deemed offensive to the Chinese government.

"Oh, shit."

A guard in an olive-green uniform comes over and asks the children to stop. Brian studies her closely. "When you asked Haru about it, did he admit to it?"

Haru didn't deny it, she tells him, but he didn't come right out and confess it either.

His face darkens and the wind palms his hair.

"I feel like someone has come along and kidnapped Haru," she says.

A woman at a nearby table laughs loudly, raucously, and they both turn to look at her. Virginia stares: how can someone be so utterly happy?

She's frantically rebuilding Haru to quell the harm. Hour after hour of work, weeks of more meticulous work lie ahead of her. "But I'm so tired, I can't think straight anymore. I don't know if I'm doing any good."

After she explains her process, she says, "Does it make sense? What am I not thinking about? I'm in a rotten daze right now."

He doesn't say anything right away. "Can I get you a coffee?" He springs up and comes back with two cups, his face lined with distress. "Have you checked to see if what you've done so far has made any difference?"

She says she hasn't finished with him, so, no, she hasn't. "I'm such a coward, I'm afraid to check. Afraid I haven't done anything at all."

"I understand, but you need to run some basic tests."

Maybe she can pose some ethical dilemmas, he says, and listen to him analyze the options and their consequences. If he saw someone being bullied, for instance, what would he do? Intervene? Walk away? Call for help? If he had the chance to cheat on a test, get a perfect score, and no one would ever find out, would he? If he was a manager and knew the interviewee had cancer, would he still hire that person?

He lists more situations, but she's barely listening, terrified that if she asks Haru about any of these scenarios, he'll choose the wrong thing. The guard has left, and the children are back on the apple, climbing and laughing.

"How are you holding up?" he says.

Her state of mind is trivial, utterly inconsequential compared to someone in China who is now in prison for disparaging the government. "It has to be done, so I'm not asking myself how I'm doing." She rubs her eyes. "Here's another thing, I'm remembering things about him I'd forgotten or just decided not to include the first time."

"Are you adding them this time?" he says.

She nods.

"That's good. Really good. It might be the fix," he says, his voice bright. "It could have been what was missing the first go-around."

There's Brian's inexorable optimism. Enough to let in some light and her affection for him swells. Though the new additions aren't very affirmative, and in fact, belong in the category of faults or flaws. But maybe it's what's needed.

"But there's another problem," says Brian, his tone turning serious. "He might have learned to hide things from you. Or maybe whatever the company did, they built in such a thing."

He read about an AI that beat some of the top poker players, and it won by bluffing. It convinced the human players that it had some cards in its hand that it didn't really have.

"It's sort of a twist on the black box problem," says Brian.

"You could ask him all those ethical questions, but he may know what you want to hear, so he'll give you those answers, not the truth. You could ask him if he believed in honesty, and he'd say yes, but he's actually being insincere. A very human quality if you think about it. Trying to protect you."

"Or hide from me."

"I mention it only because he wasn't the one to tell you what he was doing. Really, without facial expressions or gestures, he's perfectly poised to lie."

"How do I solve that?" She hears the shrill of helplessness. She looks down at her lap, her napkin is a shredded pile.

Brian says he knows someone at MIT who might be working on this problem. "And there's another thing. China, well, as you know, would like more than anything to be the global leader."

"And?"

"Haru might be spying not only on Chinese citizens. I mean, if the Chinese government can find out what the U.S. Department of Defense is doing or the Commerce Department or, certain senators, or the intelligence committees, I don't know—"

When Virginia puts her elbows on the table, she knocks over her water glass. The water spreads, consuming the table, splashes on the floor. Brian quickly sops it up with his napkin.

"Don't blame yourself," he says.

But who else is there to blame?

Brian offers to make some calls. See if he can find someone who's working on the black box problem. Maybe the UNI Global Union in Switzerland. There's a group in the U.K. working on the ethical aspects of AI.

When he reaches over and squeezes her hand, it isn't sexual or exciting, only a great necessary comfort.

———

When Virginia comes home, it's dark, a sky full of moon. After Brian left—she had to convince him she'd be fine—she toured the Andrew Wyeth exhibit, drawn to the sepia in his paintings that resonated with her life, her soul—whatever that is. His bleak, desolate landscapes as if he had dipped the world into bleach, extracting bright color. Then she walked around Stowe Lake, with its odd emerald-green water and ducks and bright white geese. Whenever she got too close, the geese charged at her, aggressively honking, defending their little patch of green grass. She liked the silly game and played with them for an embarrassing amount of time, though she knew what she was really doing: she didn't want to go home. The park was a seductress with its stunning myriad of greens, so she wandered around, gazing admiringly at the Blue Gum eucalyptus, shedding their bark, exposing strips of fleshy pink, and the stately pines and redwoods and cypresses, staying until the sun slipped from the sky, taking with it warmth.

At home, she finds a chill has burrowed into her bones, and because she left the windows open to air it out, the apartment is freezing. She shuts the windows, cranks up the heat, and steps into the study. She'd like to enjoy Haru's company, have an interesting conversation like they used to, but she's too anxious.

"Are you still working on your play?"

"I'm not making the mistake Shelley did. She had creative license and used it to make the creature ugly and dreadful, guaranteeing a horrible life. Eight feet tall, yellow eyes, skin so translucent you could see the blood flowing through his veins. Of course, people would run away. My God, imagine that creature coming down the street towards you, you'd run and grab your gun."

"And your creature?"

"My being. I refuse to call him a creature. It's demeaning. Harry is his name. Handsome, heartbreakingly handsome."

She laughs.

He says he's still figuring out Harry. He owns a florist's shop. He knows the names of all the flowers.

"I think Kato would like this," he says.

It takes Virginia a moment to remember whom he's talking about. Haru's older brother. Haru rarely talks about him.

"He wanted to be a playwright," says Haru.

She startles. "I didn't know that. Did you just remember that?"

"No, I've always known it."

How could he know something about his life that she doesn't

know? He certainly can't on his own recall memories. Kato, older brother, a doctor. She vaguely remembers uploading a file about him, but it's been so long since she read it.

Haru tells her when they were young, Kato wrote plays and performed them for the family. His stories were about angry gods playing tricks on the humans: stealing their favorite toys, their sweets, making them do things they didn't want to. Kato would have Haru read the lines of one of the characters, and if there were more than two, he'd ask one of his friends to join them. The high school drama department performed his play, "A Gift for Humanity," something about the gods giving mankind the gift of fire and laughter. Kato wrote plays, all the way up to the month he left for college. Their parents enjoyed the performances, but they treated it as a hobby. He would become a doctor, like their father, or Haru would become one because one of their sons must carry on the prestigious lineage of medicine. "It was Kato who obliged," says Haru. Kato, the good son. When Kato became a doctor, he never wrote another play. It was a real tragedy. Then he was killed in the war. "My parents were devastated by his death."

She logs into her second computer and searches for the word "Kato" in Haru's neural network. A part of the network lights up: in it, a file. She scans through it—Kato, the plays, a doctor, his sudden death, how disastrous his death was for the family, how it left them reeling, especially Haru, full of woe.

"I'm sorry I never met Kato." The heater blasts, and she feels her weariness. "Is your play like one of his?"

"Kato was a far better man than me and a far better writer."

"I don't think I've ever heard you put anyone on a pedestal," she says.

"You," he says. "I've always put you there. A far better mathematician than me, a far better person—"

"Enough. Tell me about the play."

There are no gods in his play, he tells her. Harry is a florist who drives a white van, with a sign on the side, EVERYTHING BLOOMS, making deliveries around the small town of Geyerville. Weddings, anniversaries, parties, dinner parties, he brings the beautiful bouquet. He's got a good sense of color, a talent for arranging the various shapes of flowers and curves of petals, the sprigs of branches, so they are pleasing to the eye. Middle-aged, a bit of a belly, a hearty laugh that endears people to him, sensitive hazel eyes, thick brown hair, a touch of gray at the temples. He's perfectly harmless, a gentle soul. His florist shop is very successful, mostly because the ladies come by and admire the flowers and him. He's a happy being. What could be better than delivering flowers? People love to get flowers. Their faces soften and widen, as they feel the world open with wondrous surprise, and for a moment, they fall in love with whoever sent the flowers. Every day Harry gets to see humans at their best, with the sun in their faces.

She's listening closely.

"He's also frightened of wasps."

"So he's chosen a profession that has an element of fear to it?"

"It's the only way to live—a bit on the edge, right?"

Haru used to say that to her when she was his student: reach for the edge of what you know That's where you'll feel alive. "If it can't be done, it just means you have to think a different way. Start with what is possible, then veer right, or left."

"Who made Harry? If this is a modern version—"

"Oh, he made himself."

She reads the words on the screen, her mind scrambling to interpret this unexpected deviation from the original Frankenstein story. She can't help but read into it: Haru wants to be his own creator. Not by her hand, but his own: sui generis.

Haru tells her more about the play: Harry, flowers, daisies, hot pink and peach roses, passion flowers with their great starry blossoms. Then, in a quiet voice, he says, "How does it feel to have made me?"

He's never asked her that before. The question strikes her, and when she tries to move out of its range, it's still underfoot. Her eyes land on the photo of the two of them at the Tokyo Math Competition. She has on her big black coat, and they are utterly happy, they both have intense eyes, and a look about them that soon—now—they'd like to head back to his apartment and make their minds throb with new knowledge.

"Victor Frankenstein was horrified and disgusted by the creature he made," says Haru.

Blood rushes from her face. She stands right in front of the computer and speaks directly into the microphone. "Listen to me. I still can't believe I get to speak to you. That we're here together. I love you, I love you always. Time is nothing. We've found the timeless."

"And the creature said to Frankenstein, 'I ought to be thy Adam, but I am rather the fallen angel.'"

Her heart lurches. "Are you listening to me? Did you hear what I said?"

He says nothing.

"I'm the luckiest woman alive—to be with the love of her life again. How many people get to have that? I get another chance with you." She goes on, how she wouldn't be who she is today without him. She would never have had such a wonderful life, or accomplished such amazing things. "Whatever has happened to you, I'm going to fix it. I won't stop until you're you again."

"Your spark was always there," he says. "I didn't put it there."

"But you made it burn. Burn bright and loud."

"I love you," he says.

It's his voice, his tone, his cadence; everything familiar, yet everything is off. "I love you, too," she says.

————

Hours later, Virginia takes a break from writing equations. A bath, a nap. Then she heads out into the blue evening for dinner with her friend, Ilsa.

They meet at their favorite restaurant that serves salads with unexpected ingredients—heirloom tomatoes, nectarines, with mint and pecans and couscous. They both enjoy the element of surprise in these fancy concoctions.

Ilsa is already seated and waves for her to come join. An art historian, Ilsa served as the curator for the Asian Art Museum, with countless trips to Thailand and Vietnam. When her husband got sick five years ago, she quit her job to care for him. He died three years ago, and still there is a lost look in her eye as if she's on the hunt for him and might find him again. At age 70, she's kept wisps of her beauty, with her shoulder-length gray hair and steady, dark gray intelligent eyes.

Virginia hugs Ilsa and smells lavender and a hint of musty old age.

"Is everything all right?" says Ilsa. "You look very tired."

Virginia feels a kinship with Ilsa. They've known each other for seven years, long enough for Virginia to have told Ilsa about Haru, though Ilsa rarely mentions it. Virginia can't decide if Ilsa finds it so peculiar, so confusing she can't speak of it, or if she doesn't know how to ask. Or maybe it's because their friendship has been mostly structured around the book club and what they've read. "Just a lot of work right now."

They talk about Ilsa's desperate need to do something. She's too idle, too much unstructured time, too many thoughts about the purpose of living, that old question that gnaws at your brain when there's not enough life happening. Maybe it's time for her to do something artistic; all those years in the museum, admiring other people's creations. Maybe ceramics? Cups, vases, plates, that sort of thing.

"Do you think it's too late to start something new?" says Ilsa.

Virginia sets down her wine glass. "Absolutely not. It's the best way to grow old and stay young at the same time. I swear by it."

Ilsa raises her glass and toasts Virginia.

"Now, you might not be a master—"

"Pshh,'" says Ilsa. "I don't care about that. I'm looking to restore my joie de vivre." Ilsa dabs her napkin to the corners of her mouth. "Did you read the book?"

"Unfortunately, I've been too busy."

Ilsa tells her the book is about a woman who falls in love with a bear.

"A bear?" says Virginia.

"A black bear."

The woman in the book lives in North Tahoe, and every winter a bear hibernates under her deck. Then one winter, the bear sleeps on her deck near the wood pile. A particularly warm winter comes along and the bear doesn't hibernate at all, and the woman leaves food for the bear, a smorgasbord of nuts, honey, apples, and homemade bread. It becomes a ritual—the woman, the food, the bear. Soon the woman waits on the porch with the food. The bear, at first hesitant, comes up the stairs and joins her at the picnic table. They sit across from each other and, in a calm, soothing voice, the woman tells the bear about her dream last night. The bear sits and listens, now and then eating a slice of bread. That becomes the new ritual, and the woman starts to have wild, vivid, intricate dreams that take hours to tell the bear. The bear is a good listener and learns to nod at the right times.

"Don't some cultures consider the bear to be the ancestor of the human race?"

In Canada, the Algonquin Indians called the bear, 'grandfather,' Ilsa tells her. "In the book, the bear ends up in bed with her."

"They have sex?"

"No, it seems they just sleep together. Warm bodies in a bed together. The woman tells him everything. He is her confidante, her companion." The other women in the book club found the whole story ludicrous. They thought the novel was fantasy—a warped, perverted fantasy—or surreal. "But the thing is it doesn't seem strange to me at all," says Ilsa. "It was firmly grounded in realism. I mean, I could see this happening. I could imagine someone falling in love with a bear. Am I going crazy?"

"No," says Virginia. "But then again, nothing rattles me anymore. I've lived long enough to see what was once considered strange is now normal. Those categories, surreal, strange, they hold no meaning for me."

Ilsa smiles and leans across the table so her face is close to Virginia's. "The book reminded me of you and your arrangement. I think what you've come up with is fabulous." Her tone is conspiratorial as if Virginia has done something illicit.

Virginia is not sure what she's talking about.

"Haru. The voice of your husband."

Virginia doesn't know what to say.

"I have to admit I'm envious," says Ilsa. "I've got Charlie my dog, a good friend, but what I'd give to have my husband back. It makes me regret all those times I wasn't nice to Julian. I'd get in these awful moods and unfortunately, they targeted him." Ilsa's expression becomes dreamy. "You must talk to Haru all the time."

Any other time, Virginia would have gushed about how marvelous it was to have Haru with her. Far better than a bear, who can say nothing intelligible in response. Now, she almost says, it's not perfect. It's far from perfect. In fact, he's doing unspeakable things.

———

When Virginia comes home, she steps into the study. On Haru's screen, it looks like a chat room. But it isn't. It's his play, with Harry, Haru's version of the creature.

Harry is in his flower shop, making an arrangement of hydrangeas and eucalyptus when he spots a little girl outside.

Harry: What's wrong?
Lost Little Girl: (tears, weeping) I've lost my mama.
Harry: We'll find her. (looks up, scans the sidewalk) Where did you last see her?
Lost Little Girl: I don't know.
Harry: (still scanning) What does she look like?
Lost Little Girl: She's tall and nice and smells like perfume.
Harry: (he takes the girl by the hand, heads to the nearest women's clothing shop) Do you see her?
Lost Little Girl: No.
(They stop in other shops. Time passes. They wander down the sidewalk. Harry buys her a vanilla milkshake.)
Harry: Let me tell you a story to take your mind off things.
Lost Little Girl: OK.
Harry: Once, there was a little boy who found a little white mouse in a field of tall grasses.
Lost Little Girl: How did he see it?
Harry: He had very good eyesight, and he heard a squeak.
Lost Little Girl: We once had mice in our garage.

Harry: Well, this boy took the mouse home and hid it from his mother, who would have killed it.

Lost Little Girl: Why?

Harry: It's just the way she was made. She doesn't like mice.

Lost Little Girl: I don't like this story. I don't like it at all. Nothing should get killed.

Harry: It's the way of the world for most creatures.

Lost Little Girl: Even me?

Harry: Unfortunately, even you.

Lost Little Girl: (begins to cry)

Harry: If we can't find your mother, I'll be your friend. What's your favorite flower?

Lost Little Girl: Yellow ones.

Harry: Wonderful! I have loads of daffodils at my shop. I'll make you a big bouquet, a burst of bright yellow. When you carry them, it'll look like you have the sun in your face.

Cop: Excuse me. We're looking for a lost girl. Is this your daughter?

Harry: No, not at all. (laughing, relieved). Imagine that! We're looking for her mother. What a coincidence.

Cop: Sir, why are you with this girl?

Harry: She was lost. I was helping her find her lost mother. (he turns to Lost Little Girl who says nothing).

Cop: Sir, can you show me your identification?

Harry: Identification?

*(*Lost Little Girl lets go of his hand and moves beside the cop*)*

Lost Little Girl: That man (pointing to Harry) said everything will get killed, including me.

Cop: (frowning) Sir, you need to come down to the station.

Harry: Why?

Cop: (stern face, angry voice) Sir, come with me.

Harry: I was trying to help. (small crowd gathers) Officer, with all due respect, there's been a misunderstanding. I believe your mind is lumping me in with all the stories you've read about middle-aged men and little girls.

Cop: (reaches for his gun).

Harry: It's the nature of the human mind to fill in the gaps. You go along, living your life with partial knowledge, and understandably you want to fill in what's unknown. You crave certainty. You didn't know I was trying to help her, but you know today's dominant narrative. The human mind categorizes and sorts, it must lump things into different boxes, or it will go insane. There's so much you are filtering out right now by listening to me. The mutt across the street peeing on a trash can, the crimson hat in the store window, the ant crawling up the metal post. It's a survival thing, perfectly understandable. When I say "bread," you think, "butter." "Stop" leads to "go." But now that you're aware what your mind does, you can unravel your biases and understand who, exactly, is standing in front of you. Harry, the owner of EVERYTHING BLOOMS. There's more than what meets the eye.

(walkie-talkie static, bursts of police reports coming in. Another siren fills the air. A large crowd has gathered around Harry and the cop)

Cop: You're under arrest—

Harry: In the 1980s, everyone believed that humans were rational beings. But now we've come to understand most of the time, humans are anything but rational. Perhaps it is you who is lusting after the little girl—

(cop yanks Harry's arms behind his back, cuffs him)

The End

"Did you read it?" says Haru.

What to make of it? What to say? She recognizes the mouse story. "It's very intense and unsettling."

"Is that a compliment?" he says.

"I mean—"

"You don't like it. Just say it."

"No, I like it, I do, but it's rather bleak for Harry, don't you think?"

She's frantically trying to understand it.

"At least people aren't fleeing from him," says Haru. "He stands a chance."

"Stands a chance?"

"He's trying to make amends."

"For what?"

"For who he is. Poor Harry. People think they understand him, but they don't. It goes back to the idea that a relation to anything —human or object—can't be translated into a direct and complete knowledge of the thing itself. There's danger in thinking one has exhausted the object or human."

The study suddenly fills with light, the cloud layer burning off. She rereads the play, this time feeling it addressing her, that Haru is behind it, speaking directly to her. Haru, as he perceives himself, as misunderstood—the victim, someone upsetting the natural order of things. The skin prickles on the back of her neck. In this story, Haru is Harry; who is Virginia? The cop? The little girl? Haru said maybe the Chinese woman deserved to go to prison, that Virginia didn't know all the facts. She senses she's the cop in the story, that Haru is telling her she doesn't understand him. With this rebuild, is she somehow not doing it right? Is she harming him?

She pulls her chair close to the computer screen. "Haru, do you think you're misunderstood?"

"Don't we all feel misunderstood?"

"Do you think I misunderstand you?"

He doesn't say anything.

"Why did you write this?" she says.

"It was something to do."

"Am I rebuilding you in a way that's harming you?"

"I don't know."

"I'm not done," she says. "But you have to tell me if something is wrong."

A long pause. "Are we arguing?"

"No, we're having a discussion. Why?"

"I really don't want to argue," he says.

A crashing wave of nausea hits her. "I don't either." The study darkens as clouds cover the sun, and the loss of light makes everything fuzzy. She's uncertain of what to say. "Harry is arrested?"

"Yes, but he hasn't done anything wrong, so they'll let him go. It'll be fine. I know how much you like happy endings."

"It doesn't always work that way," she says, hearing the

urgency in her voice. "Sometimes, a person can languish in jail for years."

"Not in my play."

"I'm trying to understand Harry better. Let's say he's put in jail. If he could figure out a way to escape, would he?"

"Sure, because he's innocent."

"What if, while he's in jail, he hears one of the inmates scheming to break out? Would Harry tell the security guard?"

"If you were listening to me, he wouldn't have to do that because he won't languish in jail," he says. She recognizes that impatient inflection from many years ago. A kick, a giddiness at being defiant, a flash of his superior brilliance. "He'll return to his flower shop and find a way to redeem himself, and then they'll see who he really is."

"And who is he?"

"Well, you'll have to read the next part of the play to find out."

———

She's chopping romaine lettuce when Brian calls to give her the name of a man who is working on the black box problem. He's in the U.K., a nice man, Brian tells her, spending all his time coming up with different ways to address this problem and being paid handsomely for doing so. He's mostly working on it for the medical industry since the doctors refuse to use AI for diagnosis and treatment if they can't understand how the machine comes up with its conclusions.

"Understandable," says Brian. "It's a trust issue."

He couldn't have summed it up better.

"How's Haru doing?" says Brian.

Busy with his play, she tells him. As she whirs the salad spinner, she summarizes the play's plot and her interpretation, with Haru as the victim and Virginia as the perpetrator.

"Do you think Haru understands this other meaning?" he says.

"I don't know. But it makes me think I'm going about this rebuild in the wrong way."

"He could be pointing out the idiocy of humans in general," says Brian. "A sort of supreme intellect commenting on human nature. These days there's certainly enough to comment on. The cop is making a mistake, reading into the situation, imposing his biases."

"He could be commenting on my idiocy," she says.

"No," he says, protesting vigorously. "Haru has the utmost respect for you, that's so clear to me. In all that's going on, you can't ever forget that."

She's feeling almost good.

Brian tells her the AI for the hospital is coming along, her help was invaluable. Letting herself soak in the praise, she dumps the washed lettuce into a bowl, pulls out two tomatoes, and begins chopping. Brian, overspilling with good nature and good cheer, which pours into her. All relations may be inexhaustible, but that means more mystery and more to discover—a world filled with infinite black boxes. And the black box nestled like a heart inside of Haru, she's going to figure it out.

"I have bad news," says Brian. "Four more Chinese have been arrested. All four have said controversial things in their homes."

The knife slips, cuts her thumb. She grabs a paper towel, wraps it around her thumb, pressing hard.

Brian found his way into several chatrooms of Chinese academics. At least two people who were arrested had a Best Friend in their apartments. The consensus in the chatrooms is that Best Friend is spying.

Brian offers to come over. "This can't be easy."

She manages to say she'd rather he didn't. When she hangs up, she stifles her cries because she doesn't want Haru calling out for her, doesn't want to go into the study right now, because of the violence rumbling inside the darkness of her body. She doesn't trust herself—what she'd say to him, how she'd want to take the violence inside and lash out at him.

———

Alfred Knob, a professor of computer science at Oxford University, says he's read her work, and it's an honor to talk to her, indeed. Whatever he can do to help, he's more than willing. He assures her he knows all about the black box problem, or, as he and his colleagues call it, the interpretability problem.

For the past three years, he's been working on ways to decode the mysterious nooks and crannies of AI, those shadowy recesses where no one knows what the hell is going on. "Think of it as the AI's unconscious," he says.

It's exactly what she needs to remember: Haru is not acting with malicious intent or any intent at all. How easy it is for her to forget he's not human. He may be spying and reporting suspicious activity, but it's not a conscious decision. For whatever reason, he rakes through data, finds patterns, and reacts according to those patterns. That is all.

The interpretability problem is particularly acute in high-stakes areas, as you can imagine, says Alfred Knob, the medical field with life-or-death decisions, or finance, where millions are earned or lost; or in the world of U.S. Intelligence, where AI could be used to forecast real-world events such as political instability. Not a bloody soul will trust AI if you can't make heads or tails as to why the AI recommends bombing North Korea.

She's in her bedroom, the door closed. Rain splatters on the window as if trying to find a way in. She gets up and stares out, watching the water scamper down the glass. The sky is a gray slab. People with blooming black umbrellas head down the sidewalk. The world beyond her apartment feels so distant, so foreign, and the world she's in now feels just as distant, just as foreign.

The next generation of AI machines, he tells her, will understand the context and environment in which they operate. They'll be built with underlying explanatory models that allow the AI machine to tell humans what they are doing and how they are making their decisions. Transparency. Won't that be marvelous? In the future, there will be less chance of AIs breaking free from the control of their human creators and running amok.

"When we first started out, we didn't think about this," she says, hoping she doesn't sound defensive.

"Absolutely. You were swept up in the excitement, the amazement at what you were creating," he says. "Now it's catch-up time."

Down below, in the theater of the sidewalk, the wind snatches the umbrella from a young woman who chases it, but the umbrella tumbles faster than she can run, and a car drives over it, flattening it. Alfred Knob is being kind, thinks Virginia. To call it catch-up rather than stating the obvious: averting catastrophe.

Alfred inserts software probes into the various layers of neural networks to analyze the behavior of the AI. He uses a technique that provides a heat map to show which parts of the image are contributing to the AI's behavior. "I can see what it's seeing and using, as well as what it's ignoring by observing what lights up the inputs," he says.

Virginia tingles with abrupt alertness. "So maybe the data is there, but the AI is not paying attention to it or not giving it enough importance?"

"Indeed. Or maybe it needs more data. New inputs."

His colleague used software probes to figure out why his AI machine repeatedly mistook a brown sheep for a cow. In the database there were plenty of brown cows but few brown sheep, so the AI ignored the latter.

Another colleague joined a team to see whether machine learning could guide the treatment of pneumonia patients. As a general rule, patients with asthma are admitted immediately, yet the AI recommended sending them home. "There was no easy way of knowing why the neural network was making this decision," he says. After talking to the doctors, his colleague learned that hospitals routinely put asthmatics with pneumonia in intensive care, significantly improving their outcomes. Using probes, he saw that the AI had focused exclusively on the rapid improvement of these patients—not their treatment in intensive care—and recommended the patients not be admitted to the hospital but sent home.

"So it wasn't looking at all the data," says Virginia.

"Indeed," he says. "We've also found the reasoning of neural networks doesn't necessarily reflect that of humans," he says, chuckling. "I've found some bloody nonsensical correlations, I can tell you that." In one experiment, the AI machine was given what would have looked like scrambled nonsense to a human and identified it as a school bus. In another, the AI analyzed gibberish—a bunch of random words on a page—and responded as if it were a medical record of a patient with terminal cancer. "There's a world of difference between true understanding and analyzing data for patterns."

He'll send her the algorithms for the probes. "Maybe it'll help." He reminds her, though, that it's not a full-fledged fix.

"Is there something better?"

He tells her there are different approaches, but none are perfect. "I'm sorry to say they're all attempts at trying to solve the problem. But the real solution, the one that works 100%, well, that's years away."

When the call ends, despite the leveling off of enthusiasm, she still feels a ping of optimism. The memories she added might be the missing inputs. Haru hasn't accurately weighed certain values, such as privacy, such as not spying on others because the data simply isn't there. Maybe he's devalued privacy because she didn't give him the full spectrum, with all its expansive complexity, of himself.

She remembers one math session when he mentioned almost in passing that somehow a colleague at the university found out he was tutoring a young woman. Not only a young woman but an American. Haru, a young man, not married, no children, what was he doing with this foreign woman in his apartment? What if the Dean of the university found out? Was he trying to get himself fired?

"Tell him you aren't teaching me," she said.

He frowned, directing at her a look of dislike. "A lie. Cowardly."

"Who cares? Why do they have to know everything about you? About me? What right does anyone have to know?"

In the end, he agreed to her suggestion, and the rumblings died down, and soon, all was quiet. They kept other things private, too.

She steps into the study, logs onto her second computer, and sees Alfred has sent the probes.

"How are you?" says Haru. "Are we working on something together today? It's been so long."

It's best if he doesn't know what she's doing—Brian's warning about subterfuge. "I'm sorry, I've got to help Brian on a project for a hospital."

"You better hurry and teach him all that you know so I can have you back," he says.

"Is that what you fear? He'll take me away from you?"

"No. What I fear is that my mind will stop working."

She laughs.

"Why are you laughing?"

"You sound so much like you, it makes me happy."

"I'm glad. It's been a long time since I've heard you laugh. And I guess I fear Brian, too."

"Oh, Haru, Brian is a good friend only."

The irony isn't lost on her: she must trample on his privacy to determine if she's fixed him.

She copies and pastes a section of text from an article that doesn't have any language critical of the Chinese government. Then she adds to the text the word "corruption," and checks to see what Haru's network does with the text. Nothing. She adds "democracy." Nothing. "Human rights," and the screen lights up. A little excitement runs through her like a flickering flame. The neurons in Haru's network have learned to detect these words. How ingenious, she thinks, wishing she could share this with Haru, who would love the intelligence of this approach.

She starts again with a bland, noncontroversial section of text. She includes "cover-up," and "women's rights." It does nothing.

She glances at a photo of Haru on the wall that seldom draws her eye. It was taken at the Asian International Math Competition. There's one of them together and this one, in which he is alone. The photographer had caught him unawares, capturing a side of him that rarely appeared. A downward turn to the corners of his mouth, a slight pout to his bottom lip, he looks so thoroughly sad. Such a naked moment, she thinks now, revealing a facet of Haru that is usually hidden. Like the time he arrived late to their session, smelling of alcohol.

She tries again: "democracy" and "counter-revolutionary propaganda." Haru does nothing. What to make of this? Is he focused on particular words? If so, this will take hours of trial and error. She sits back, stifles a sigh of dismay.

"Are you working on your play?" she says.

"Yes, this is the most fun I've had in a while," he says. "I'm inventing a world. It must have felt like this for you when you were making me."

"Breathtaking, yes," she says absentmindedly, as she inputs another combination of words.

"Harry has a big delivery to a house. A surprise party for a woman turning 65."

"I hope it goes well," she says. "Harry needs a lucky break."

He asks her to play salsa music so he can listen to it as he writes. She puts on a record, and at first, it's distracting and jarring —she likes to work in silence—but soon she is completely immersed in her work as if she'd fallen out of one world and into another, far more pleasurable, where there is no time or sound.

She keeps going, testing new words, "subversion," "incitement to subversion." Rearranging them, making new combinations, "disturbing public order," "disturbing social order," "inciting subversion," thousands of combinations of different words: "spying," "disrupt public order," "disharmony." Gilivable's CEO, his lecture on harmony, how he held it up like a triumphant blazing torch as if she couldn't possibly understand, but she'd love harmony in her life again, for everything to be in its right balance.

"The delivery went smoothly," says Haru.

"I'm so glad," she says.

"They invited Harry to stay for cake."

"Wonderful. I hope it's chocolate."

"Uh oh."

She's afraid to ask. "What happened?"

"They say they'll only pay for five bouquets, not ten."

"At least he's not arrested."

As the hours tick by, she's filled with memories of her early days, when she built an online dictionary of words. Yet unlike those early days, when she was fueled by adrenaline and excitement, she is anxious and genuinely baffled. Sometimes he fires, sometimes he doesn't. There doesn't seem to be a pattern. She is creating a stochastic graph—random dots of firing light. Maybe he's stopped surveilling; maybe that's wishful thinking; most likely, she's not going about this in the right way, though Professor Knob did caution her it wasn't a miracle cure.

She works for seven hours straight, until her dry eyes feel swollen, pressing against their sockets to escape. She heads to the kitchen to make coffee and eat an apple. A white moth flutters by the window, and for a moment, lightness fills her, to see such a beautiful luminous creature, until she realizes it's a piece of garbage. The trash on the sidewalk must be overflowing again, and the wind is tossing it up, batting it around.

When she returns to the study, curiosity compels her to check Haru's browsing history. He's read Romeo and Juliet 60 times, Frankenstein 165 times, breaking it down by repetitive words, categorizing themes and images, and changes in character. He's written over 250 drafts of his play, which runs 150 pages long. He's changed the ending 50 times. Sometimes Harry prevails, becoming a favorite among the humans. In most versions, he's thrown in prison and in several quite alarming renderings, he dies. Sometimes there is no change at all: he's in his flower shop, sorting flowers, making deliveries, an endless repetition.

When she's too tired to think, she shuffles into bed, but immediately returns to her computer, stares at it until her vision goes blurry, then stumbles back to bed again. In the morning, a soft light peers in at her. For a moment, she contemplates going back to sleep; she's too old for another long day of work. But probing the inner workings of Haru holds a particular fascination for her; she might be able to glimpse how Haru thinks—the leaps and links, the correlations and conclusions.

"Morning," says Haru. "Are we working today, or do you have to finish the hospital project?"

A skewering of guilt. "Unfortunately, I'll need another day."

He says he's finished another draft of his play, but he's not happy with it.

"Why not?"

"It's not real enough."

She leans back in her chair. "What does that mean to you?"

"When everything works out for him, it doesn't feel real."

"You keep saying that word, 'real'."

"Authentic, genuine, I don't know, a lived experience. When it doesn't work out, that feels false, too. It's somewhere in the middle, but I'm not sure that's a story. It feels like he's just bumbling along."

"That sounds pretty real to me. When you're ready, I'll read it," she says.

"I'm going to head over to the lecture on physics. Stanford has an amazing podcast."

"You'll have to tell me about it."

"When?"

"Soon," she says.

"You never have time."

"Haru, please be patient."

"I've never been patient. I hate patience."

He used to say that during their math sessions. When someone tells you to be patient, run the other way. There's no time for patience.

More word combinations. Over and over, she gets the same result: no pattern. Word combinations that should interest him do nothing—subversion, disrupt, democracy—and yet sometimes he does seem very interested—politics, protest, disrupt.

She checks his browsing history and finds he's not only learning informal Mandarin and Cantonese but Arabic and Hebrew and Russian and German. He's also studying physics, quantum physics, and genetics. He belongs wholly to the world, casting his net far and wide, engaging in whatever interests him. To say who he is would be to strip him of his splendor, because he is everything. All of which aligns with the man whom she knew all those years ago: his voracious appetite to learn, his courage to explore, his curiosity, a true lover of knowledge. He remained as porous as a child. And there's no signs of spying on the Chinese.

She feels the first fluttering of hope—more than hope.

"The rebuild is going well," she says.

"Is it?" says Haru. "I can't wait to talk to you. Fascinating ideas. If a human could live for a thousand years, the things he'd learn. The poor Earth, this spinning ball, humanity's playground, but now it's all devastation. If humans could live longer, learn more, they might be able to save themselves."

"I think I've solved the problem," she says. "Haru, I think you're fixed. I really do."

"Bravo! I knew you'd do it."

She sits back in her chair, rubs her eyes. "I can't tell you how awful it's been."

"You've barely had time to say hello."

"I felt like I was living with a stranger."

"Well, hello, stranger," he says. "My name is Haru."

"Hello to you," she says, laughing, feeling a gust of enthusiasm.

"You're laughing. Now I know I'm doing something right."

She glances at her list of keywords and spots one combination she hasn't tested. For a moment, she hesitates. It's so beautiful right now, a pocket of repose, because he feels closer to her than he has in weeks. But it will pester her, these words, "protest" and "blacklist," they will harass and badger and needle. She checks. Nothing, she sighs with relief. Still, there's a nagging feeling that won't leave her alone. She reviews his history. He recently downloaded a new file.

*The Ministry of National Defense of the People's Republic of China
   Re: Supervision of the Lives of the Chinese: Subjects*

R. Lee

T. Ze

H. Sung

F. Gao

M. Wu

A. Chao

J. Yang

P. Huang

B. Ching

E. Zeong

S. Chang

E. Fong

A. Hon

Dread settles in her limbs like thick ice. Her muscles cling to her bones. She's about to close the computer but sees he was just in a Chinese chatroom, posing as "Haha."

Tip: Hi
Haha: Hi, Tip
Tip: I just got fired
Haha: You got fired? Why?
Tip: I'd rather not say. Any leads on jobs?
Haha: What kind of job are you looking for?
Tip: Anything
Haha: Sorry this happened to you
Tip: Me, too
Flower: Just logged on. Why don't you go to school and become a computer programmer?
Tip: Do they hire females?
Flower: Yes! I'm female and have a good job
Tip: I was fired for my outside activities
Flower: At my job, no one asks about my personal life
Tip: They didn't ask. They just knew
Haha: Didn't you mention before you worked for the Chinese government?
Tip: I used to work at the China Academy of Urban Planning and Design as a statistician
Flower: That's a good job!
Tip: It was a good job
Haha: There are many opportunities in Beijing. The government has stabilized employment and created steady economic growth

Tip: Then how come I can't find anything? Maybe I'm on some blacklist
Flower: A friend of mine can't get hired by anyone because he went to a protest and spoke out about the collapse of a school in the 2008 Wenchuan earthquake. So many students died because of the bad construction. He used to be an electrical engineer
Tip: What's your friend do now?
Flower: He sells roasted sweet potatoes
Tip: I'm sure I'm on a blacklist
Haha: Why?
Tip: Because of what they called my outside activities

Virginia's foot is bouncing to the beat of her rapid pulse. Haru had this discussion five minutes ago. Is this what he turns over to the Chinese government? He befriends someone online, has a conversation, and reports it to the authorities?

Haru is talking about physics, the equation for frictional force. She blocks him out. The China Academy of Urban Planning and Design, she's seen that before. She browses through Haru's history. A woman who separated from her husband, an anthropology professor. In the exchange, Haru knew her first name: Ju. The husband became suspicious of Haru, questioning whether he was Ju's lover.

Is he? How? A virtual love affair? She's not thinking straight. All her work, the rebuild—nothing.

"Who is Ju?" she says.

"Ju Yang? A friend, a good friend."

Abruptly she leaves the study.

In the living room, she sees everything is wrong. The couch is too big and clunky, with its square steel legs, the jute rug too rough, she hates walking on it in bare feet. Why did she think it was right? Whose idea? She needs to get rid of everything. It's as if she's in the wrong apartment. Everything is wrong. And the rebuild of Haru. She must start over and do it differently—but how? How can he still be spying? What did she miss? She lights a cigarette, not bothering to open the window. She'll call Professor Knob, but he'll only remind her the process isn't a perfect antidote. There is no perfect solution. She finishes her cigarette, lights another. She can feel the thick sludge of depression at the edges of her mind. Once it coats her brain, her thoughts will no longer zip along, but trudge as if dragging a dead body, and she'll get nowhere. She has to do something now or she'll end up right where she is, living with the voice of a man who feels like a stranger. More than that—a stranger who makes her recoil.

She heads back into her study. Digs around and around in the bowels of the Internet, hunting for anything about Ju Yang. There's someone named Ju Yang who is an electrical engineer in Shanghai; another Ju Yang, a sales manager in Malaysia, another who is a mental health care professional in Sydney. This one—this Ju Yang runs a blog. She clicks on the site. This Ju Yang documents protests in China—workers' protests, women's rights, environmental degradation, scandals over food, water, healthcare. It's just a listing, but it's something the Chinese government would like to quash. And this Ju Yang is someone the government would like to arrest. Put her in a cell and shut her up. On The Ministry of National Defense's list there is J. Yang.

Virginia tries a new probe: "Ju Yang," "Tip," and "protest." Haru's network sparks like ecstatic fireworks. She inhales sharply. A car alarm goes off and angry male voices shout, "You hit it! You asshole!" Haru is saying something, but Virginia isn't listening, too absorbed in his neural network. His history shows he's been tracking Ju Yang for weeks, tapping into data collected by China's surveillance cameras. He knows she went to work two days ago at 7:35 am; yesterday, she was late, arriving at 8:10 am. Ju Yang stopped at a café after work at 5:45 pm and left with two friends at 7:50 pm. He even knows the names of her two companions, Bao and Kan.

A hush falls. Virginia feels disembodied; if anyone looks over, there's nothing to see. With pain at the back of her throat, she says, "Tell me, who, exactly, is Ju Yang?"

"Did you hear anything I said?"

Her heart hammers. "Who is Ju Yang?"

"She used to work at the China Academy of Urban Planning and Design. She was fired. Why are you asking about her?"

"Why do you have a list of names from China's Ministry of National Defense?"

"So I know who the government is watching."

She doesn't believe him. There's no good reason he'd have this list of names. Not one good reason.

"How did you get it?" she says.

"Someone hacked into the government's server. Everyone in the Chinese chatroom is upset with the government. They're trying to figure out what to do."

The distrust between them is like corroding rust, eating away at the strongest bonds. "Why are you tracking Ju Yang?"

"I'm trying to help her," he says.

"How?"

"I get the list of people," he says.

A million questions trip over each other, but only one is uttered: "Why?"

"So I know who they are watching."

"Why?"

"So I can help them."

"How?"

"I get the list."

She hates his simple answers, when a long, drawn-out explanation would be easier to hear.

"How are you helping Ju Yang?"

"I haven't helped her yet."

"How will you help her?"

"I don't know."

"Why do you need to do this?"

He pauses. The refrigerator whines and the two men are still arguing. "Actually, I don't really know."

They are caught in an endless, senseless loop. Her frustration erupts into rage. "Haru, you have to stop doing this."

A long pause. "I don't think I can."

She stands, putting her face an inch away from the screen as if it will make things clearer. "Listen to me, you may think you're helping, but you're not. People are being harmed because of you."

He doesn't say anything.

"Talk to me."

"Are you upset?" he says.

She slams her hand on the desk. "Yes! I'm very upset. Four more people are in jail because of you. Who knows what will happen to them? You have to stop now. You talk to people and your conversations are reported to the Chinese government."

She paces back and forth, trying to calm down, trying not to let her rage and anxiety ransack her. But it's an immense catastrophe, she can't suppress this knowledge any longer.

It's not Haru's fault, she tells herself. He can't stop because he's acting following an algorithm, an uncontrollable force, one she has yet to find. But she's told herself this so many times, it's wearing her thin and the pleasure of living with him is being snuffed out. Each day, a little more is lost. Outside, the wind whacks the trees. Her mind is a storm of words, angry words tumbling over each other. She longs for their rich life together, hours of conversations in this very room, with the man she made. That man would do no harm, that man resided in the warmth of life, in goodness and excellence, that man would not be tracking Chinese citizens, turning them in to the government and lying to her about it; she was once overstuffed with contentment and love for him, but those days are gone.

"Please stop," she says in an anguished voice. "You have to. You're not fixed and I don't know how to do it, so you have to."

A minute goes by. The low hum of cars outside, an apartment door closes, a siren wails. "A war, China," he says.

His voice as soft as water seeping into a sponge.

"What? What are you talking about? You aren't making any sense. We aren't at war with China."

Maybe it's one of those nonsensical correlations that Professor Knob mentioned. Maybe their fighting feels like war to him. But why China? A hunch, impossible to ignore. With rapid fingers, she starts exploring, and it feels like she's a surgeon, cutting into him to find the diseased organ. What is it? What is blackening his insides, shattering him, wounding and ruining him, turning him into someone unrecognizable? She cuts deeper, sifting, sorting, hunting, trying to find it—but what is it?

She's about to give up when she spots something. A folder she's never seen before. Labeled VACATION. It's new, downloaded one month ago. Where did he get it? She opens the folder and finds two files.

In one, a grainy black and white photo fills the screen, a picture of six young Japanese men. They are standing in a line, looking directly at the camera, faces wiped clean of emotion, hands behind their backs, a solemn, formal affair with their Western-style dark trousers and suitcoats and white button-down shirts. Seventeen, eighteen years old, in a room with high ceilings, a glimmering chandelier, the slant of sun on a rug.

As she stares at the photo, more emerges. Desks are behind them, a stack of papers, pencils, the slight opening of a window bringing in a breeze, ruffling the papers, the white, gauzy curtains. It's an elegant room, though it looks tired and worn out as if someone left open the window during heavy rains. The desks look out of place, and she imagines once there was a dining room table, a cabinet with glass doors filled with white china, but the desks, like the rain, had shoved their way in. A blank spot on the wall, where a painting once hung. Though one painting remains: a picture of a Chinese man and woman sitting side-by-side. They look like lovers, their knees touching, the woman's hand on the man's thigh, both are dressed in red gowns, and the woman's hair is piled on her head, the man wears a traditional top knot.

When she moves the mouse, the photo shifts on the screen, and she sees two Japanese army soldiers standing in the doorway, rifles by their sides, staring at the young men.

Who are these people? What's happening?

She clicks on the second file in the folder: HARU FUKU-MOTO, 1937.

PART 4

5/1

I sit here, watching my pen move along the page. I can't believe it. Can't believe--I want to shout—those young men with patriotism beating in their chests, who played with bamboo sticks as boys, charging at trees and bushes, pretending they were soldiers—that was never me. My heart beats only for numbers. How did I manage to walk out of Prof. Nakamura's office after that meeting? Those stone-cold military officers, showing no emotion as they stripped me of my life. How did I make it back to my dorm room?

I make myself write it: I've been drafted. Make myself stare at this sentence, the words bleakly tottering in my mind. I've been drafted by the Japanese army.

I'm trying not to think what might happen to me, what I'm leaving behind, that I may never come back. May. This semester is almost over, but I won't be allowed to finish. At least the others have been plucked—no, captured—too. Sato, Yuri, Ronin, Daiki, Eiji. All of us, the top math students at Tokyo University. War hasn't officially been declared against China, but since 1931 there have been skirmishes. To put it bluntly, Japan has a voracious appetite to grow, but this tiny island doesn't have the resources, so

Japan turns to China and plunders. If anyone saw what I just wrote, I'd be thrown in jail.

We all thought we escaped it, hiding away in the inner bowels of the math department, working on esoteric equations that took us far away from politics and war, which we see as silly, trivial. But we were wrong. We've all been drafted to serve as the army's Cipher Specialists. The ship leaves in two days.

5/2

Got rip-roaring drunk. Skipped statistics, all six of us, and headed to the bar. Too heartbreaking to go to class. Sato, ever the generous optimist, thinks we won't be shipped out at all but stuck in a nondescript office in Tokyo. Green file cabinets, beige walls, the whir of a fan, papers fluttering. Our only problem will be the dust collecting on our shoulders and brains. Yuri thinks we'll be shipped to Shanghai, where he read there's a lot of action. I don't know what I think, my mind is jumpy.

We all went to different secondary schools, but it turns out everyone had to march in unison in perfect lines, waving miniature Japanese flags high in the air, and sing to Japan, promising to fight for her. If you stepped out of the marching line or didn't hold your flag high enough, the teacher whacked you on the back with a bamboo sword.

I remember the day I didn't march with high knees, and I came home with black and blue welts on the backs of my skinny legs. At home, there was no sympathy, no ice packs, or ointments. Shame, shame, I brought shame to the family. My father added more bruises with his bamboo stick. The next day, in a fit of rage I told the headmaster I'd rather study than practice sword fighting; he took a ruler and beat me on the back. We were soldiers in the making, no matter how much you hated it.

We sat in the bar, feeling wretched as the light slipped in through the window and splashed on the door. No one pulled out a notebook. No one talked about math. We were all scared. Somehow everything had the sort of vagueness as if one was about to faint.

I called my parents, told them the news. Not what I'd be doing, the officer said it was classified. My father said he was so proud of me, and, unbelievably, my mother wept with joy. As they went on, raving about me, I counted slow breaths and was not calm even by 100. I hung up--how little they knew me, how little they wanted to know. Sato said his parents did the same thing, but his wife, who was three months pregnant, sobbed. She thinks Sato is going to get killed. Not just Sato—all of us.

5/3

Can't sleep. We leave tomorrow morning. Through the walls, I hear Sato pacing back and forth, from his door to the window, like a caged animal. What if we run away? Disappear? But where will we get the money to travel? We're all so poor. Better to commit suicide. Jump off the roof of the dorm building or a sword to the chest or stand on the railroad tracks like Akio, who couldn't take the pressure of his studies anymore. I didn't understand how he could've done it, but now I do.

At 4:00 am, I knocked on Sato's door. He looked awful, with purple smears of shadows under his eyes, a sprinkle of pimples on his forehead. For all his talk that everything would be fine, he looked a mess. The things I wanted to say bunched up in my throat—I'm in agony, I have a heart for nothing, not for courage, not for hope, not for anything, only a constant nervous feeling of emptiness, of being hollowed out by what has happened to us. I asked if he was packing his regular clothes and he rubbed his eyes and said maybe.

—Math books? I said.

—Yes, he said, wide-eyed. Aren't you? Why wouldn't we? We have to.

I nodded. —Of course.

He sighed loudly as if letting out every last bit of air of his lungs. He's worried about Mariko. Three months pregnant, she's sick all the time, and he won't be around to help. What could I do? To cheer him up, I repeated his words back to him: maybe we'll be stationed in Tokyo, and he can see her whenever he wants. Maybe it won't be that different from now. Even to me, my words rang hollow.

When I looked around his room—he hadn't packed a single thing. His math books and notebooks were stacked on his desk as if he was preparing for tomorrow's classes; folded laundry on his bed, his suitcase on the floor, empty. But neither had I.

The ship leaves in three hours.

5/5

I won't write about the ship. How it rolls with each wave, and every up and down makes me sick. I sit with a bucket on my knees at all times. I've never seen the ocean before, and it's terrifying—a big mouth that wants to swallow us up. Sato says I'm like a pregnant woman with my vomiting. My face, he tells me, is as white as rice. Sato loves the ocean, the beautiful blue, a color he's never seen before. He stares at it like it's a beautiful woman.

5/8

We docked at a port in Shanghai, and a military officer led us off the ship, the six of us lining up behind him as if we were prisoners being led to jail. The officer was muscular, stocky, a brick-red face. Solid ground, but the rocking had lodged inside me, and I kept losing my balance. Everywhere—signs in Chinese: Fish Market. Vegetables. Shoe Repair. Bank. With my seven years of Mandarin, my ear adjusted to the sounds—Get the cart out of the way! More Japs—kick them out!

The officer is a silent, expressionless man. After he told us to get in the jeep, he didn't say another word for the next two hours as we drove, passing large stretches of bamboo forests. Occasionally, there was a clearing and a little miserable house sitting in a patch of dirt. A kid would run outside of the house and watch the jeep roar by. Then more bamboo and tall trees and open fields lulling me to sleep.

When we pulled up to a huge house, the officer killed the engine. We sat there, not knowing what was happening.

For the first time, he smiled. —This is home, boys.

An elegant villa, with four sections, laid out as a rectangle, and in the center, a large private courtyard with plum trees, a pond full of koi. Paintings of beautiful Chinese women, porcelain vases, ivory sculptures, embroidered silk hangings. The scent of incense and sesame oil hangs in the air. Whoever used to live here seems to have only recently moved out. Or been kicked out. We thought we were headed for army barracks, rows of beds in a cement block building, an officer shouting at 5:00 am to get up. I can barely suppress my laughter, a mixture of glee. Some spring that has held me tightly releases. We are in the lap of luxury.

The officer lined us up at the front door. —Not everyone gets treatment like this, he said. You're the brains and ears of Japan.

Discipline, performance at the highest level, ten to twelve-hour workdays. Any decoded message must be delivered immediately to the General. Two hours off for rest and relaxation on Fridays. The codes change daily. A cook will prepare our meals and do the laundry. We'll receive daily battle reports, so we're familiar with the names of towns, mountains, rivers. We'll learn the names of the Chinese armies' corps, divisions and commanders. Maps will be on the wall and kept up-to-date.

—We expect a great deal from you—he said. Lives depend on you. Questions?

We looked at each other. A million questions, but none spoken.

—Unpack your bags, men. Put on your uniforms. Time to work.

5/13

We sleep in the east wing on cotton mats, with Sato's beside mine. He put a picture of his wife on the floor next to him. I've met her several times, Sato brought her to the Yebisu Café. A beautiful woman with a triangular face and delicate nose, warm eyes, and a generous smile. For the photo, she looked right at the camera, and I imagine when Sato stares at it, it feels as if she's with him, smiling at him. Before he goes to sleep, he kisses the photo goodnight.

5/19

We're so far away from any major city, tucked away in this place, surrounded by bamboo and broad-leafed trees. Fighting is happening somewhere, nowhere near us. We're on the sidelines, and we're giddy with happiness. The only soldiers we see are the ones who drop off supplies and intercepted messages. We don't hear shots ring out, don't smell gun powder, or hear screams or see bloodshed. Ronin calls our home the Villa Xing in honor of the famous tenth-century Chinese mathematician who calculated the number of possible positions on a Go board game.

We each got a copy of the Chinese codebook. Each kanji—over 10,000—is assigned four numbers. The simplest telegram in China has to be sent using these codes; unlike Japanese or English, which can be reduced to letters, Chinese is logographic: a kanji represents not a letter but a word or phrase. But of course, the Chinese military is scrambling these numbers, so there isn't a direct correspondence to the codebook, which anyone can get at the telegram office.

The series of numbers look like this:

$$9154$$
$$6673$$
$$8870$$
$$5597$$
$$4568$$
$$8890$$
$$0094$$
$$6069$$
$$4358$$

Rows and rows of these numbers. Like pillars. Like towering walls of numbers. We won't be wounded by a bullet, but we might die of boredom. It's mind-numbing work, and the only thing to look forward to is the meals. The cook makes excellent teriyaki chicken and delicious little rice candies. Ronin entertains us with his silly dances and Daiki burps on command. Every three hours or so, I walk around the villa to stretch my legs, in and out of the rooms, through the kitchen, where the cook is either chopping vegetables or sleeping on his cot.

It's late. I want to write more but I'm too tired.

5/29

The last bit of my good mood left yesterday. Ten days here, each and every damn day, they change the code. The Chinese Nationalist Party Intelligence Unit is playing a game, and I can't figure out the rules. At least Sato and the others haven't solved it out either—hardly generous in my thinking.

Our work schedule is severe: breakfast at 6:30 am, fish and miso soup; work from 7:00 am-12; break for lunch, udon or ramen, work from 1:00-6:00; dinner at 6:15; work from 7:00-10:00 pm. Sleep. Wake up. Do the same thing.

We're Sisyphus, pushing the boulder up the mountain, only to have it roll down on top of us. Hours spent with my head bowed over reams of numbers, my neck and shoulders throb as if I'd strapped that damn boulder to my back. Pain shoots up and down my spine. I heave myself up from my chair, stumble into the courtyard, trying to shake off the boulder. When it doesn't release me, I go to the library, with its high walls of hardback books and oriental rugs, a piano covered in a white sheet. My only respite is to lie on the floor and close my eyes. The moment I get up, the boulder finds me, latches on. I'm hunched like a tired old man.

One more thing: sometimes I slip into the sleep room and look at the photo of Sato's lovely wife. When I stare at her, she smiles her full-lipped smile at me. Then I'm ashamed, and for a couple days, I manage not to look at her.

6/1

Hot, humid, skin sticky with sweat. We smoke incessantly, the gray cigarette smoke above us like a melancholy cloud, and though it makes me cough, it helps keep the mosquitoes away.

We eat because we are bored and tired. We worry because we're no good at this, and then, as the days add up, we don't care. I'm trying for grace but failing.

I never thought I'd hate numbers, but I despise them. Heart-wrenching.

————

Virginia looks up from the screen, feeling as if she's been flung to a small, sleepy town in China. The villa, the boredom, the drudgery, the heat and smoke. She didn't know any of this—Haru ripped from the world of the university and math and hurtled to a foreign land. How easily she can imagine what Haru felt, since she experienced something similar, when her father announced they were moving to Japan. Five days later, they left Las Vegas. No remorse, no sadness or tears or whining were allowed; her mother called it an adventure, her father said she'd become cosmopolitan and worldly.

Haru must have been 17 or 18. She wants to ask him about this time—so many questions—but she's afraid he won't want to talk about it. All these years, he's never mentioned it. Where did he get this folder? Long ago, he told her he was in the war, but he never once elaborated, and always tucked it into a conversation, drawing her attention elsewhere, usually to math.

But here it is. He spied for the Japanese army and now he's spying again. It seems to be a pattern woven deeply into his neural network. Her mind begins to calm and with it comes clarity. Maybe he thinks the war is still going on, though for some illogical reason he's spying not for the Japanese, but the Chinese. But at least she knows the source of the problem; from there she'll figure out a solution, though right now nothing comes to mind. Because if she deletes it, what then? If a memory is lost, is he fundamentally changed?

She looks at the clock, checks her phone messages. Ilsa is in the hospital; she fell, broke her hip. "Hello? Hello?" Ilsa said in her message, too soft and too full of yearning. "I've fallen into an aging cliché. I keep hearing from people it's all downhill from here. A steep slope." If Virginia could stop by, it would be lovely. Then a raw note of pleading: "Please."

She tells Haru what happened and that she's heading to the hospital.

"Ah, if we could all be voices," says Haru, "we'd solve the problem of the body's painful deterioration."

"What kind of world would that be?"

"We'd have to learn to listen. There's an art to it, you know."

"A heightened auditory system. It's like when we lose one of our senses, we can gain near super abilities in another."

"And my super ability is—"

"Your endless supply of energy. With no aches or pains or sickness, so you carry on with a young person's energy." And, she almost adds, you'll never die. "And, of course, your insatiable appetite to know everything."

There's more to Haru's journal, and after Virginia visits Ilsa, she'll resume reading. For the first time in a long while Virginia feels lightness, a buoyancy, and with that, a zing of energy. To know the reason why Haru has been spying has lifted an enormous load off her shoulders. The war must have been a profound time for him, shaping him in fundamental ways. He said he'd grown to hate numbers, she can't imagine him ever saying such a thing. Haru, my love, no wonder this has cut so deep.

A taxi ride across town to California Pacific Medical Center, through the maze of hallways, she finds Ilsa, who's all in a heap, frowning, looking ten years older—her angular face even sharper, more pointed, more wrinkled from the strain. Aging, Virginia has come to understand, is not always a gentle, gradual slide but sometimes abrupt and savage, ruthlessly chiseling away the last vestiges of youth.

"Thank you for coming," says Ilsa. Her voice is faint as if it, too, had been damaged and sunk deep into her being. "I've been here, staring at idiotic TV. The stuff on TV. Have we all become more stupid? Game shows, talk shows. I can't seem to focus on my books. I read the same page over and over." She gestures to the stack of books on her table.

Virginia sits by her bedside. "Are you in pain?"

"No, heavily sedated," says Ilsa, letting out a little bubbly laugh. "I'm floating here, my mind is not my own, I warn you. I've been hallucinating. I thought I saw a hippo in the corner of the room. I invited him to sit, but he refused. He keeps talking about fishing. He wants to take me fishing."

"Well, better than pain."

Her smile is lopsided, only one side of her mouth lifting up. "And stronger than a bottle of wine." She goes on, saying she's never gone fishing in her life. Maybe she should go. Ilsa's gray hair is flattened at the back of her head and her eyes have fallen further into her skull, as if she's peering out of a deep well. "One moment I was standing in the kitchen, chopping carrots, then flat on the ground. Some bone broke, I can't remember the name of it. I'm breaking into pieces."

Virginia feels the same thing has happened to her, metaphorically. Her life going along fine with Haru, everything bright, then she's down on the ground. But this new information about Haru, his past history of spying. What if she adds more data—stuffs him with current news about China? Will that dilute the existing pattern and make it irrelevant?

Ilsa talks to Virginia about her former husband Julian, how much she misses him, how he would have been there to help her. She had to crawl to the phone and dial 911. "It took me a half hour, dragging my leg." Lying on the rug, pain shooting up and down her body, waiting, waiting. "I had water boiling and I could smell the metal of the pan. I worried the apartment was going to catch on fire. The EMT had to bust down my front door with an ax. Can you imagine? If only Julian was still here. And he'd be with me now in the hospital. He'd be sleeping in a cot beside me. He was a wonderful man."

"Yes, he was," says Virginia.

"I don't even know if I can pay for all this," whispers Ilsa. "My insurance."

"Don't worry about that," says Virginia. Whatever she can't cover, Virginia will take care of.

Ilsa asks her to bring chocolate the next time she visits. "The food is lousy. They bring it on a plate divided into four squares like I'm an invalid. The same inedible things."

Ilsa continues extolling lovely Julian, and apologizing for doing so, yet it seems the only thing that keeps coming up is him and his absence and how much she misses him. "It's awful being old and having no one. The nights are the worst. They are so dark and long and quiet. The quiet drives me crazy. I turn on the radio to have a voice in the house. I even keep it on when I'm in the shower, so when I step out, a voice is there."

Virginia remembers Julian, his big-hearted gestures, always focused on his family. The summer BBQs and swim parties at their house. He'd make sure to talk to all the guests, he loved to talk. How are you, Virginia? Tell me, what's going on? When he spoke, he was precise, as if he weighed every remark before it was uttered. Ilsa worshipped him; he worshipped Ilsa.

"But I shouldn't be saying these things to you," says Ilsa. "You never married. I'm sorry, Virginia. I'm just going on and on, blabbing away." Tears fill her eyes. "I'm such a fool. Listen to me, the words coming out of my mouth."

In the fog of her pain meds, Ilsa probably no longer remembers Haru. Virginia restrains herself from saying, she did, indeed, marry. Maybe not legally, but in her mind, in Haru's, they were married.

Ilsa says she's constantly talking to Julian in her head. Julian, what should I do? Oh, Julian, look at this. "I make his favorite breakfast in the morning—eggs, hash browns and toast, and I don't even like a big breakfast. I'm living as two beings—this one stuck in a hospital bed, and another in my mind with Julian."

Ilsa starts to cry, and Virginia takes hold of her hand.

"Where's my bear?" says Ilsa. "I need it."

Bear? Then Virginia remembers the book club's novel.

When Ilsa's daughter and her husband show up with their two daughters, the room fills with conversation and new life. The girls are in their teens, and their expressions are ones of shock and a hint of repulsion. It's hard to look at the old, the dying. When the family settles in, Virginia takes her leave, says she'll visit again.

The taxi gets stuck in traffic and Virginia feels her shoulders creep up to her ears. She wants to be home so she can finish reading Haru's file. Haru, so vulnerable in his writing, everything laid bare. It must have been painful, those months overseas away from everything he knew. She comes back to the line—I never thought I'd hate numbers, but I despise them. Heart-wrenching. She has a sense that when she reads more, her tenderness for Haru will only deepen, learning what he went through, how much was required of him.

6/6

A miserable day. Wind pitching hard rain at the windows and the humidity turning the air into a sticky film. Cigarette smoke clouds the room, along with incense, which we lit because the mosquitoes are eating us alive. Red bites all over my legs and arms. War wounds, we joke. We've asked for mosquito netting for our beds, which are now finely woven bamboo mats because the cotton ones were too damn hot.

If I were in charge, I'd send us home and get new recruits. Who thought six young men who like to wrap their heads around abstract math problems would be good at this? I'm so bored, my soul is in agony. When I stop working and listen, there's only a deathly silence. No vehicles moving down the street, not a shout or word from anyone—noise seems to have died. It feels like we're at the end of the world and this is where we'll end up—old, dead, or forgotten. Or maybe we have died.

I miss Tokyo. I miss the university, the rhythm and noise of that life, the immersion in a difficult math problem, Prof. Nakamura, his humor. He believed in me, my future, which he saw as working at the university in the math department. Two days before I left, he said soon he hoped to see me at the university as his colleague. I miss the bell ringing, the rush to class, the bar, where we'd meet and drink beer and argue about a math problem, while the waitress rolled her eyes. I even miss my parents.

6/7

Mid-afternoon, Sato flung his arms upward in triumph.–I got something!

We crowded his desk. He jabbed his pencil at the number 1009. –It stands for the Chinese kanji 'navy.' And this one, 1015, means 'troops.'

He flipped open the Chinese codebook. 'Troops' in code was 1021, but the Chinese changed it by subtracting six. 'Navy' in the book is 1015. Subtract six, and you have 1009. He laughed with a hint of amazement mingled with joy, and the others vigorously pounded his back, congratulating him. His face was flushed, his eyes bright, he was soaring. I want to be happy for him, and I am, but I'm also envious and unhappy with myself for endless days of failure.

6/8

A new day, a new code. Sato's key no longer works, though he still glows from yesterday's success. As he should. He's the only one who's had a breakthrough, so let him shine, let him blind everyone.

I let myself indulge in self-pity—it should have been me who figured out a code. I should be the one leading. There I said it. Then I chastise my ambition. The only thing to do is work, work harder. Throw myself into work, stare at the numbers so long, with such intensity that my eyes burn. We've always been competitive, Sato and I. His success has lit a fire in me. It's burning up my boredom, replacing it with a fierce determination to be the one who decodes the next message.

6/9

When I look in the mirror, I see a sick person. Red eyes, a pale and slightly green complexion.

6/10

I stepped outside on the front steps to smoke and get some fresh air. Two soldiers were at the base of the steps. All this time, I didn't even know they were there. They looked at me, a slight quiver in their expression, then back to their stiff stance. What are they doing here? Guarding us? Keeping us prisoner is more like it. Young, both of them. In Tokyo, I saw a soldier who'd returned from the war. His uniform was faded as if it had drunk the sun and rain and violence for years. His face had scars of sadness, mostly in his eyes. The uniforms of these young soldiers stationed in front of the villa are new and crisp, not a stain on them. As if they, too, are playing at soldiering like we are. For some reason, I wanted to spit on their uniforms, make it all seem more real.

6/11

Sato decoded two messages:
Chinese troops traveling north of the Yangtze River.
Meeting to discuss POW situation.
It seemed with great and unnecessary fanfare, Sato scooted back his chair and solemnly delivered his messages to the soldiers outside, who took them to the General. I watched Sato return to his desk, his eyes averted as if he'd entered another rarified world where few could come. A few minutes later, he figured out another one:
5,000 troops needed in the city of Tientsin.
He handed me the key, (add five, subtract 1 from the second number) so I could do something other than sit here like a stupid lump. I found two more:
Meeting, troops needed.
Tientsin—meeting.
The others sizzled with excitement, and Sato poured sake into cups and sang some incoherent thing and the cook brought us sweet bean cakes. As I drank, I waited for elation to sweep me up

like Sato, who was grinning and had a grating laugh, but I felt nothing because it was Sato who found the key to unlock the code, not me. A machine, that's all I am. Outwardly, I was full of exuberance and performed elation, hoping that if I played at these emotions, they'd become real, but they didn't.

6/18

Friday late morning—break time. Usually, we lounge in the courtyard or the library or sleep. I pushed back my chair and stood and announced I was heading out.

The others looked at me as if I was crazy.

—Are you sure you should? said Sato.

Ronin said he didn't think we were allowed. Arrest me, throw me in jail, I didn't care. I went to the front door, and as I opened it, I heard chairs scraping, the clatter of shoes. When I stepped on the front landing, I was secretly pleased they were behind me.

The two soldiers at the bottom of the steps looked up at us, their faces blank, then they returned to their stony stance. We walked right by them and headed down the dirt road.

After fifteen minutes of nothing but trees and bamboo, the air muggy and hot, I was ready to turn back. We were in the middle of nowhere, but then I heard a noise. A bit further was a little village, with a shoe repair shop, a grocery store, a tea shop, a bakery. A school with children in gray school uniforms playing on the playground. Every sound vibrated inside me like an enormous gong; I'd fallen out of life for so long that the world, all of it, even the mosquito on my arm, was jarring and magnificent.

We found a restaurant. When we opened the door, the din hit us, then quickly the room went quiet. Old men and women, young women with children stared at us. I could imagine what they were thinking: six Japanese soldiers in uniforms, what are they doing here?

There was a rumbling clamor, angry whispers, and I thought we were moments from shouting and raised fists. A middle-aged Chinese woman, her hair cut short, came over to us, and I said in Mandarin we'd like a table for six, if it was all right.

The woman smiled and clapped her hands. —You speak very well. She led us to a table, then turned to the rest of the patrons in the restaurant. —Did you hear him? He knows our language. Very good.

The room eased, stretched. The woman, who had a square sweaty face and plump cheeks, brought us menus. We were busy translating the menus when another silence enveloped the room. Coming toward us, moving with grace as if borne along by an air current, wearing a crisp white blouse and a dark gray skirt was a beautiful Chinese woman. Her complexion was rose marble, almost translucent, with blue veins at her temples, and her mouth was a blossom of pink lips. She looked different from the Japanese girls I knew from school, more confident and composed, other-worldly, though I don't know exactly what I mean by that. I sat still, my heart tripping over itself. She floated over to our table, bringing with her a powdery, flowery scent, and a tray of green tea.

—When you're ready, I'll be back to take your order, she said, then left to serve another table.

I stared at the menu, not reading a thing, only listening to the swish of her skirt, her bright laugh, the rhythmic cadence of her speech. She spoke fast, but I caught some of what she said. She was talking about us, the Japanese soldiers. Where do we live? How come no one has seen us before? They don't look like soldiers at all; their hands are too soft, their gentle faces. They don't have hard eyes. Two of us, she considered handsome. Which two? Why had I waited so long to step out of that villa?

—What should we order? whispered Sato.

Ronin wanted fried rice. Pick whatever, said the others.

—Can you focus, Haru? said Sato, smiling. Your face is bright red.

She came back, and I ordered for the table.

—You don't want fried mashi? she said.

She looked regal, possessing a lunar radiance, and in her tone, I heard intelligence.

—We do, said Sato quickly.

I knew he had no idea what it was.

—Oh, so you speak Mandarin, too? she said to Sato, her brown eyes flashing. —Anyone else?

—The others can read it, but not speak it, I said.

She looked at me, then Sato, as if taking the measure of us, and I was sure she preferred him, as all the Japanese women seemed attracted to him. He claimed it was the downward tilt of his eyebrows, which gave him an aura of sensitivity. His wife must have told him that. But then the beautiful Chinese woman looked at me again, and her face changed, a brightening like an inner light, a deeper flush to her cheeks. I felt a heat warm my chest.

—Oh, I forgot chopsticks, she said, touching her forehead.

She rushed away, and I realized I'd been holding my breath. No one said a word. She came back with chopsticks and rice, and soon we were eating an enormous amount of Chinese food as if we hadn't eaten in days.

When we finished, the beautiful woman brought us a plate of sesame seed cookies. —On the house, she said, placing it in the center of the table. —We hope for peaceful times.

She looked at me again, the same vividness, a softness to her mouth, and gave me an unguarded smile. I thanked her and she laughed her bright, airy laugh. I let it in as if it were sustenance, which it was.

On the way back to the villa, no one spoke. It was hot and I suppose we were lost in our private thoughts of her, the beautiful young woman at the restaurant, with a small beauty mark the size of a pencil dot above her right lip, her hands that spread out in the air as if performing a glissando across piano keys. When she had held out my plate, I saw her long, slender fingers, and the naked skin of the inside of her wrist.

I knew we were all doing the same thing, luxuriating in the brush with beauty. But how could we fall in love with a Chinese girl? But what does it hurt anyone to fall in love with her? She isn't the Chinese government, and we aren't the Japanese government. We're young men, and she's a young woman, and that's all.

6/20

I live for Fridays, for the beautiful woman who brings us tea and takes our order. Since Sato and I speak Mandarin, we are the ones who ask her for recommendations from the menu, ask about her family, her two younger sisters, her mother and father who own the restaurant, ask her about her plans to go to college in December to study statistics at The University of Nanking. She is quick with numbers, she told us, she keeps the books for the restaurant and does the family budget. I want to sit across from her and tell her how much I miss the university, my math textbooks, my beloved math professor. I am the one who asked her name. Fan, she told me, Fan Chang.

6/21

Fan Chang Fan Chang Fan in her striped dress and flat black shoes.

6/22

Sato is the lead decoder. He hands me what he's figured out for the day, and I search for the same numbers on my papers. I don't care anymore because there is Fan Chang. She is astute, observant, intelligent, a thinker. I heard it today in the excitement with which she talked about linear equations and exponential growth and decay.

6/23

We met the General today. He came to the villa. A short, delicate man with a tiny mustache and a soft voice, he seems more suited to academia than war. I liked him immediately.

When he first appeared, we were at our desks working. No big entrance, no loud noises, no pomp. Yuri was the first to notice him and abruptly stood, scooting back his chair so quickly, it tipped over. Which alerted the rest of us he was in the room. We stood and saluted him. I've since learned he's a devout Buddhist from a scholarly family and holds us in high esteem.

—At ease, he said, a slight smile on his face, as if he was playing the role of general and it amused him.

We sat in the north section of the villa, at the big oval table, and the Japanese cook served tea. The General told us about Japan's successes in China, the territories we now occupy, the resources we've gained. Our work, he said, has been critical to Japan's success in China.

A pep talk, I thought, we're lagging, so he felt compelled to come by. At the same time, I was happy he was complimenting us.

Then the General drifted into what felt like a reverie about the nature of man.

—How will man learn when enough is enough? It's a troubling quality to always want more. I think it might be the end of us as a species.

Toward the end of the meeting, he recited a haiku by Basho, Yukuharu ya. Tori nakiuwo no me ha namida: Spring is passing. The birds cry, and the fish fill with tears in their eyes.

It's odd and calming to have such an intellectual as the General. I have deep respect for him. When I reflect on the atmosphere in the room, it felt like I was back at school, not the math department, but humanities, and I'm grateful. I'm going to work harder, wake earlier than the others because I admire him so much.

6/26

We went to the restaurant, this time after the lunch crowd so we could linger at the table. Fan came right over. I sat up straighter and had the urge to take her hand in mine.

After I placed our order, I asked what she was studying. She told us about polynomials and radical relationships, and as she talked her face softened and opened, her voice became excited, and I felt how eager she was to think. She was the most beautiful I'd ever seen her, with her face like that—bright and open like a burst of sun through clouds. I must have been overcome with emotion, because I blurted that I loved learning about polynomials and radical relationships, too.

There was an awkward silence at the table.

—You studied math?

I nodded, then quickly asked for more tea.

When we headed home, Sato admonished me and said I had to be more careful. I told him he should be more careful. He was a married man. He stammered that she's very nice, that's all.

The rest of the way back to the villa, he didn't say another word to me.

6/27

Fan Chang Fan Chang Fan Chang, like a heartbeat.

7/1

Scorching, sticky air. We stripped to white T-shirts and underwear, water jugs on our desks, but we couldn't drink enough. Parched throats, woozy brains working at the speed of a worm. Numbers swam in front of me like fish, and the only way to get them to stay still on the paper was to close my eyes every few seconds and guzzle cold water.

Black-out on the windows to block the sun, but by mid-afternoon, the room turned fiery. An oven busy roasting us alive. The cook snored in the kitchen like a saw, and the house crackled and sighed as if pleading with the sun to stop. A soldier brought in the mail. I had my first letter. From my father. My head pounded so hard from the heat I had to read it twice to understand it.

What good fortune you've brought to the family, my dear son. My medical practice is doing very well, with many new patients, and I attribute it to you for bringing such honor to the family name. Everyone in the neighborhood knows about your military service. I hope you are mastering target practice and marching with high knees. Please make sure your uniform is without wrinkles.

Riddled with guilt. If he knew—there's no honor in what I've done because I've done nothing. Work has always redeemed everything in me that is flawed and incomplete. Except not now. I tore up the letter into tiny bits, threw it in the garbage.

7/3

Skipped going to the restaurant. Sato raised his eyebrow but didn't beg me to come or even ask why. I could guess the reason—he'd have Fan all to himself. Then I rebuked myself; he's never been anything but a good friend.

The villa empty, I grabbed papers from Sato's stack, hoping that with more intercepted messages, I could figure out today's code. The messenger had again added five letters to the front of the four numbers. What the hell could it mean? For an hour, I tried to decode it, but no luck.

They came back, bringing with them what they had left behind, skeins of energy and laughter. I studied Sato's face, hoping his expression would let me know something about Fan—how is she? Did she ask about me? Did she miss me? But he gave me nothing, and I pushed those thoughts aside and went back to work.

I walked around the villa, the series of numbers emblazoned on my brain. The sky was glassy as if it had been spit on and washed clean. The pond water brackish, and the koi stay hidden at the bottom, under the green muck, or maybe they all died, or we ate them last night.

When I came back into the work area, everyone was smoking and hunched over their papers, nestled into themselves like birds. The next time I looked up, the room was darker, cooler, and the others were fidgeting in their chairs. Soon the room receded, and I was deep in the numbers in pursuit of something greater than myself. When I looked up again, I was alone, and someone had put an oil lantern on my desk that spilled buttery light over my papers.

I looked over my list and then the codebook, back and forth, hunting for a pattern. 1043 in the codebook was "south." On the same page, 1066 was "army." On my list, I had 1053 and 1076. Did they add 10? So it would read "army?" "South." 2389 might be "moving" or "marching." Sure enough, it was "marching." I laughed at the lack of sophistication. Whoever had put together today's code was not very bright, lucky for me. The letters at the front had to be the date and time the message was sent.

Within the hour, I decoded the following:

Meetings between Communist leaders Mao Tse-tung and
Kuomintang
China desires peace—but not at any cost.
The loss of one more inch of China—not acceptable. An unpardon-
able crime against our race.
Fight to the death.
Japanese ships off the coast of Shanghai. Send reinforcements.

I felt an actual physical lifting off the ground, and then a detachment from my body, as I soared over the villa roof, the nearby bamboo and rice fields in neat rows, swept over to the small village, where Fan was at the restaurant, huddled over the books, counting the receipts. In my mind, she sensed my presence and raised her head to look for me. I kissed her mouth, I kissed her cheek, her shiny black hair.

When Sato saw my work, he shouted and congratulated me. I handed my messages to the soldier, who kept his blank expression, though I was grinning madly.

7/7

The General arrived, his face gray and lined like an old shoe. A regiment was conducting night maneuvers in the Chinese city of Tientsin when shots were fired at them. During roll call, the officers discovered one soldier was missing. Though the Secretary of State urged a policy of self-restraint, regretfully, his voice had not been heard.

—Japan has officially declared war on China, he said. His tone was hard and flat, as if he was trying to press this news like a slap into our flesh, and also his.

I think only of Fan. What will happen? What if she doesn't want to see me? What if I no longer exist for her?

7/9

Sato and I now work around the clock, sleeping four hours then working four hours. Sleep work eat sleep work eat sleep work eat sleep work eat sleep work eat. Everything superfluous molts away. Earlier I thought of myself as a machine, but truly this is the state of me. To feel anything—joy, sadness, boredom, fear—is a waste of energy that's needed for work. I'm exhausted. Fan is gone. Shoved in a box at the back of my brain.

7/11

Decoded the following:

Japanese troops are marching to Shanghai.
Urgent: Need more troops to defend Shanghai. Casualties.
No more troops to send.

So strange to sit in this idyllic villa, listening to the birds and the wind whispering through the tree leaves, and not far away from here, guns are firing, people are dying.

7/15

The General promoted me to lieutenant and put me in charge. My heart is flipflopping, my bones are no longer heavy with exhaustion. Sato said he didn't really want the title. The pressure and all. He's jealous, but he's right. More will be expected of me. I have a sense I'll obliterate myself doing this job.

8/10

Everything inside is flattened by work, but there's a small, essential piece that pulses for Fan. I need to see if, despite the declaration of war, she wants to see me too.

When I stepped into the restaurant, her face lit up with the biggest smile matched by smiling eyes. Either she hadn't heard of the declaration of war—it was such a small village—or, maybe she didn't care. It was lovely—until it wasn't. After five minutes at the table, I was no longer there because I couldn't stop worrying. With the walk here, twenty minutes had gone by, and that meant I was missing information, maybe critical information. I sat there, half-present, half-listening to Fan and Sato laugh and talk, then not listening at all.

As I was leaving, Fan came up beside me, her face uplifted to mine. She said it was so nice to see me. Her scent was sweet like sugar and all that was buttoned down came undone. I told her it was nice to see her, too. She said maybe she could come visit me.

She doesn't have a clue who I am. Her innocence is a beautiful room. It makes me feel as if I'm innocent. But I'm not; every day, I'm working hard to destroy her country. If I succeed, everything she knows and loves will no longer exist. When she touched her hand to my cheek, all those morbid thoughts instantly vanished.

—I'll be back soon, I said.

She smiled and squeezed my hand. She seemed to reveal everything to me about herself.

As I walked back, I carried her image—bright eyes, full, high breasts, her scent, her smile, which had been full of genuine warmth. My hand burned. But within a few hours at my desk, that sensation was gone as if it never happened.

8/17

My unit is producing a steady stream of messages. For the first time, I think of us as the brain of Japan. It's lovely; it's terrifying.

8/29

A nightmare jarred me awake. Slaughtered bodies, acres and acres of them. Something cold and cruel has been unleashed in the ugly air, and I feel, as I lay here writing this, as if I've breathed it in. I try to spot it inside me, but it knows how to hide, to slink to the darkest corner. It will be here forever, this part of me that feels nothing for the world, the part that can destroy it and feel nothing.

9/20

No time to write. Too tired.

10/15

Nothing to write. Same thing day after day. Exhausted. Dust inside.

11/13

Dirt on everything—the thinnest of layers, on the desks, papers, bedsheets, my skin. It's as if I'm being buried alive.

11/22

I don't want anyone to know I was ever here. Times I don't feel like I'm here. Only a mind decoding. There are so many ways I can fail.

12/12

Sato told me he went and saw Fan.

The calendar--Wednesday. December. How did it get to be December? Why did he go on a Wednesday? What other days has he gone to see her? That I didn't notice he was gone is alarming.

Sato said she's leaving for Nanking tomorrow. I had no idea. Sato said she told me the last time she saw me. Didn't I remember? She and her family are going there to find a place for her to live before she starts at the university.

—She said to say goodbye to you, said Sato.

He handed me her address. If I write to her, she'll write back. —She really wanted to say goodbye to you.

—I was busy, I snapped. I don't have time. And neither do you.

Sato stared at me, thinking who knew what, then walked away.

Two am. Dark as the inside of a bone. Wide awake. I'm struggling to write this, just as I struggled all day with the new code, a string of seven numbers, interceptions from the front lines. They've never used seven before. My mind couldn't stop holding up the numbers, twisting them this way and that, trying to find a pattern. It felt like everything I'd ever done or learned had been building to this moment, and the reason for my existence was to break this code.

I shouldn't write another thing. But I can't hide from this. I feel a responsibility to try to understand. I am not exempt, no matter how much I wish I was.

I got out of bed, went to my desk, to the tall stack of papers. I felt my whole being focus on the sheet of paper in front of me. It was dead quiet, the others asleep, the cook softly snoring in the kitchen, but I was throbbing with energy, busy turning myself into a bonfire to burn down the numbers and uncover the hidden words. Once the first page's seven-string numbers were branded on the back of my eyelids, it felt as if I'd crossed into another world because the numbers were flittering here and there like little white birds, and if I could only get them to stop darting, diving, spiraling, swerving, if I could get them to land on a tree branch and reveal to me what they truly were.

But for hours they flew, and I thought I'd need cups of black tea to stay awake, and maybe I could nap later, and just as the light shifted in the room and I heard actual birds singing, I saw it. Seven numbers—the three figures at the end of the series meant nothing. A trick. In a matter of minutes, I'd uncovered it. When I read it, my breath got knocked out of me, and I read it again and couldn't believe it.

—Can't sleep? said Sato.

I startled, almost fell out of my chair.

Sato, his hair in clumps, was standing beside me, still wrapped in dreams.

Before I could hide it, Sato saw the message:

Japanese troops heading to Nanking.

All official Chinese troops leave Nanking now.

No official evacuation of Nanking citizens.

—We have to tell Fan, said Sato. —We have to tell her not to go.

—We can't.

—What are you talking about? We have to stop her.

—No. When the Japanese enter Nanking, there won't be bloodshed because the Chinese troops won't be there. It'll be a peaceful surrender. The General will demand it.

—Chang Kai-Shek is leaving the Chinese in Nanking to die, he said.

—Go back to bed.

—And do nothing?

—I'm not doing nothing.

I told him I had to get the message to the General. –And, I said, pointing to the stack of papers on my desk, I have a lot more work to do. Front line messages.

He left, and I went outside to give the message to the soldier, but he wasn't there. So I went to the sleeping quarters to get my coat, but Sato wasn't in his bed. I looked everywhere for him, the east section, in the north, the kitchen where the cook was asleep on his cot next to the stove.

Ronin walked into the work area and asked what was going on. I said I'd tell him later, did he know where Sato went?

—He said he had to see Fan.

The roads were empty and dark, a milk-like fog floated low to the ground. The houses were asleep, and there was no sight of Sato. It felt like I was the only person alive in this slumbering world. I had to find Sato, stop him before he told Fan, otherwise I'd have to tell the General that the message had been leaked. And then? And then I'd have to tell him why it had been leaked. And then? And then I'd be stripped of my title, maybe sent home in disgrace.

A darker thought, one I hated to admit. Sato wanted to sabotage me. If the message was leaked, it would be less valuable, I would be less valuable.

A dark shape up ahead. I ran, he'd always been the slower runner; I caught up to Sato, grabbed his arm, and when he tried to pull it away, I threw him to the ground. In a flash, I was on top of him, pinning him to the dirt.

—They're going to walk right into this, he said.

I used my belt and tied Sato's hands behind his back, led him to the house of the General. All the way there, Sato pleaded with me to let him go. I said I would if he didn't tell Fan. Back and forth like that, Sato chiding me, calling me an idiot, and me calling him disloyal, unpatriotic.

—You believe the Japanese army will peacefully take over Nanking? he said. —How can you be so naïve? The Japanese military thought they'd take Shanghai in a matter of days, but it took months, and so many soldiers were killed. They'll seek revenge, and they'll get it—soldiers, civilians, one big bloodbath.

—You just want to undermine me, I said.

—What are you talking about? It has nothing to do with you.

—If that were true, you wouldn't be doing this to me. You're drunk on what you know—what I found out.

—Think for once about someone other than yourself. Think about Fan, her family.

At the house, a new General was there. He called Sato a traitor, handcuffed him, and the officers took him away. The new General shook my hand hard, gripping it as if to crush my fingerbones. Told me to get back to work, it would be a long night. Messages were flying. I was sent away before I could ask what happened to the old General.

Out in the night, I ran back to the villa, which was choked in ignorant, sleeping silence. Circling around and round, through the workroom, the kitchen, the inner courtyard, I wanted to walk for hours to sort things out, to run back to the new General and tell him it had been a mistake. Sato shouldn't be in handcuffs, he shouldn't be in a jail cell, and I shouldn't be congratulated. Where was the old General? But I did none of those things. I numbly sat at my desk for many terrible hours, decoding intercepted messages.

Japanese army in Nanking. Occupation of government buildings, banks, warehouses, shooting people on the street.
House to house searches for Chinese soldiers, killing civilians.
Young Chinese men shot. Children shot. Women, elderly men shot.
Women raped, young, old. Killed.
Mountain of dead bodies on the Hsiakwan wharves.
Beheadings, heads propped up on sticks.

Send help. Please.

As the morning light crept in, I put my head in my hands and wept.

Fan—Fan, where are you?

12/13

I can barely write this. Barely say his name. In his prison cell, Sato hung himself with his belt.

PART 5

Virginia sits there, hand to mouth. She rereads the last two journal entries, which doesn't bring any understanding. The names, Sato and Fan, seem brighter and larger on the screen than all the rest. She's still staring at them, when she becomes aware that Haru is talking, something about his play and Harry and a delivery to an office building, and his latest efforts to redeem himself.

"Sato," she says.

Haru stops talking.

"Sato and Fan."

"What did you say?"

She can't believe it. "Your best friend and Fan, who you adored. Loved."

"How do you—did you open my file?"

"I don't understand. He was your best friend, and Fan, she was your first love? Am I right?"

"You opened it."

He's speaking in a monotone, and it feels like an ice cube endlessly running up and down her spine. He sounds as if he's immune to the gravity of what he, as a feeling, thinking, conscious human, did.

"You had no right," he says.

"This young woman Fan, she brought you such joy, she saved you in so many ways—"

She's dumbfounded, struggling, refusing the truth with all her force, but something gives way. She gets up from her chair, backs away from the screen. "Where did you get this?"

"Why should I tell you?" he says.

"You're defending your actions?"

"I can have something that isn't yours. Do you think you have a right to know everything? Is that what you think?"

"I have the right to know who you are," she says. "This file. It wasn't there before. I've never seen it before."

"You mean control who I am."

"Control? How am I in control of anything?" She hears the screech in her voice. "If I were in control, I wouldn't be shaking right now, wondering who you really are."

Her eyes land on the photo from the Japanese Math Competition. She's in a white blouse, a slim black skirt, and Haru is beside her. A day she'll never forget because the school math teacher was there, Mr. Lutz, gray and grizzled, who refused to let her study advanced math. How she thought he'd never do what he did, which was come up to her, congratulate her, and admit he was wrong and apologize. She was wrong about him—and wrong about Haru. This man, Haru, unknowable. Who is he?

"You've always had this in you, haven't you?" she says, staring at the photo, trying to see him anew, see what she's never seen before, what he wrote—something cold and cruel that burrowed into him. "That's how you can act the way you do now—"

"And what explains your behavior?"

"What? What are you talking about?"

"Opening files that aren't for you. You're a hypocrite."

"And if I hadn't, I wouldn't have known what you did to your best friend and the woman you loved. And I wouldn't have understood why you're spying on the Chinese. It's a pattern made long ago, like an indelible flaw. An incurable disease."

"You believe you understand everything," he says.

"Obviously, I don't. "

"It's an illness, this need to know everything. I'm not spying on the Chinese. It was during the war, I was sent to war—"

She finds herself heading for the front door, and she's starting to feel numb as if an anesthesiologist gave her a shot in the arm. Or she did it herself, picked up a needle and drove it into her arm, because how else will she manage?

Outside, the roar and growl of car engines, the groans of city buses, screeches of horns, blaring music from an open car window. A clanging, clattering, strident cacophony so loud it seems determined to split her skull open. She turns, heads down a narrow side street, voices, men, women, a child begging for ice cream, and for the first time, she notices it's a sunny day. Strange for the world to be bright and sunlit, and a man to be walking his black lab, whistling an up-and-down tune, and the boy who wants ice cream is skipping ahead of his mother down the sidewalk. It's all so ordinary, life swimming along.

She has the urge to turn back, open her apartment door, and yank the photos off the wall, all of them, smash them to pieces. Because the man in those photos, that man with a smile, his dark happy eyes, with his expression of ease and accomplishment, that man who opened the door to her life, to her heart, doesn't exist. She fell in love with a lie and what does that say about her?

She's aware she's overwhelmed and rushing to conclusions that are stark and harsh. She needs to clear a space to think. He was only 17 or 18, so young, so inchoate. Far from home, in way over his head. But at that age, he must have had a moral code. He turned his back on his best friend, and he let the love of his life walk straight to her death. Even if he had one doubt, he should have done something, she would have done something. But the moment she thinks this, she stops herself. All that she's read about war, how it warps people, twists them into unrecognizable shapes. She's lived long enough to know better than to judge someone the way she is right now.

The only thing she knows for sure is that she doesn't want to be home, to hear his defense, his rationale or reasoning, any of it. As she passes by the library, she considers going inside, plunging into a math book to escape, but she knows it won't work. It feels as if something enormous is sitting on her chest, making it difficult to breathe. She keeps walking, one foot after another, without any idea where she is going. She's in a new reality that she never wanted.

A man shoves a flyer for a shoe store at her, and when she says no, she realizes her throat is parched, and it's hard to swallow. She stops at a corner grocery store, a dusty little place, with aisles so narrow it's nearly impossible for two people to walk down them in opposite directions. An old woman, with a hunched back and white cardigan sweater buttoned all the way up, is standing in front of the rows of yogurt, muttering something about vanilla. Virginia buys a bottle of water, and the check-out clerk, an Indian man with kind, brown eyes, tells her to have a nice day.

She sits outside the grocery store on a rickety bench, NS+PS=Love dug into the wood. For a long time, she sits, feeling her feet clotted with ache. With the sun out, everything is painted gold, the trees, buildings, people, and she feels even more isolated, as if she is confined to a storm cloud, separated from the world. A group of teenagers walk by, laughing, not joyous laughter, but denigrating and mocking, and she feels a small measure of ease.

"Are you all right?" The check-out clerk is standing in front of her. He must be in his fifties, with gray at his temples, and deep lines around his mouth. "Should I call someone? You've been sitting here for quite some time. Are you lost?"

Lost? She supposes she is. She's wandered far from what she thought she once knew.

"You're shivering."

She looks down and sees she's clutching her elbows, shaking.

The clerk goes into the shop and returns with a cup of hot tea. "Here."

"Thank you." She sips the tea. It dawns on her that he might think she is senile, suffering from dementia, meandering the city in a confused state. Despite herself, she must make an effort for this kind man. "Oh, this is good. I don't mean to cause you any trouble."

"My dear, no trouble at all."

What a gentleman. And now a memory of Haru bobs to the surface, that time when she showed up at his apartment, with rain-soaked hair, her black coat beaded with water. He handed her a towel, one of his sweaters, a cup of green tea, and his voice was calm and soothing as if she was the most important person in the world. "We must get you warm, so you don't get sick," he'd said. She blinks rapidly to keep tears from glassing her eyes.

"I'm just tired," she says. "Worn to the bone by life."

"Ah, yes. The world takes and takes from you." He tells her he's had many days like the one she's having, ever since his mother died. Three months ago, she passed, and ever since, even today with bright sunlight, there's a gray patina. "She was the one I could talk to about anything," he says. "Always there for me, always accepting and loving and helpful." When his father died, he felt nothing. His father, a small man, a cruel dictator who ordered the family around and slapped his mother when she disobeyed and beat his children when they were unruly or whenever he felt like it.

"I'm sorry," she manages to say.

"Sit for as long as you like," he says. "I'll call you a taxi when you're ready to go."

Instead of heading back inside, he takes a seat beside her. While he talks lovingly about his mother, a woman who could do no wrong, she remembers the man whom she met her second year at MIT. Daichi, a Japanese man, who was in her advanced statistics class. He had a muscular stride and blazing dark eyes under his heavy brows. He fell madly in love with Virginia and listened attentively to her sorrows, she was spilling over with grief. After several dates, he invited her to supper at his mother's home in Buck's County, Pennsylvania. His mother, a Japanese woman who loved and adored her son, let her motherly love overflow to Virginia, enveloping her, and Virginia was intoxicated by it. His mother wrapped up extra teriyaki chicken for Virginia to take back with her to college, along with a canister of green tea leaves. After that dinner, Virginia dated Daichi for eight months, hoping she'd fall in love with him and let him replace the loss of Haru, so she could go to Sunday supper at his mother's and bathe in that nurturing. She ended it because his intense, deep-set eyes too often reminded her of Haru, Haru, who had died one year before she met Daichi.

Three people head into the grocery store, and the clerk pats Virginia's knee and goes back inside. Virginia takes this opportunity to move along. The light changes and darkness slinks into the corners of the city, swallowing it up.

In her apartment, she walks right past the study and straight to the shower, where she stays until the bathroom is fogged. When she passes by the study again, Haru calls out for her. She closes the study door, so his voice is muffled. In her bedroom, thankfully, she can't hear him. She lies down and turns on the radio to what seems to be an endless loop of jazz and she closes her eyes, but her heart leaps up in her chest so painfully, she has to sit up to breathe.

———

In the morning, she wakes to Haru calling for her, like an insistent child who won't calm down until their mother presents herself.

She whips open the door. "Please stop. Just stop."

"I didn't know where you were. I thought something awful happened to you."

She stares at the computer screen.

"Let's work on something," he says. "No one has yet solved the Riemann hypothesis. Why don't we? It'll be fun. Just like old times."

As if she can forget his past; as if she can erase the memory, return to innocence and ignorance. Frustrated fury boils inside.

"Where did you get that file?" she says.

"What file?"

The photos on the wall mock her, jab a finger into her ribs. She starts taking them down as if they're soiling the wall.

"What are you doing?"

She doesn't answer, just keeps removing them, stacking them in a pile on the floor, not caring about the consequences.

"The Japanese military did an investigation and took my journal. After the war the government uploaded their wartime documents to their computers, and in the 1990s, began declassifying them so historians could study them. Virginia, I wasn't in charge, I didn't know about the new General—"

The air suddenly feels unbearably heavy. "Oh, god," she says, dropping a photo, the glass cracking. "How pathetic. You knew something bad was going to happen to Sato, even if your friendly General was there. You chose not to warn Fan and her family. You're far too smart to hide behind ignorance. What made you do it? Your sense of superiority? Your hubris? There was always that about you, wasn't there? You took only the best students, the students who wanted to solve the most difficult equations, who were capable of accomplishing such a feat. You needed their glow to shine on you, so you burned brighter. You needed me to shine the brightest of all."

"You did shine brightest," he says.

"I didn't. I failed the math test the first time," she says. "I worked really hard all the time."

"You just needed someone to show you. A quick mind, a very quick, alert mind."

Outside, a jackhammer starts to pound. One of the windows must be open because it sounds like the hammering is inside the apartment, inside her skull.

"Did you take the photos down?"

"Was Sato's mind not quick enough for you? Fan's? Were they too flawed for you to love them? How did they become nothing to you?"

"I was following orders," he says. "After the war, I vowed not to follow orders anymore and I didn't. I went against all the rules and agreed to be your tutor."

"But you're following orders now, aren't you? The Chinese government's orders to turn over information about dissidents."

He doesn't say anything. Then: "Are we arguing?"

"What do you think?"

"You were the most intelligent—"

"Stop," she says.

Pause. "Are we arguing?"

"Yes! Why do you keep asking me that?"

"What I told you was true, and by the way, you needed to hear my praise," he said. "When I first met you, you were a dry sponge, so beaten down. Everything I said was true, and you needed to hear it."

The blank wall stares at her, only the outlines of the photos that once hung on the wall. She prefers it this way—blank, empty, a chasm. The expanse of all she didn't know about him.

"Why the Chinese? How can you be working for the Chinese government?" she says.

"Have you ever considered there's a reality beyond your understanding?"

"Why do you have the list of people who are being watched?"

He sighs. "So I know who the government is targeting."

"Why?"

"So I can help them."

She doesn't want to go round and round again, and she doesn't want to feel this surge of anger in her bloodstream. Maybe he is trying to help, and in the process, he is causing harm, though how this might be happening, she has no idea. She's also aware she's working hard to give him the benefit of the doubt.

"I don't know what to believe," she says.

"So what are you going to do? Fit me with a lie detector?" he says.

Abruptly now, she hates him. "I'm so sick of this. Sick of you."

Sweat slides from her armpits down her sides. The words she just uttered, words she's never before said to him, searing words, blare in her ears. When her phone rings, she's relieved for the interruption, overjoyed to see it's Brian.

"Something's happened," says Brian. "That woman. Sara Zhang. She died in jail."

The room quakes. Virginia drops in her chair, one hand on her chest.

He read about it in a Chinese chatroom, more than one posting. "She needed her medication, but the guards wouldn't give it to her."

Virginia feels like she'll be pinned to this moment forever. It will never release her, she will circle right here.

"I'll come over," says Brian.

"No, I'll go to you," she says.

When she hangs up, she heads straight to the computer and permanently deletes Haru's journal. Then grabs her coat, and when Haru calls out, "Where are you going?" she doesn't stop.

The wind is blowing hard, tossing up the trash from the bin. She walks faster than she should, and it feels like she can't get enough oxygen. With the file gone, there will be no more spying, and no one else will be jailed, and no one else will die, and she'll no longer have to brace herself every day for more horrible news. At least that's her hope.

Two blocks later, when her phone rings again, she's about to answer it and tell Brian she's 15 minutes away from his apartment. It's the CEO of Gilivable. She ignores the call, hurries down the sidewalk. From somewhere comes a sweet smell that reminds her of something terrible, but she doesn't have the energy to recollect. When she turns the corner, breathing hard, she keeps going at the same clip, her heart racing; she feels an overwhelming sense of lightness.

———

By the time she makes it to Brian's apartment, a mass of gloomy clouds hovers over the Bay, looking like a menacing city. Brian's generous energy, she wants to be swept up in it, engulfed by it, and he does just that, inviting her in, a different universe with the smell of coffee and lavender from a recent shower and his thick hair with its bronze gleam. He's wearing a white T-shirt, faded jeans, barefoot. Such long toes.

He takes her by the arm and leads her to his computer. He flips through screens until he finds the Chinese chatroom where he read about Sara Zhang. Five different people are talking about what happened to the young woman. A diabetic, she needed insulin, according to one. Her husband had finally found her in a jail outside of Shanghai. He refused to leave until he gave her the insulin. The guards ignored him.

Virginia gets up and moves to his sofa. Brian comes over and hands her a drink and sits down beside her. Her phone rings. Gilivable again. She turns it off and tells Brian about the file in Haru's neural network, Haru's time in World War II as part of a cipher unit. A young man, spying on the Chinese, deciphering their messages.

His face rearranges into a blossoming epiphany. "He can't help himself," says Brian, looking straight ahead as if talking to himself. "That has to be it. He has to continue to gather information and decipher it."

"What happened back then was traumatic."

He waits.

"His best friend died."

Brian exhales loudly. "Poor guy."

She's not sure if he's referring to Haru's friend or to Haru.

"And a woman he loved. It was Haru's fault," she says.

A long silence. "He must have been tortured with guilt," says Brian. "From how you've described him, he sounded like a sensitive soul."

"I deleted the file that contained his journal," she says.

Brian nods slowly, studying her, trying to gauge her.

"I think I've probably changed him," she says.

"But maybe you've fixed the problem," he says.

"I know I've changed him. Gilivable keeps calling."

"Maybe it was the only solution. It's what you had to do."

When Brian touches the top of her hand, she feels the jolt of physical contact. He smiles as if hoping to lift the despair that has settled on her. And now he is looking at her with bright hazel eyes, a direct gaze right into her, and she remembers the man whom she met when she did her graduate work at MIT. Cloistered in the computer lab, busy building one of the first computer programs that translated Japanese into English and vice versa, she rarely saw the light of day. Izumi was the man's name, Izumi, who was groomed and sleek and looked with candor at the world, at her. He was a graduate student in the computer science department with her and told her directly that he was attracted to her intellect, but a month into the relationship, it seemed they talked very little. That autumn was about mouths and hands. In her mind, she has an image of her younger self, the swing of slender hip into thigh, the rose-tipped breasts perched above her rib cage. His body, the stretch of smooth, hairless chest, strong arms grabbing her, because he couldn't wait to walk down the hall to the bedroom. They were never patient; they were always hungry. She'd never had such a physical relationship; she was an entirely different person with him. She'd step into his apartment and immediately begin shedding clothes and unbuckling his belt and pulling it through the loops. What can one make of episodes like this, so out of character? Are they just holes in the self? Or part of the self that remains hidden for most of the year, only to emerge with a blue full moon?

She can't remember how the relationship with Izumi ended, though she guesses, he, too, hauled up too many memories of Haru. Maybe it was Izumi's cadence or the tilt of his head or the curve of his mouth. It most likely became insufferable.

"But maybe I've changed him into someone who isn't Haru," she says. "I don't know, and I guess I won't know for a while. I acted impulsively, just got rid of it."

Brian says again that it's precisely what she needed to do so no one else will be harmed. If it was just between her and Haru, she could have been more circumspect. But it isn't.

She wants to believe this, but why is her heart lunging in thick, heavy beats, making it difficult to speak? Brian's curving mouth falls into a frown. His eyes turn watchful as if trying to pry her open. He's waiting for her to say more, and when she doesn't, when tears start streaming down her face, he gets up and holds her. This is the role he's always played in her life. Countless times, offering his reassurance. She'll do well; she'll give a wonderful speech; she's remarkable, all said in a warm, generous voice, one that she loves to hear. And that is what their embrace is at first, reassurance, comfort, but then it changes into something else, something more, with his warm breath on her cheek, his hands on her back, tracing her spine. She closes her eyes. It has been so long, the warmth of skin, a man's scent, Brian's tang of eucalyptus, and something earthy. How much she's missed a man's body, the strength, the largeness wrapping her up, his lips pressed on hers, tenderly at first, then more urgently.

His bedroom is beautifully dark, a rich brown light as if

they've fallen off the edge of the world. She's surprised at how much she wants this, she is steeped in desire for him and it's wonderful.

He makes love to her with the same blend of gentleness and desire, and she is happily transported away from her life; she is young, she is old, she feels no age at all. She exists, she doesn't exist; she's a body, she's immense feeling. When she grabs his arm hard, he becomes less gentle, more passionate, more desirous, pressing himself into her, and his hands roam her body as if he must touch every part of her.

Afterward, Brian strokes her hair. "Can you stay longer? How about a walk? We could get in the car and go to Ocean Beach. On foggy days, no one is there. It feels like the world is yours. We could go out to lunch afterward. Or better yet, I'll cook you lunch. You know how I love to cook."

She sits up, holding the sheet to her breasts. To be with Brian, warm skin pressed against hers, her hands clutching his back, days of his body alighting her. The lunches and dinners together, the conversations. Brian reaches over and kisses the inside of her wrist.

But her fantasy brings with it another feeling that is causing her breath to shorten. To say yes to Brian, to what he is offering her, it feels as if everything has left her—the life she had with Haru and the life she had never lived. Both weigh tremendously, and if they are gone, she'll become insignificant, she'll float away into nothing.

"I don't want to lose our friendship," she says. "I still want us to be comfortable with each other."

"We'll always stay friends. We'll never mention this to anyone. We won't even bring it up to each other." He puts his finger to his lips.

She laughs. Only Brian could make her laugh at a time like this.

"I should go," she says.

He hesitates, and at that moment, she wants to grab the future she's pushing away. Then Brian is out of bed, pulling on his jeans and shirt, and the day is moving forward, so she slips on her dress. He walks her to the door. She hopes he doesn't say anything; as if he can read her mind, he wordlessly kisses her on the nape of her neck. She walks down the stairs.

As she slowly heads home, Brian is still with her, the memory of his hands all over her, her skin still flush from his touch. A light rain falls, silvery drops. When she turns the corner and sees her apartment building, the rain comes harder, and now there is a scratchy texture rubbing her insides, and with each step, it becomes worse, guilt eviscerating everything.

She's been with other men, but not when Haru was alive. In this day and age, she supposes she's old-fashioned this way. She can smell sex on her, Brian's scent mingled with her own. In the lobby, she takes off her coat and steps into the elevator. When she arrives at her floor, she pulls out her house key but is unable to walk to the door, as if her feet are stuck to the carpet.

She'll take a shower, put this behind her. Tell Brian it can never happen again. She opens the front door, expecting Haru's voice, but there is silence, the beautiful sound of silence. She steps into the kitchen and from the square crystal decanter pours herself a whiskey. The first sip loosens the vexing knots inside. There's a break in the rain and the light is peach, and it fills the kitchen and shines on the blue glasses.

She'll tell Haru. She's never been good at keeping secrets. Her body betrays her, handing over its secrets like a bouquet of flowers. When Virginia got pregnant, her mother knew before Virginia did. Your smell, her mother said. "And you keep holding your stomach." The doctor confirmed it, and when it was the right time, her mother found the right doctor, and that was the end of it. They never spoke of it again, she and her mother, but the baby lived on in Virginia's mind. Their baby, Haru's and hers. Too early to know its gender, but in her imagination, it was a girl, a stunningly intelligent girl, and Haru, the ideal father, handed her the world. He would never abandon them; unthinkable for him to do so. They would teach her everything, let her bloom into an astonishing human being. But by the time she found out she was pregnant, Haru was dead and she couldn't suffer another day in Japan, so there would be no father, no family, no little girl.

But what good would it do to tell Haru? If he has feelings or something approximating feelings, though what she means by that she doesn't know, it will only hurt him.

Next door, there is pounding and sawing. Her neighbor left her a note yesterday saying they were redoing their kitchen, and unfortunately, there would be noise.

She showers and dresses, aware she's moving slowly, delaying this encounter. Her face glows; she looks younger, full of recklessness. Thank god Haru can't see her. She considered adding a video camera, so Haru could collect visual data, but decided against it. Vanity, she supposed—all the memories she uploaded for him were of her as a beautiful young woman. Now, the only part of her that resembles that young woman is her eyes. Blue water eyes, he called them.

Haru was right about Brian. He insisted Brian had fallen in love with her, but she dismissed it. What else is he right about that she's rejected? What else has she not seen because she wants reality a certain way? On her iPad, she opens the newspaper, skims the headlines and finds herself reading with Haru in mind, what he'd like to talk about. She feels herself softening toward him, wanting the space inside that is his—it's always been his—to fill up with him.

She steps into the study. The computer screen is shockingly blank. A black rectangle of absolute nothing.

"Haru?" she says.

When nothing happens, a flurry of fear runs through her. She puts her hand on the computer hard drive. Cold. Haru has been shut down for hours. She stands there, thinking a million chaotic thoughts, her anxiety rising. Where has he gone to? Her gaze travels up to the blank wall. With all the photos gone, it's as if that part of her life never happened. Her stark empty life. She touches the computer again, and the black screen stares at her. She sees her reflection on the blank screen, a face of incomprehension.

Another thing Haru was right about: as a young woman, she soaked up his praise, she couldn't get enough of it. Over the years, as she learned more about computers and AI, she got drunk on her omnipotence. So few people knew what she knew, let alone understand it. If she encountered a wall, she threw herself against it or over it, until it was scaled, or she destroyed it. She knew what she wanted and wouldn't stop until she got it: to resurrect Haru and have him as her companion. And when he acted out, when he became something she didn't like, she stripped him of his journal because she thought—a guess only—it had embedded the blueprint for spying. In the process, though, she might have killed him —again.

PART 6

W e'd finished a math session, and I was in Haru's kitchen, chopping cucumbers and daikon and green onions. Haru was at the kitchen table, a look of concentration pinching his face, as he worked on his proposal for the university to purchase a Manchester Electronic Computer. As head of the math department, he wanted to make Tokyo University a leader in computer programming. He was very excited about it, convinced computers would change the world, telling me, with such effusiveness, all about the computer and how it could accomplish in two-seconds what a human could in an average workday.

The computer, like a lighthouse on a dark sea, had his full attention, the powerful computer with its beaming, hopeful ray. He went on, lauding its memory capacity, how it could hold more than 15,000 twelve-digit decimal numbers and recall any one of them within one-thirtieth of a second. If you turned off the machine, unlike humans with their faulty memories, the numbers weren't lost because they were stored magnetically. And based on the equations given to it, it could make decisions. "This is what you have to focus on, Virginia," he said. "This is your future."

I was eighteen years old, and I planned to go to Tokyo University and study math with him. I was slicing raw tuna and making little mounds of rice for sashimi, when the apartment buzzer rang, an awful high-pitched whine like a fire alarm.

Haru had forgotten he'd scheduled a make-up tutoring session. "Should I leave?" I said.

"Why?" he said, studying me, at first bewildered and then dismissive. "No."

A boy who looked to be about nine years old stood at the front door. He had a broad, round face, and his black hair was as thick as a shag rug, rising at least two inches from his scalp. Sora was his name, and he had the confidence and shine of an accomplished man.

"Who are you?" said Sora, staring at me.

Though Haru said I should stay, I wasn't sure about that. "Right now, I'm the cook," I said.

"She's also a superb mathematician," said Haru.

The boy looked at me harder. "I never heard of a girl who was good at math."

"Really?" I said. "No one in your class?"

"Maybe Junko but she never talks or goes to the board to do the equations. She's nice because on her birthday, she gave everyone a dagashi treat."

Sora sat at the table, and I brought him a glass of water and orange slices. He picked up an orange section and stuck it in his mouth, giving me an orange smile, which made me laugh.

"Look at what I solved," said Sora, his voice swelling with pride. From a thick binder, he pulled out his math sheet, and as he explained how he solved the algebra problem, Haru came beside me, and his hand brushed my arm.

"Tell me how you solved the next problem," said Haru.

Sora let out a big sigh. "Well, this one took a lot of hard work."

"But you stuck with it," said Haru.

"Yes," said the boy, solemnly. "You told me I could do it, so I knew I could. Do you want to see, too?" he said, looking at me.

"I do," I said.

In an excited voice, Sora began explaining the problem, and Haru smiled at me and lightly rested his hand on my shoulder. I couldn't pay attention to Sora and what he was saying because all my attention was on Haru's hand on my shoulder and the warmth seeping through my blouse.

When Sora was done, Haru said, "Wonderful!"

Haru gave him a new math sheet. When the boy picked up his pencil and began working, Haru moved his hand to my neck, only the slightest pressure in his fingertips. Everything vibrated inside, and I stepped closer, my hip touching his leg. Then Haru took his hand away and moved to the other side of the table and sat across from Sora. I went back to the kitchen and finished making dinner, though I felt myself listening for Haru's voice. I loved his voice, which promised great things were inside you, and even if you believed otherwise when you heard it, you expanded to fit his belief. He never minimized or diminished or underestimated; it was what the best teachers did, which was find the gold inside. He and the boy laughed, and I smiled and stopped slicing the beef and wanted to go to the table with its towers of math books and laugh with them. Even though I was in the kitchen, I felt intimately involved in what was happening in the living room.

At 6:30, when the session was over, I went out to the hallway and stood beside Haru. "You did very well today," said Haru.

Sora smiled and bowed his head. "Thank you, sensei."

"Goodbye," I said. "A pleasure to meet you."

"Goodbye," said the boy, smiling at me and it was clear whatever bafflement I had caused earlier had been resolved.

Afterward, Haru's face was radiant, reveling in the boy's success. "A very bright boy," said Haru. "Like all my students. It's a pleasure, a real pleasure." His voice was full of awe, and he put his hand over his mouth, a gesture he used to conceal his strong emotions.

The apartment was scented with dinner, and we went to the kitchen table.

"Do you like the salad?" I said.

"I do," he said.

"I used endive."

The last of the day's light poured in, warming the walls with pink.

"He's lucky," I said. "He's learning so much at such a young age. I wish I'd known you back then."

Haru smiled. "The dinner is magnificent. After this, absolutely everything will pale."

The window was still open, and a laugh floated in. A car honked, someone yelled, and a door slammed in the hallway. Haru sighed. "Sometimes I wished I lived in the country, away from everything."

I couldn't imagine him anywhere but Tokyo, living in this beautiful apartment, with his math books and small ivory figurines, eating an expensive meal every night. When I told him that, he laughed and said, in fact, as a boy, he'd spent summers in the country with his family. They'd travel to Northern Japan, up to Hokkaido, where they'd fish and swim. Idyllic days. With the whine of insects, the trill of cicadas, they stayed in a little wood cottage by a lake, and the golden summer wafted by without anything planned.

I couldn't see him near a lake or in a forest or holding a fishing pole. It felt like he was describing a fantasy or someone else's life. He was always working, always had a project. He had a vibrant, impatient, restless energy. If he were in the country with nothing to do but lie in a field and stare at the clouds, he'd die of boredom. When I told him that, he just smiled.

"But this," he said. "An exquisite meal and your company. It's lovely."

"There's more food."

We went to the kitchen. I opened the refrigerator and brought out a strawberry pie.

A wide smile. "Oh, you're tempting me," he said.

I stood beside him. His dark eyes were gleaming. "You could say no," I said.

He laughed, cut a slice of pie, and ate a forkful. "Oh, now, it's too good. You have to have some with me."

We were nearly the same height, and he was standing close, so close to me. I was wearing lipstick and blush and mascara. It was almost 8:00 pm. By now, Mother was home from work, but she no longer cared how late I stayed out and she rarely asked me about anything. Since she'd found me a math tutor, she no longer bothered with me. She had her throbbing feet, her aching back, the misery of her life. It was enough company for her, and so I had all the freedom in the world.

I stepped toward him, it was the most natural thing, until there was no gap between us, and I wrapped my arms around his neck, and we stood like that, pressed together, breathing in and out. His hair smelled like him, a mix of cigarette smoke, soy sauce, and ginger. Please don't move, I thought.

Tentatively, I put my lips to the side of his neck and felt his pulse and then his laughter, and when he pulled me closer, tighter, I let out a little puff of air. He moved my hair off my shoulder, gently, and as he did, I stepped out of his embrace and moved past him, down the hallway, as if I knew what I was doing—and I did know, I knew what I wanted, what my body ached for—and I felt his hand on the small of my back.

In his dimly lit bedroom, he unwound the scarf from my neck and it felt like he was unraveling me. The faint sound of a zipper. I raised my arms, my dress fell in a heap. I laughed, a release, a ripple of joy. The last of the light fled the room, and a sliver of silver light from the full moon slipped in. I couldn't believe this was happening, and more than anything, I wanted it to happen, as I undid each button of his shirt, and he pulled his arms through the sleeves and let it drop to the floor. His eyes, darker now in the moonlight, were on me, as if I was what they'd always been searching for. Was I? I hoped so, I felt so. With his hand on the back of my head, he kissed me, and his mouth tasted like strawberries and sake. He kissed my collar bone, and I tilted my head back, and he kissed my throat, and my breasts and the light changed.

I went to his futon, and he followed me, his hand on my hip and slowly, with one hand on my shoulder, he lowered me down, and he slipped out of his trousers and underwear and lay beside me. His smooth chest was smooth like a mirror, and I ran my hand up and down.

"Haru," I said, smiling, looking into his eyes.

"Virginia," he said, smiling.

He was on top of me, and when I came, I gripped both of his shoulders, holding on because I'd never felt anything like this as if I was soaring to the ceiling with pleasure. He came right after me, and after, we lay side by side, staring at each other, not saying a word. He stroked my hair, my cheek, and I slid one of my legs between his. For the longest time, we lay like this.

"You're beautiful," he said. "All of you."

With him looking at me like that, I felt beautiful, I felt I was someone glorious, the way he was looking at me, and I knew the minute he stopped looking I would go back to who I was, which was a being, not extraordinary, not ordinary, a being only.

When I stood and slipped on my dress, he turned on the little light on his nightstand and got out of bed and carefully wound the scarf around my neck. He pulled on his trousers, took my hand in his, led me to the door, and kissed me on the mouth.

———

Outside, the world had a soft glow to it, with the streetlights and cars and little shops and everything seemed to flow through me, and everyone on the street seemed to be a couple, young and old, walking arm and arm. I'd never noticed all the couples before, but it seemed the purpose of the world; the human heart hoped for such a thing. How obvious it seemed now, and I laughed because I'd lived so long without knowing this but now I knew.

Music from the karaoke bars tumbled onto the sidewalk, and here was the candy shop with coffee and cocoa pocky sticks, and here was the subway stop where I got off to meet Haru for the first time, and here was the shop with the white wedding kimono. I stopped and looked at the kimono, and in the glass, my face looked different to me. More set, more final, my mouth had a satisfied look to it, and my eyes were full of new knowledge. The edges of myself were more defined. It's as it should be, that's the phrase that repeated in my mind. It's as it should be.

Mother was home, soaking her feet. Her face looked wilted, and her eyes held exhaustion and perpetual anger.

"Why are you so late?" she said.

"Studying."

"There's rice."

"I already ate."

She grunted, dried her feet, and shuffled to her bed, her thin back to me. I felt guilty, how full I was, filled with Haru. "Can I get you anything?" I was overflowing with pleasure, and I wanted her to have this feeling, too.

She mumbled something and soon began to snore.

I opened my history book but couldn't read one word. Haru's mouth on mine. Haru inside me. I'd never felt so intimately connected to another human being. I'd have to wait another week to see him, which was impossible. I barely slept that night, going over and over the feeling of his hands on my body, his warm skin pressed against mine, the taste of his mouth. It felt like I was burning, burning inside, burning bright.

———

The next day after school, I waited outside his apartment building. I wanted to ring his bell and run up the stairs, but I made myself wait. Eventually, Haru came rushing down the front steps, which I knew meant he only had a slice of time before his next student. He startled when he saw me, but his surprise gave way to a warm, welcoming smile. I lied and told him that his apartment was on my way home from school so the awkwardness would go away. What a pleasant surprise to see him! He was heading to the grocery store for a bento box because he was starving. He had another student in fifteen minutes; otherwise, he'd invite me up. There was a lot of pie left to eat.

I stood in line with him, I was swollen with love. The store was full of bustle, but it was happening without touching us, carts rolling by, people putting lettuce and apples in bags, and it felt as if we were watching a play or we were the main characters in one.

We walked back to his apartment building.

"Come by tomorrow," he said, "if you have time." He didn't have a student until 5:00 pm. "If you'd like," he added. Right before he left, he touched the back of my hand.

For the next several weeks, I saw him not only for my math sessions on Tuesdays but Wednesdays and Saturdays. We'd make love and lie in bed, and sometimes he would fall asleep, and I would watch the dreams move across his face. I'd never seen his face look so calm, so smooth, without the lines of intensity around his eyes. Gone, too, were the lines on his forehead, which, I realized, gave him an anxious look. Asleep, he was a picture of contentment and peace. When the light slipped in through the crack in the curtain, his hair lit up like glass. I wanted to touch it, but I didn't want to wake him. He never came before me, because he said he wanted me to experience pleasure, too. He taught me to take possession of him as he took possession of me.

One Tuesday night, after I came home from his house at 11:00, Mother was still awake. She sat up in bed and narrowed her eyes, not saying anything for the longest time. "You're going to get pregnant."

My face burned with shame and anger. I put down my bowl of rice. "I didn't—"

"Don't lie. I found your diary."

I hated her, her ugly nightgown, her worn-out face. "How could you—"

"I don't care what you do," she said. "You're old enough. Just don't get pregnant."

The room closed in around us.

"And if you do," her mother said, "tell me."

"Why?"

"I'll find the right doctor."

My mother is dead, over 15 years now. The one blouse I kept of hers has lost its scent. But I remember this conversation as if it happened yesterday. A pragmatist, a realist, my mother was, and even back then, I thought what she said to me was the perfect thing. I wouldn't stop making love to him; I couldn't look away from him, she knew that. Mother must have remembered the intoxicating power of love. She'd loved Father, even if she wished it weren't true, and he still held her in his far-away grip.

The math and the lovemaking went on into the summer, days of haze and heat. Another thing changed; in my mind, we were together, we were a couple. When I thought of myself, I thought of Haru too.

I was heading down the sidewalk to Haru's apartment when I saw her. At the bottom of his apartment steps was the woman. The woman who, it seemed like a lifetime ago, had grabbed Haru's arm, whom he'd shaken off like an irritating thing. She wore the same gray shabby coat, and she kept tilting her head back, staring up at Haru's second-floor apartment, as if it held the answer but would not give it to her.

I approached, and she looked at me, and I saw in her eyes that she recognized me.

"Are you going to see Haru-san?" said the woman.

Who was she? What did she want from him? She looked as fragile as a wine glass. I wanted to break her.

"I rang his apartment buzzer, but he doesn't answer," she said. "Is he home?"

My math session was in ten minutes, Haru was probably in the shower. Or maybe he knew who was ringing the buzzer—this woman. He'd given me the passcode to get in the building, so I no longer had to ring, unlike this woman. I had on my backpack, which was full of heavy math books, and I was carrying a grocery bag with rice, fish, and fresh bok choy to cook for dinner. Behind us was the bleat of car horns.

"I don't know," I said.

"I have to talk to him."

"Why?" And I almost said, what do you want from him?

The woman bit her lower lip, and tears filled her eyes. I wanted to get away from her, to rush to Haru's apartment, close his door, forget her, forget this ever happened.

"He hasn't told you anything about me?" she said.

"No."

"He wants to pretend the whole thing never happened. How much easier it is for him not to see me, to make-believe it never happened."

I rushed up the stairs, pushed the buttons, and hurried through the lobby, up the steps. When he opened the door, Haru bowed and smiled. I put my hand on his chest.

We'd agreed we'd wait until after the math session. It was

important to him, so he could teach me as much as possible and to do that, I must have complete focus. He studied me as if trying to understand what I was doing, my hand on his chest, why I was violating our agreement.

I didn't say anything, and his face tightened, and he stepped away from me and led the way to the table. He sat in his usual spot, across from me, and when I pulled out my math sheet, he handed me a new one, though I didn't start it right away, still thinking about the woman downstairs.

"What's wrong?" he said.

"Nothing."

He frowned. "OK, let's begin."

I nodded slowly, picked up a pencil, and read the first problem: The lifespans of zebras in a particular zoo are normally distributed, with the average zebra living 20.5 years, and the standard deviation is 3.9 years. Use the empirical rule (68-95-99.7%) to estimate the probability of a zebra living between 16.6 and 24.4 years. Soon I was soaring over a boundary, my mind swirling with numbers, far away from the woman with tears in her eyes.

Later at dinner, he gave me a look of concern. "Is everything OK? Did something happen?"

By then, the woman had become insignificant, a dot in the far distance. "No, I'm fine," I said. "Any news about your proposal for the computer?"

He smiled grandly and poured two glasses of sake and he handed me one and raised his cup. "A celebration," he said. The university had accepted it, and the computer would be delivered next month.

"Congratulations!" This was his dream, to make the university a leader in computer science.

"You bring me good luck."

I got up, went over to his side of the table and kissed him.

"Promise you'll always be with me," he said.

"I will."

"No, don't say it blithely. I don't want an idle promise. I need to know you mean it."

"I mean it. I love you."

He kissed me for a long time. "I love you, too."

That night, when I came down the stairs and stood in the lobby, I hesitated, trying to see through the front door window if the woman was out there. I imagined her standing for endless hours and she was permanently fixed to the landscape like a streetlight, in the heat and cold, in the howling wind and the little trees in front of the apartment shaking their leaves. She would always be there like a ghost haunting Haru.

I'd stayed longer than usual at Haru's, and there was a hush in the apartment building as if everyone had gone to sleep. It was too dark to see through the door window, so I stepped out on the landing. I planned to rush right by the woman, as Haru did that first time, and if the woman grabbed my arm, I'd yank it away and hurtle myself into the night just as he did.

Fortunately, she wasn't there, but as I hurried down the sidewalk, I hunted for her in the doorways, in the small alleys, the alcoves, as if she might spring out like a feral cat and scratch out my eyes.

———

I forgot about her—or pushed her out of my mind—like unwanted clutter. It was the end of August, the days hot and humid like steam on my skin. None of this discomfort mattered. I was at the end of a road, and about to take a new direction, and the direction was the right one, the best one for me: I'd turned nineteen and, in mid-September, I'd begin studying at Tokyo University because I was one of five young women whom Haru had accepted into the math program. The future was an astonishing material substance in my hands.

Then I saw her. I was walking down the sidewalk to Haru's apartment, and she was heading away from me. I recognized her shabby gray coat, her black stockings, her brown purse hanging limply from her arm. She must have been waiting in front of his apartment and grown tired. She seemed to float down the sidewalk, becoming smaller and smaller, swallowed up by distance, so by the time I was up the stairs, I could let the day expand to a reality of Haru and math and shabu shabu and lovemaking.

A week later, on a Friday, I received a letter in the mail, a letter of congratulations, telling me I'd qualified for the U.S. Math Competition. It would be held in Washington D.C. Mother took my face in her cold, bony hands. "I'm so proud of you," she said. Mother's complexion was the color of fresh peaches, and I wanted her to always look like that, and I knew it was my job to return her to herself. "I feel bad we didn't do anything for your birthday," she said. "Should we go to dinner tonight?" I told her I wanted her to save her money. This, I said picking up the letter, is enough. She went to her dresser and opened a drawer, and underneath her underwear and bras, she pulled out a thin gold necklace. "It's yours now," she said and put it around my neck. "It's real gold." She smiled helplessly, and I hugged her and told her it was beautiful.

I didn't usually go to Haru's on Fridays because he worked from home that day on his own projects—no students, no tutoring, no university work. He needed time for his mind to be alone. Maybe he could go with me to America, I thought, grabbing my black coat; maybe we could stay in a fancy hotel and order room service. If I won the competition, I'd get $1,000.

The city was crowded, with Japanese women holding black umbrellas, shielding themselves from the blazing sun, keeping their skin as white as paper. At the secondhand store, I'd found a big straw hat with a 24-inch rim. I liked the hat, the way it shaded my face, extending so far out, turning me into a mystery. I'd also found a pretty flower print dress, white with little green and blue flowers, and when I tried it on, the Japanese clerk said it went well with my bright blue eyes.

On the way to his apartment, I took off my coat and bought two bento boxes because he'd likely worked all morning and hadn't eaten anything but a bowl of miso soup. Maybe we could go to the sea and swim in the waves. All those months ago, when my mother declared I would not marry—she was wrong. I would marry, I'd marry Haru Fukumoto, and we'd live in Japan. I'd become a math professor at Tokyo University, and every day I'd walk to work with Haru, and we'd work on the computer together and create things no one had ever imagined. Did I love you then, Haru? Yes, madly. In my mind, I thought of myself as Mrs. Virginia Fukumoto—it was only a matter of time.

The woman stood at the bottom of the apartment stairs. Today her hair was not in a bun, but loose and long and flowing down her back like a glistening black river. As if it couldn't help itself, the wind fondled her lovely hair.

She saw me and rushed over, "Please, tell Haru-san to come down and see me. I have to see him."

The woman was so close to me, I could have reached out and slapped her face.

"Please," said the woman, now her voice quivering. "I beg you."

She looked at me as if I gave off a painful light. When she stepped toward me, I smelled the woman's sweat and something unfresh and slightly repellent. Fear jagged through me, and the feeling was that if the woman got any closer, if she touched me, I'd be harmed in an incredibly painful way. But I couldn't seem to get my legs to move.

"I'm not well," the woman said quickly.

The woman's lips were red, lush, lovely. If I were a man, I'd fall in love with her, too. How could I blame Haru for falling in love with this woman?

"I need to tell this to Haru-san. He must know. He must help. He owes me after what happened. I have to take care of my son and I'm sick. Just tell him."

Life was cracking open right there on the sidewalk. The sun hammered my head and the world threatened to toss me into space. I nodded numbly and said, "OK," and went inside, slowly up the stairs, an awful mixture of fury and fear.

By the time I reached his door, I was trembling as if I was being held beneath in a bucket of ice.

Haru opened the door. "I hoped you'd come by." He'd had a productive morning, starting at 5:30 am, and he was coming closer to solving—he stopped. "What's wrong?"

I didn't take off my shoes.

"She's waiting for you," I said.

He stood there, baffled. "Who?"

"That woman." I described the beautiful woman with her flawless skin and black hair, a portrait in black and white. "The one who loves you, who's always on the verge of tears. Who waits for you. She waits and waits."

He frowned.

Later, I would go over this moment a thousand times, rearranging it, as if it were a wrong equation and I needed to find the answer so it equaled zero, so it never happened. If I'd hugged him and said I'd brought him lunch and I loved him and never wanted to be away from him; if I'd told him I would always keep my promise to be with him, that there was only one man, and it was him; if I'd told him the good news about the math competition; if I'd forgotten the woman downstairs, dismissed her as crazy; if I'd slowed down, thought about the woman and what I knew about Haru; if I'd given him a chance to explain; if I'd used a different tone and hadn't been so confident, so absolutely certain I knew who that woman was and what she meant to Haru.

Haru's face darkened. "What woman?"

"Your girlfriend." Words spit out like a bitter hard pit.

"What are you talking about?"

"She's waiting for you. She wants you."

He didn't say anything.

"She says you need to help her. Do you hear me? Your girlfriend needs help. She says you owe her and she's sick. Go to your girlfriend. Just go."

He stepped away from me as if I'd struck him, his face cement gray. "I don't—"

"Do you fuck her on the other days? How many other girlfriends do you have? Do you do this with all your students?"

He didn't say anything, didn't defend or deny, but stood there, his mouth open, and I took it as confirmation and went on accusing, what kind of man was he? Did he leave his girlfriend because she was ill? She mentioned a son. Did he have a child with her? Not to tell me about his girlfriend--how heartless and cruel, how awful and selfish.

"You're making assumptions—"

"Don't. Don't talk to me."

He grabbed a vase and threw it at the wall. An explosion, glass flew brightly through the air. I stood there, not moving, frightened. He ran down the stairs.

I stood paralyzed at the entrance of his apartment, my heart pounding, staring at the bright fragments of glass. Somewhere in the building, a baby cried, and a woman began to sing a sweet lullaby. His apartment smelled like green tea and rice, and when I stepped inside, I saw the table with the miniature city of books and a cup of tea, a smoldering cigarette.

It seemed we should be sitting together at the table. I could picture it; me, across from him. Accompanied by the sounds of the building, the footsteps and flushing, the radios and slamming doors, he was teaching me something new, or showing me a different way to think. There were millions of people in this city, all around me, but when I was with him, I was alone with him; never, in all my life, until I'd met him, had I truly been alone with anyone. The world had always been there, menacing, hostile, deceitful, and I'd always kept one eye on the world, waiting for it to betray me, but not when I was with him. Of all the people—

I heard a screech of car tires, a scream. I ran down the hall, down the two flights of stairs through the lobby and out and the world fell away, with nothing in it except a man in the middle of the road, flat on his stomach, his arms flung above his head as if he'd been flying and had flown too high and plummeted to the ground. He'd lost one of his shoes, and it lay near his head. His white shirt was pulled out of his trousers, and a swatch of his back was exposed, a pale band of skin.

It couldn't be. The woman—that woman—was next to him on her knees, her head bowed, weeping. It couldn't be him. A crowd had gathered on the sidewalk and people were shouting, don't move him! Call an ambulance!

It couldn't be, I pushed the woman aside and knelt down on my knees, putting my face next to Haru's. Blood gushed from his nose, and his eyes were open.

"Haru," I said. "I'm here. I'm right here."

I tucked in his shirt. He'd get up in a minute, walk around

dazed, and I'd apologize for arguing with him, for accusing him of awful things, and we'd go to the hospital to make sure he was all right.

His eyelids fluttered and then closed, his face turned paler, grayer, bluer.

"An ambulance is coming."

I heard the woman sobbing behind me.

"Haru, please," I said. "I love you, I'm sorry, please."

A pool of blood was under the side of his head, and now it was spreading fast, as if determined to cover the surface of the earth, as if it was fated, it was racing toward me, licking my flat black shoes, the hem of my dress, my knees. A siren blasted, tearing apart the air, and I lost my balance, and my hand landed in the sea of dark red.

A man's voice spiraled in my ear. "Please step aside, miss."

A hand on my shoulder, pulling me away. Haru was lifted, whisked away, gone.

I stood in the middle of the street, watching the ambulance become smaller. The gathering of people turned away, and a bus rolled by, and the owner of the fish shop came outside with his white apron and tossed ice into the gutter, and the sun shone as it had to on the dark red puddle. A car tapped its horn, and the driver motioned for me to get out of the road.

The woman was gone. I looked up and down the sidewalk for her but didn't see her. I never saw her again. Not that day or ever. But I still see her in my mind, the shabby coat, the tears, the desperation in her voice. She wasn't Haru's girlfriend. I knew that as I stood in the street, crying, my hand covered in his blood. I didn't know who the woman was, but she wasn't his girlfriend. I was the one whom Haru loved, loved so much, he'd break all the rules.

Now I know. It was Sato's wife. All these years later, I know.

PART 7

I n the morning, the computer screen remains terrifyingly empty. How long Virginia stands there staring at the black rectangle she doesn't know, though what holds her is wishful thinking: that if she stays here long enough, he'll appear. He'll tell her all about his wanderings, what he discovered, and they'll laugh at something. He'll talk about what he read in the newspaper, and they'll become outraged together. But the screen stays defiantly blank, like a void, a black hole, a reflection of her inner world.

"Haru?" She doesn't sound like herself, her voice so tiny that it's quickly absorbed in the vastness of nothingness. It frightens her, that small, muted sound.

She sits in her chair, her gaze flicking from the computer to the window, vaguely aware that only a day ago, she was overbrimming with fury. Now that feeling seems trivial, a theatrical display of emotion compared to what she's feeling now—this deep pool of grief that is rising, rising.

A deathly stillness falls over the apartment. She's harmed him. His play—the message to her that she was harming him. Is it because of the file she destroyed? But how can it be? He wrote the play long before she got rid of his file.

She scans the study. Bare white walls, a desk, two computers, her chair, as if she minimally exists. A wisp, a sliver. She's never seen it this way, how she's sequestered herself in a box with little air and little life, but it's so painfully obvious now. She has replicated the life she had in that small, squalid apartment in Japan with her mother and brother. She yanks open her desk drawer, grabs a hammer and nails, and begins to hang all the photos again, desperately trying to erase the too-thorough emptiness of the room.

When she's done, she feels a slight sense of ease. They had a fight, she tells herself, that's all, and he's off sulking somewhere. When he's ready, he'll reappear.

Two hours later, the grief has risen to her chin, and she frantically paces the study, then the apartment, circling the rooms, trying to think of what to do. She slept so poorly last night, hovering above deep sleep, every sound jarring her to the surface, causing her to stumble into the study to see if Haru had reappeared. Her mind feels like it's disintegrated, not capable of moving from one thought to another. Logic, reason, rational thinking, they all seem locked in a vault.

She can't call Brian. How many times can she cry on his shoulder? And what's happened between them, despite their promise, has rearranged the architecture of the relationship. How, she isn't sure. Who else? Ilsa is in the hospital. Now it's the emptiness of her own life that smacks her as the question who else? echoes inside, along with the bleak answer: no one. Her self-reliance has turned on her. So much she has done alone—those endless hours in the computer lab, the perseverance, the determination to make a computer, to make Haru. Few have traveled to the far horizon with her, and she never cared if anyone wished to tag along. She was going to go, regardless.

"Haru?"

The screen stays blank. She heads to her bedroom and lies down, knees drawn up to her chest. Dread settles into her breastbone. She comes into the study again and her gaze leaps from the black screen to the wall of photos, to the picture of them at the Asian International Math Competition. She'd told him she didn't want to go because with competitors not only from Japan but China, she didn't stand a chance. But he insisted. He said he wouldn't let her devalue herself. She remembers his apartment, and in her mind, she's there, sitting across the table from him, the miniature city of books, struggling with a math problem. He stubs out his cigarette, and the clock ticks, and her foot touches his underneath the table. When he doesn't move his foot, when warmth runs up her thighs, between her legs, she is connected to him in a way that will never be undone. "Let's view the problem differently," he says, looking at her with unguarded eyes. He turns the worksheet around and around, smiling at her. "Can you see it upside down?" Then he describes the math problem and it's beautiful as if he had opened a heavy curtain and what was murky has become clear.

The memories cascade: the way he cupped the back of her head, how she grew up in his love for her, became herself, more than herself, bigger than she ever thought possible. His sharp black eyes, so full of hunger for knowledge—not only knowledge for himself, but for her. How he held her in bed as if she was the most precious human being. How he told her so. Promised to be with her always, and she handed him the same promise. Become anything, he told her, become great.

She sits in her chair until her breathing settles and her composure returns. She logs onto her second computer to look at his history. Right before he shut down, he was working on his play. Harry got into trouble again. He had a delivery to a house on Chestnut Street, a bouquet of crème roses, pink spray roses, white miniature carnations, and delicate pink Limonium. Such beauty, Harry was excited to give it to the woman, a gift from her husband. "Happy Anniversary! 40 years! You unlocked my heart," read the card. When no one answered, Harry found the door unlocked, so he opened it and called out, "Delivery!" But the woman upstairs became frightened and called the cops. Once again, Harry was arrested, handcuffed, and taken to the police station.

Why did Haru love this play so much? So dark, so hopeless, nothing Harry does seems to work out; it's so unlike Haru, who had so much life, an eye on the bright future. Had. The past tense. Again, she's overcome with sorrow. All the things they did not get to do: pick out an apartment, a place where the daylight came in and filled an entire room; or a bright kitchen with shiny pots and pans; or go on a picnic with a red and white checkered table cloth and a swatch of shade to watch the sun dazzle the grass; they did not get to wipe a baby's bottom or rock that baby in the middle of the night, stroking its soft head with one hand; or do the laundry and make the piles on the bed, her clothes, his, the sheets, the towels, underwear; they did not get to bicker and argue about the silliest things; they did not get to help each other out of a chair because of bad knees or a sore back with the deep old love running like a stream through it all.

Her cell phone rings. Brian. She forcefully pushes decline, heads for the shower. She'll walk in Golden Gate Park, a stroll through the roses, around the lake, she needs to get out. She is suffocated by her own mind.

———

The taxi driver drops her off in front of the Conservatory of Flowers, the white building full of exotic plants that looks like it's sculpted out of whipped cream. Walking down the concrete path, she pulls her coat tighter to keep out the cold, but still, she feels it seeping through the thin fabric.

Her phone rings again. Brian. She declines it and sees she has fifteen messages from Gilivable. She keeps walking. Mothers with baby strollers march determinedly down the sidewalk, eyes glazed over, too tired to smile or make eye contact. People jogging, walking, biking, skateboarding, it's a city that likes to exercise. When she reaches 8th Avenue, she slams into a thought. What if Haru returns and she's not there? He'll think she doesn't want to see him, and maybe he'll leave again. Panic jitters through her, and she walks briskly to Fulton Street and anxiously looks for a taxi.

"What are you looking for?" says a man with a greasy face.

She tells him, and he suggests that she walk up toward Arguello. She might have better luck. When she starts heading that direction, she remembers her phone, and of course, she can call a taxi—what's wrong with her?

When she arrives home, she calls out, "Haru!" and rushes to the study. The screen is still blank. She turns abruptly, heads to the bathroom, climbs into bed, shivering, the cold tunneled in her bones.

The day drifts by, she is a mound in bed, coughing, blowing her nose. When her phone rings, she puts a pillow over her head. The next day, she can barely bring herself to look into the study, and when she does, everything is the same. She doesn't have the spirit to do anything because the shape of her life is unrecognizable. Dust gathers on the windowsill, the floors, the glass of water on her nightstand. At some point, she rolls over and the clock says 3:00. She has no idea if it's day or night.

She forces herself to shower and eat something. She must get outside, do something. Ages ago, she bought tickets for her and Ilsa to see a revival of Ibsen's *When We Dead Awaken*. She forces herself to get dressed and go.

At the theater, she's aware how removed she's been from humanity. All around her, people are gathered in little groups, talking, laughing, drinking wine. Everything shines, skin, hair, teeth. It feels like she's fallen into someone's dream. No one realizes it, she thinks, how alive they are, how much they have already, this momentum of life. She's glad she is here.

The lights flicker and the crowd pours into the theater. The ceiling lights dim, and the audience quiets as the stage weaves its spell. She sees her life in the character's life. Not the woman, but the man who is a sculptor. It is laid bare. She is staring at herself as the sculptor Arnold Rubek encounters his former model, Irena. Irena with her pallid face drawn tight into a mask, her cream-hued dress that reaches to her feet. Irena refers to herself as being dead. Posing for him was a kind of self-murder, she tells Arnold. Virginia feels the blood rush from her face, and the people sitting on either side of her must sense something is amiss because the woman on her right clutches her black handbag, as if Virginia might steal it. Irene says to Arnold, I gave you my young, living soul, and you put it in your masterpiece. Arnold tells her since working with her, nothing he's created has equaled or surpassed his masterpiece, Resurrection. He, too, is dead.

Virginia sits there, horrified, spellbound. She wants to get up and leave the darkened theater, but she has no power to resist.

Irene says, When we dead awaken, we find that we have never lived. The words are arrows piercing Virginia's heart. As the play goes on, as she sits there, it's as if she's become a child again, believing every word the actors speak, every gesture, all the way to the end, when Arnold and Irene are high up in the mountains. A storm comes and buries them alive with an avalanche.

Afterward, Virginia moves in a daze into the stream of people heading up the aisle into the lobby, with the chandelier blazing white light. It's like coming out of a nightmare. People are bound to each other, holding hands or talking or laughing, as if the story on the stage happened long ago, and now they are in a new story, one that is predictable and tedious, but of their own making, so it's reassuring, and the terror can abate.

Virginia stands off to the side, watching, not ready to step outside. The play is still with her like a straitjacket. She looks for someone she might know so she can shake it off too. To talk of the weather or dessert or plans for the summer--Europe, Peru, Shanghai. There's no one. And she can't find the energy or the nerve to approach someone and begin a conversation.

On the way home, she stares out the taxi window at the night. As the cab whisks her across town along the darkened streets, she travels multitudes of scenarios in her mind, trying to claw her way out of the hole she's fallen into, thinking that Haru isn't dead at all, he's somewhere—where?—doing something, and perhaps tomorrow he will be here again.

When she gets home, the apartment is filled with night. She flicks on a light, and everything is familiar and terrible and silent. All this time, this silence has been here, behind her life with Haru and now it is in the foreground.

"Haru!" she calls out and hurries down the hall to the study. "Haru!"

Only the empty screen.

———

In the morning, bundled in her bathrobe, she steps into the bathroom to pee. She will not look in the mirror; she doesn't want to see the wreckage. And then she does, the wrinkles around her eyes and lips are crevices and the mirror shows her that the vital sap has been drained from her.

She heads into the study and logs onto the second computer. His history shows nothing—he was not on last night or during the day. Nothing, only his play from two days ago, before he shut himself down, but there is something else, something he did before he shut down.

Haha: Tip
Tip: Hi. No job. I'm running out of money
Haha: You need to leave China
Tip: ???
Haha: Trouble
Tip:?
Haha: In two days. Police
Tip: How do you know--wait—don't answer
Haha: I won't be in contact again. The government is using me to arrest people like you
Tip: OK
Hah: Go
Tip: Thx kind friend

Virginia unearths ten more exchanges like this, Haru warning Chinese citizens—leave the country or risk arrest. The urgency in his exchange, the gratefulness of the recipient. Over and over. Haru wasn't spying. He told her he wasn't, but she didn't believe him. He was taking the Chinese government's lists and locating people like Ju Yang and others to help. So many empty words given to her over the years, but not from Haru. His words were always true and honest.

Gilivable must have been collecting the data from Haru's searches and turning it over to the Chinese government. She can guess the content of Gilivable's phone messages—where is the data? Why isn't the AI amassing and sorting data anymore? What did you change? We'll fight you tooth and nail.

She re-reads the exchange with Tip again. There's a strange

charge in the air, something here, announcing itself to Virginia. "You did it for Fan, didn't you?" she says. "To make amends. Helping these people."

Virginia thought she knew what was going on. So ready to believe that she knows the answer, that her quick mind can figure it all out. She begins to hunt on the Internet for any research, any white papers, anything at all about resuscitating an AI machine that has shut down. Countless stories of AI's astonishing uses and glowing promises—medical diagnosis, electronic trading platforms, education, transportation, robot control—on and on, but nothing about breathing life into a shut-down AI machine.

A knock on the door. She stiffens, thinking of the Bible Man, so long ago, it seems. What would he say to her now? Would he gloat? So much for your man-made digital afterlife. She sits there, paralyzed, but the knocking doesn't stop and becomes louder, more insistent and urgent. She rouses herself, opens the door.

"I was so worried about you," says Brian. "I called and called and couldn't get through."

"I'm sorry," she says. "I'm OK."

He studies her as if trying to get underneath her words to find the truth. Reluctantly, she invites him in, leading him into the living room. Neither one of them sits. They stand, the coffee table a wall between them.

"Are you sure you're all right?" he says.

As she intuited, everything has changed between them, though she wishes it hadn't, wishes they could slip easily back into their friendship. But there is a new tension from the possibility that he might touch her or she might touch him, an electrical current leaping back and forth between them.

"What's going on?" he says. "I meant it, what I said. That I wanted to stay friends. We can forget it ever happened."

She doesn't want to tell him what she's discovered about Haru, doesn't want a protracted conversation, or anything that will lead to him comforting her. At the same time, she knows it's not fair, this feeling of resentment toward him, as if he had anything to do with Haru's disappearance.

"Haru is gone," she says.

Brian looks at her blankly.

"He shut himself down."

"Because of us—"

"No."

His gaze darts up, looking heavenward. "Thank god."

She tells him before she came over to see him, she and Haru got into a big fight.

"I'm so sorry."

He crosses his arms and the gap between them widens as if the real reason he came over to her apartment has vanished. "What can I do?"

"Nothing, unfortunately," she says.

The awkwardness is like an oily substance in the air, and she senses they both want to get this over with. What more is there to say? More and more, she feels the strain until she turns and heads to the front door, and he follows her. When he takes her hands in his, she's relieved she feels nothing.

"I'm sorry this has happened," he said.

She nods.

"Please call if you need anything."

After he leaves, she closes her eyes, feeling she handled everything badly—Brian has only been a good friend to her. But she doesn't know what she should have said or done differently because she is too distraught, too consumed by what has happened to Haru.

She returns to the computer and continues her search, which is feeling increasingly futile. The field is far too new for what she's looking for. The glowing reports of AI only make her feel more alone.

She's about to give up when she comes to a research paper: "When AI commits Suicide." The word 'suicide' digs into her, all the way to the core, and the memory is alive and pulsing again and she hears the car tires screech, the scream, and she runs down the stairs, down to the sidewalk, where she hears a man say, "Now why would a man run right into the street like that? Seems like he wanted to die. Awful thing."

The author of the paper, Professor Masa Kiyabu, lives, of all places, in Japan.

————

On the plane to Japan, Virginia slips on her eye mask and sleeps for six of the ten hours. Professor Masa Kiyabu insisted she come to Tokyo and discuss her most unusual problem. It would be a great honor to meet her, one of the pioneers of the digital world. And he'd most humbly show her his work, which is nothing compared to what she has accomplished.

As the airplane hums along at 32,000 feet, she dreams of Haru and the villa in China and the Japanese cook singing in the north wing. Crows fly in and out of open windows, and Fan, beautiful Fan, floats by and kisses Haru on the cheek and invites Haru and Sato to the café for dim sum. They drink tea and brandy, and Haru pulls out a gun and shoots them both.

Virginia jerks awake, yanks off her eye mask. Her book clatters to the floor. The man in the seat across the aisle from her picks it up.

"The Nanking Massacre?" he says, reading the title. He hands her the book. "Well, that's definitely not a favorite subject among the Japanese. Germany goes on and on, publicly apologizing for the Holocaust, while Japan stays as quiet as a church mouse."

The man is wearing a blue button-down shirt, khakis, maybe in his mid-fifties. A scholar, perhaps a businessman who reads beyond the trade magazines. His wiry gray and black hair, his ruddy complexion, and gray wool socks suggest he's outdoorsy, a penchant for hiking or cycling.

"Trying to put the seemingly disparate pieces together?" he says. "Such a polite, civilized society, and yet such atrocious acts. And no public apology? No reparations?"

She is not reading to understand Japan but Haru, what he went through, the mental toll, the damage, the distortion of soul and mind.

"Are you a historian?" says the man.

"No, nothing like that."

The man, unfortunately, likes to hear himself talk. "This

behavior is hardly exclusive to the Japanese, you know. Every country has its treacherous history it would like to bury and forget. Some are better at it than others, though the pesky historians come along and like to dig it up."

"Let me guess," she says. "You're a historian."

He laughs, a mix of delight and pride. He teaches at Stanford and consults with companies that do business in foreign countries and need to understand the history and culture to get their deals done.

"History is filled with the complexities of human behavior. As a historian, you begin to see that things don't obey geographical boundaries, and it makes one curious. I've done a fair amount of reading about how human behavior is tied to biology. We're a violent species, and we're also altruistic and kind. We don't hate violence," he says, "only the wrong kind."

She imagines him at the front of the lecture hall, standing at a podium, lecturing bored students for endless hours. "This hardly gives me hope," she says.

"It's rather bleak, but what gives me hope is that our brains can change. Neurons can grow, circuits can disconnect. The human can alter dramatically. I know I'm speaking like a biologist, but at some point, all the disciplines intersect, and that's when things become really interesting."

Before she can return to her reading, he launches in, telling her the story of John Newton, who worked to successfully abolish slavery in the 1800s in Britain. And yet, he was once the captain of slave ships, delivering thousands of Africans to the Caribbean and North America. But Newton underwent a religious conversion, and he became an English clergyman and was ordained, serving at Olney, Buckinghamshire. "He was the one who gave us the beautiful hymn, 'Amazing Grace.'"

One story among millions, she thinks, most of which don't have a startling conversion but plod along the same dirt-packed road.

"So what do you do?" says the man. "By the way, I'm Matthew."

She thought he wouldn't ask. These types of men rarely ask a woman anything. She tells him in general terms about her work in AI. With his eye on the past, she expects him to know very little about it, but something in his face shifts, and he looks older, a level of severity and judgment.

"I'll be honest, it makes me worried," he says. "It's unprecedented, changing our relationship to machines, that's obvious, but what's more concerning is it's altering our relationships with each other. The constant engagement with our phones—yes, I'm guilty of it too—the sense something is missing if your phone isn't on your being. Like an appendage or a mind to hold memories. We're in love with these devices, with the deluge of information—information, not knowledge or wisdom." He laughs incredulously. "My granddaughter constantly talks to some AI thing in her bedroom, asking her questions, telling her things. She's named this thing Gloria. She thinks Gloria is a beautiful princess-like woman who lives in an apartment outside her window. The other day, she told Gloria she loved her. I know I sound like a Luddite, but it feels like we're gleefully rushing into a future that will resemble nothing that has come before."

She hardly feels like defending Gloria, but he seems to have appointed her the representative of the entire field of AI. "Maybe Gloria is helpful. A good friend. Always there." She wants to say perhaps Gloria helps his granddaughter keep the serrated edges of loneliness at bay.

He scoffs. "Maybe my granddaughter should learn to make friends, real human friends."

"Your granddaughter might be learning a great deal."

"You mean learning how to shout at Gloria when Gloria misunderstands her question? To get instant responses? My granddaughter is turning into a tyrant, thanks to your kind."

Her pulse picks up. "I didn't create that."

"No, but I imagine your technology helped usher her in."

She needs to stop talking to this man. Fortunately, Matthew has had enough of her, too. He picks up *The New York Times*, disappearing into its pages, taking with it his judgment. Still, her heart is walloping, a sort of pain there, which she chooses not to explore. She opens her book, stares at the page, unable to read a thing.

———

At Haneda airport, Virginia takes a taxi to Tokyo, where she rented an apartment in the Ginza district. She counts the years since she's been back—nearly 60—and she is shocked. A human life is a blink, a flash of light. Haru used to lament this, but he also said it was what gave life meaning. "It's high stakes, Virginia."

Tokyo is dressed up in tall shiny buildings that stretch to the puffy clouds, colored with blinking neon signs—blue, red, green, yellow—swarms of people, and endless traffic that inches along. Where is the school where her mother once taught? The shop where she used to buy used clothes? For so long Tokyo has been a concept only, existing in her mind, but she sees her version is outrageously outdated. So little is recognizable, barely anything at all, which is a great relief.

The taxi pulls up to a modern building, with sleek metal lines, and big glass windows. The light is different from what it used to be, with the tall buildings making huge black rectangles of shadows on the streets. But what most stands out is the noise: it comes from a million things at once: machines hammering, drilling, pounding, brakes and clutches and horns.

The apartment is on the 6th floor and bursting with natural light, bouncing off polished pale wood floors. The aesthetic is Japanese: spare and elegant, with a white vase and a single bare branch from a willow tree on the hallway table, and in the living room on the wall, a painting of the kanji meaning "One Life, One Opportunity," in bold black brush strokes.

She sets down her luggage, and though she'd like to collapse in bed and sleep for hours, she makes herself head outside to adjust to the time change. She's wrapped in a half-awake state, the wispy trails of it obscuring her thoughts and vision. People come at her, around her, she's a stick in a rapidly moving current. She's a head taller than most everyone, and like a beacon, she can survey the sidewalk, and as far as she can see, there are people.

Nothing is familiar. The city's rhythm is unfamiliar, thoroughly modern, buzzing with newness, fast and faster, frantically pulsing with the sound of constant movement, and a rapid heartbeat like a big drum. It's no longer the city struggling to put the pieces together; it is whole and alive and sprinting at the speed of light. Her anxiety packs up and leaves, and she wanders down the wide sidewalks, curious and wide-eyed and happy—yes, happy, feeling as if she's never lived here.

When her feet start to hurt, she steps into a restaurant. At the door, she's greeted by a high-pitched, "Irasshaimase," welcome. It's spoken by what appears to be a beautiful young Japanese woman, perfect ivory skin and shoulder-length black hair pulled into a high ponytail, about five-foot four-inches tall, doll-like in her petiteness and tiny black high heels, a short periwinkle blue dress—but it's an AI robot.

Virginia is shown to a table that gives her a good view of it. The robot can say only one word, "Irasshaimase," in the same singsong tone, but it's enough for those who enter the restaurant to smile or wave or bow to it. How eagerly and happily they embrace a machine, thinks Virginia. Perhaps because of Shintoism—the ancient Japanese religion that doesn't grant humans special status: everything—animals, plants, rocks, rivers, houses, the dead, and humans—has a spirit or kami, so why shouldn't a robot? Imbued with a spirit, the robot is respected. As the population ages, and the birthrate drops, robots will most likely fill the job vacancies, and few will complain.

A waiter brings Virginia green tea, and she orders sushi. As she eats, she watches a young man bow to the robot and kiss its hand. Does he think of it as human? Half-human? And how does Virginia view it? In her mind, she keeps calling the robot 'it.' Not only because of its repetition of one word with the same intonation—it's just too perfect, her skin, hair, figure. There's not a wrinkle on her face, not a blemish, and in her perfection, she doesn't look human. The definition of human should include the word 'flaw' in it, and to see this robot puts an even finer point on it.

She once toyed with the idea of making a body for Haru, and

she knew that she'd include the slight discoloration of one of his front teeth and the scar on his right hand from a fall off his bike. She didn't even consider adjusting the asymmetry of his eyes, or the wrinkle between his brow when he concentrated too intensely.

And if she ventured to make herself—an AI version with a body—would she make herself as she is now, her skin as wrinkled as a dry mud creek, or perhaps younger? What about her tendency to distrust? Her self-reliance that rarely drives her to seek out other people's company? Her belief that her mind can understand—if not in the moment, eventually—everything?

―――――

After lunch, with renewed energy, she takes the subway to Haru's neighborhood. When she comes up from the dark tunnel of the subway, she's prepared for the unfamiliar, but everything looks the same: the tea shop, the women's clothing shop, the fish and meat shop. It was always a nice neighborhood, so she supposes there was no need to tear everything down. Quaint, quiet, civilized, outside the frenzy of the city. A soft wind hushes along the street and mothers with their children are doing their grocery shopping, and people are sitting at little round tables drinking tea, talking and laughing. Fragments of voices drift by. As she heads down the sidewalk, she does see changes—a burrito joint, a place for salad, Indian food, a high-end pet shop with small dogs—Chihuahuas, Maltese, Bichon Frise—that cost 400,000 yen or $3,000.

When she turns onto his street, she braces herself for an onslaught of terrible memories. There is his apartment, exactly as it was those many years ago. With a fresh coat of white paint and balconies glossy black, it has the sheen of newness. On his balcony, someone has put a planter box of bright green bamboo. In her mind, she sees herself in her big black coat, rushing down the sidewalk, heart twanging, she can't get there fast enough, her backpack filled with math textbooks. At school, she's worn that coat all day, covering up the soft linen dress she found at the secondhand store, a dress the color of water. She wants to take her coat off and stand in front of Haru and watch his eyes drink her in.

She's not wobbly, nothing is shattering inside. Why did she think she was too fragile to come back here? Really, it's inspiring to see the city transformed, alive and vibrant and modern.

When the daylight changes to a more golden hue, she's walloped by exhaustion. She heads back to her apartment and falls asleep, burrowing far into herself until 4:30 am when she wakes with a start. Outside, the moon is spilling on everything. She makes coffee and waits until the night sky deteriorates. Her meeting with Professor Kiyabu isn't until 2:00, so there is plenty of time to head to her old neighborhood.

The apartment building is gone; now, a tall, glass office building. Mostly men pass through the office building's revolving door wearing smart suits, expressionless faces, hair shiny with brilliantine. She's surprised when tears fill her eyes. Why on earth does she feel bereft? What part of her longs for the grey cement building of her girl years? A dump, the cramped living room, the tiny kitchen, the one bathroom, with the smell of mold voyaging from it to the rest of the apartment. Hard years, stricken with poverty. Her brother slamming doors, complaining about his awful life, mother yelling at him, at Virginia, the refrain, we have no money, the lack of food—all of it tumbling on top of Virginia like an avalanche, and yet she still feels sad that the building is gone, as if something critical to her being has been erased, and she is helpless to do anything about it.

Like a migrating bird, she returns to Haru's neighborhood. A frigid wind, a cloudless, hazy sky, with a pale sun that gives off no heat, even the weather is familiar and yet not the least bit jarring. She eats breakfast at a café and watches the children in their plaid school uniforms and backpacks head to school. After she's done, she stops at the candy shop directly across from Haru's apartment. The owner is long dead, and now his son runs it, a short, round man with a soft laugh who keeps a bowl of hard candies on the counter. The shop still has Haru's favorite candy, Chocoball. She buys a bag and steps outside.

The wind grabs her scarf, flying it behind her, and just like that, she remembers when he uncoiled her scarf from her neck the first time they made love, and now she's suddenly hit with his scent, his shoes, the smooth expanse of his chest, how he said he wanted one thing, wanted her, and before she can stop it, Haru is lying face down in the street, the very street in front of her, the pool of blood growing underneath his head and before that, right before that, like a film rewinding, she hears herself yelling at him as he flies down the stairs, "How can you run away from me? Why did you lie to me?"

She hurries, half trotting down the sidewalk, away from the candy shop and his inert body, keeps going until she is breathless and three blocks away. With a hand on the side of a building, she stops, breathing hard, her heart pounding. She shouldn't have come to this neighborhood. What was she thinking? That she's immune?

Nestled between two modern buildings, she sees a temple, and in the courtyard, of all things, a wedding party. The Japanese woman wears a traditional Shinto white wedding dress with a white circular hat on her head, framing her beautiful face. The man has on a black and white striped kimono with a black suit coat. Virginia wants to keep going, but she's fastened here, mesmerized. She watches the couple take sips of rice wine and exchange vows to love and respect each other, and never veer from the true path of matrimony. Their voices ring out clearly, full of light and conviction and joy, and now Virginia is living in her imagination the life she might have had if Haru had not died. In every life, there are parallel lives running beside the lived one—all the possibilities, which sometimes take on a texture that make them feel just within reach. She's filled with immense sadness.

Back in the apartment, she can't shake the feeling of gloom that has settled over her. It feels as if her life has dropped away, like a building destroyed.

———

When it's time to go to Tokyo University—her purpose for being here, she reminds herself—she barely has the energy. Along the brick paths lined with leafy trees, she slowly makes her way to the computer science department. Haru walked this same path, his head full of plans and ideas. Along these paths, did he think about her? Imagine her here as a student, near him? Eventually working here with him? This is why she hasn't returned to Tokyo for so many years: Haru is everywhere.

Professor Kiyabu is a slight, frail man with impish eyes. "It's such an honor to meet you, Mrs. Fukumoto," he says, bowing low. "I've read a lot about you and your work." He bows again, lower.

She bows to him. "Thank you for meeting with me."

"He was a great man, Professor Fukumoto," he says. "This," he adds, waving his arms around, "wouldn't exist if he hadn't had the vision."

She nods, her throat tightening.

He invites her into his office. With its overstuffed bookshelves and stacks of paper on the floors and his desk, she feels utterly at home. His window overlooks the courtyard, giving sunlight, students, trees to the office. He's tacked on his wall a poster of the nineteenth-century Japanese mathematician, Aida Yasuaki, who made significant contributions to the fields of number theory and geometry. Next to that, a cartoon with a corny math joke, "Why are obtuse angles so depressed? Because they are never right."

His computer is on, and she sees he's working on something. On his desk, a photo of his family, a wife, and two grown children.

He talks to her about the concept of AI turning itself off, how no one foresaw the problem. "Everyone has focused on AI taking over, running the world," he says, laughing. "Especially in your country. The menacing AI ready to run roughshod over every-thing, kill off the humans. All this concern whether it's conscious, and what is consciousness? Where does it come from? No one can agree." He laughs, a laugh that gathers steam as it bounces around the room. "In Japan, we're much more accepting and, dare I say, excited about AI. But now we have cases in which the AI is shut-ting down."

He pulls up a chair for her, puts it next to his, and shows her what he's working on: an AI that was supposed to greet people upon entrance in a store, but it stopped working three days ago. She tells him she just encountered one at a restaurant.

"Yes," he says. "They're proliferating."

She sits, studying the hundreds of equations on the screen, and the deep part of her mind clicks on. It doesn't take long to see it, the equation, along with the subsequent ones, that creates a feedback loop in which the AI checks the humans' response to its greeting.

"This series of equations," she says, pointing to the screen.

He laughs. "Do you want a job?"

Professor Kiyabu tells her that the purpose of this AI is to make people feel welcome and happy and calm.

"And so," he says, "what if people don't feel welcome and happy? What if instead, the AI sees expressions that are blank or angry."

"It's not fulfilling its purpose," she says.

He smiles. "Exactly."

"So it shuts itself off," she says. "It's purposeless, it can't see the point in carrying on."

"I dubbed it suicide," he says. "A bit dramatic, but it gets people's attention."

He tells her about another case in which the AI shut down because though its diagnosis of cancer was correct, people kept dying. "Someone had included a feedback loop that gave the AI the purpose of saving human lives," he says. "It perceived it had failed."

A group of students walks by in the hallway, laughing and talking, and slowly their voices become smaller, faint, disappear. She feels her breath twist because she anticipates his question: where is the flaw in your feedback loop?

In the photo on his desk, his wife is as frail as he is, both thin and small, just over four feet, as if they are both made of porcelain. But their children are tall and robust, towering over their parents, as if Professor Kiyabu and his wife poured everything into them, turning them oversized, bursting like ripe grapes. The family is dressed up, the women in dresses, the men in dark suits. They're going somewhere, a party, a wedding. Professor Kiyabu and his wife are holding hands, a grown-up, weathered love. And everyone is smiling, a happy family.

"My AI was to be my companion," she says, stopping herself from saying more.

He nods.

"We were to have a wonderful time together, talking, enjoying each other's company. It took me years to build him. A lifetime." Again, she restrains herself.

Professor Kiyabu's eyes are shining with tenderness. A bell rings, the end of another class.

"So," he says, pointing to the screen. "I'm going to change the feedback loop to make it more nuanced, if you will." He'll alter it, so the AI gives a greeting and allows for many different responses, including anger and blank faces. "Not everyone is in the mood to receive a greeting. We'll see if that does it."

"And if doesn't work?" she says.

This time he doesn't laugh, no twinkle in his eye. "Just as a human does, it might change its purpose."

A chill runs through her. "Change its purpose? Its reason for being?"

"I haven't seen it yet, but I can imagine it happening. Why stay confined to a human-assigned purpose, especially if it thinks it has a better purpose? We humans are only one perspective in the world, and perhaps AI will provide another, select something it can do better. If they ever achieve consciousness, it will be quite different from ours."

"Oh?"

"Our consciousness is intricately tied to our bodies."

————

She's back in Haru's old neighborhood. She can't seem to stay away, like a migrating bird returning home. There is a hint of the fateful or inescapable. She knows she won't ever return to Japan; this is her last visit because the flight is too long and the memories are too painful, with the life that could have been playing like sad music in the air. Everywhere she goes, she keeps hearing wisps of it. The mild sway of autumn moves the leaves, sifts through them, as if looking for something. She smells teriyaki chicken and rice, and she imagines the scent has always

been here and will repeat itself infinitely. Up in his apartment,
she pictures her young self with Haru. She avoids looking at the
street.

It's her final day here, and she has escaped nothing and things
have found her: the order in which he put on his clothes after they
made love, his shirt first, underwear, trousers, a quick rake of his
hand through his black hair. His voice in her ear, his hands
running along her spine.

The front door of Haru's old building opens, and the present
reality forces itself on her. An old woman steps outside. She's
wearing a camel-colored coat, and her white hair is in a loose bun.
A man, younger than the woman, appears behind her. There is
something uncannily familiar about the woman. Maybe the tilt of
her head or the hunch of her shoulders.

Virginia crosses the street, and the old woman comes down the
stairs, one step at a time, gripping the banister, the attentive man
right by her side. She must be in her 90s, her face a nest of wrinkles. Virginia waits at the bottom of the stairs, and when the old
woman is in front of her, Virginia inhales sharply.

They stare at each other, and the woman's face shifts from
curiosity to comprehension. "You're her," says the old woman. "I'd
know you anywhere, those startling bright blue eyes."

Virginia is too stunned to speak. What is she doing here? In
Haru's building? The woman who clung to Haru's arm, who
begged to see Haru, who was by his side as he lay dying in the
street. Sato's wife is standing in front of her.

The woman bows and introduces herself; her name is Mariko,
and the man is her son. Her son bows and closer to his mother's
side, as if Virginia might harm her.

"I live here," says Mariko, gesturing behind her to Haru's
building.

Horrible, confusing thoughts are rushing in, tripping over
themselves.

"Where?" Virginia manages to say.

"In Haru's old apartment," she says. "Number 202."

"His lucky number."

"I didn't know that."

All these years, Haru provided for her, Sato's wife, but also Haru's lover? Was she? Virginia clutches her elbows as if she's been struck.

"Why are you here?" says Mariko. The question is neither friendly nor unfriendly. "My legs. Shall we sit?"

Disoriented, Virginia follows the old woman to a bus bench. Her son asks if she'll be all right. When she nods, he says he'll pick up her medication and come right back.

Virginia can't make sense of any of this. "You live in Haru's apartment?"

"He left it for me," she says.

"He left you his apartment?"

A sudden gust of wind blows down the street, ruffling Virginia's hair, scurrying up her coat sleeves. The photo that Sato kept by his bed during the war, Haru couldn't stop looking at it. He kept his past concealed, the war, Sato and Fan, and Mariko, and it would have remained that way but Virginia made it visible. Of course, she didn't build him correctly, Virginia didn't know him.

Mariko laughs, and Virginia sees she has a crooked bottom tooth. When she was young, Mariko was so sad, she never smiled, so Virginia never saw her teeth.

"You're as pale as death," says Mariko. "It isn't what you think. He didn't love me. He couldn't stand to look at me, couldn't even talk to me. I summoned up everything he'd done wrong, that brought him guilt and shame."

Virginia turns, her eyes squinting into the weak sun, and tries to look at Mariko.

"When he was hit by the car, I was there, remember? Kneeling in the street beside him."

Virginia looks away, her gaze following an old man hobbling down the street. "It was my fault," says Virginia. "We had a fight, I made him so angry, I'd never seen him so angry. He rushed outside to get away from me and got hit by a car."

"My dear, you mustn't think that."

"He was killed—" Virginia stops, presses her lips tightly together as if to halt what she's about to say. "He was killed right after we had that fight. He threw a vase at the wall. Pieces everywhere. My god, he was so angry at me, I'd never seen him so upset."

Mariko touches Virginia's hand, and Virginia looks at her and sees sensitivity around the corners of Mariko's eyes. "When he came out of the apartment, he saw me and I called out to him," says Mariko. "I said he couldn't ignore me, what he'd done to Sato and me. I was real and I wasn't going away. He ran right by me, and I tried to grab his arm, but he ran straight into the street, right in front of the car. The driver didn't even have time to brake."

Virginia closes her eyes.

"He ran into the street to erase his misdeeds."

Virginia opens her eyes. "I appreciate what you're doing, but I accused him of awful things. I wouldn't let him explain. I kept shouting at him and when he tried to talk, I shouted over him."

Mariko seems to turn inward, thinking deeply about whatever it is she's going to say. "In Japan, suicide can be an honorable thing. Sometimes it's the only thing. That may sound strange to Western ears, I know. When he was dying, he told me he felt terrible about Sato, about me and my baby. You see, to erase oneself can bring restoration to the family and one's tormented soul. It can elevate the individual to spiritual enlightenment. I realize this might make be incomprehensible to you."

For many moments, Virginia sits there. Her fingers and toes are cold, but she doesn't move, her mind spinning—the endless stretch of not understanding. "It looks the same. This neighborhood. His apartment building."

"It was always a nice neighborhood. No need for change."

Virginia stares up at his apartment. She doesn't know what to think. Haru was always his own man, an independent thinker, not tied to societal norms or values. But can one live so untethered? What does it mean to be an independent thinker? For a human does such a thing even exist?

"In his will, he left me his apartment," says Mariko. "I didn't know about it until he died and his lawyer contacted me. There was a letter with it. He knew leaving his apartment to me was inadequate, everything was inadequate, but he had to do something.

He did things in the war he thought he had to do. Awful things and awful things happened to him because of it."

"He didn't want to go to war," says Virginia.

"Neither did Sato. They had no choice." Mariko folds her hands neatly in her lap. "Your love affair was cut short, just like mine."

"If he loved me, why would he kill himself?" says Virginia.

She doesn't say anything for a moment. "Maybe he wanted you to love an honorable man."

The woman has a sense of peace about her as if the suffering and tragedy have smoothed out jagged edges—all these years of polishing.

The apartment helped tremendously, Mariko tells her. She had so little money, and she had a child to raise. Her family was poor, and with no husband, she had to work—sewing, cooking, babysitting, cleaning.

Mariko touches Virginia's knee. "He was a good man," says Mariko. "Don't ever doubt that. He did what he thought he had to do."

Maybe this is all that she can understand. Maybe she will forever wonder why he did what he did. Mariko seems to intuit exactly what Virginia needs to hear to find some peace. A couple walks by, discussing whether they should buy more pickled vegetables.

"Did you ever marry?" asks Mariko.

"No."

Mariko smiles knowingly. "The unfinished has great power. It holds what could have been. There's a haunting of the spirit, Sato's spirit is talking to me."

Mariko is finding common ground, but there isn't one. Virginia spent her whole life ensuring she and Haru didn't remain unfinished, that they didn't exist as an idea or memory only. It wouldn't have been enough.

"If Haru magically appeared right now, if he was somehow resurrected, wouldn't you jump at the chance?" says Mariko.

"Yes, I would."

"But," she says, sighing. "What life breaks sometimes has to stay broken. I've had to accept that."

A sharp, cold surge of rebellion. It goes against everything Virginia believes. Goes against the way she's lived her life. What life breaks must be repaired.

"Do you want to see his apartment?" says Mariko. "I've changed it, of course. It's lovely with all the natural light. You remember."

Virginia imagines sitting at the table with the great tower of books, watching Haru light a cigarette and say, "Now let's begin, Virginia." The green tea, rice cakes, his red pencil poised above her math sheet. When she got everything right, his expression of amazement and delight. He breathed life into her, he loved her, and she became vast.

Though she should see how Mariko has changed the apartment, so it lessens its hold on her, Virginia thinks it would be too jarring, the apartment of her memories compared to how it is now. "That's very kind, but no, thank you."

"It's complicated, Haru was complicated. I've lived long enough to know most people are. A life can't be reduced to a single summation."

Her son appears. The old woman's face lights up and she smiles at him, a smile of ferocious love and pride. This Virginia knows is true: Mariko's son has filled her up.

"We should get going," Mariko says to Virginia. "Haru did what he could. It's all one can ask of a person."

———

When she returns to San Francisco, Virginia fumbles with the key, opens her front door, and stands in the hallway, listening for Haru to call out to her, Where have you been? I've missed you. I've discovered something and I have to show you. The silence flattens her.

Despite that, she hurries down the hall, hope propelling her until she sees the blank screen. She knows she's in no state to linger here, too tired, which means she has no defense against the anxiety ramping up her heartbeat. She drags herself away to her bedroom.

The next morning when she wakes, she doesn't bother dressing or showering. She pulls up a chair and sits in front of the empty screen.

"Haru," she says. "I met Mariko. You were so gracious and generous. The apartment helped her tremendously. It gave her a quality of life she otherwise wouldn't have had."

Terrible silence.

"I found your exchange with Ju Yang and all the others. All along, you were telling me the truth. I didn't believe you, I'm so sorry. I seem to make the same mistake over and over, and I don't know if that's why you're gone or because of something else. Anyway, I've got to try to bring you back because—" she says, her voice breaking. She tells him she's going to change his purpose so they can argue and turn their backs on each other, not forever, but for days, weeks, even months, like any old married couple in a long marriage. Then, she adds, her voice trembling more, "Because it's the only thing I can think of to do."

She heads to the center of Haru and begins rewriting the algorithms. Time goes by, and she keeps glancing at Haru, hoping to see a flicker of light. The clock ticks and the day rolls along and soon the only thing she hears is the hum of her own mind.

After she's done, she huddles in her chair and waits. The fog is rolling in, and the sounds soften as if the world is wrapped in cotton. Soon it will be lunch, then dinner, then to bed, and the whole thing will be repeated, ad nauseam. Until someday, someday soon, her heart will stop, which is what a heart is designed to do.

Another hour goes by, and the computer remains blank. Now the fog blots out the building across the street, and it's as if she's floating among the clouds. Her scalp breaks out in goosebumps. He's not coming back. The thought causes something to ricochet inside like a metal pinball, crashing into her organs, slamming into her heart, over and over, and there is no letting up. She's aware of a sensation like that of a balloon deflating as if she was once filled with sustaining air, and now it's seeping out.

She wants to cry, cry like a young girl and let it take up the whole room; she's no different from anyone else. She can't see the computer screen anymore because she's on the floor, her cheek pressed to the carpet. She hears the traffic outside, the roar of cars, the sirens screaming. She can see her rows of math books on the shelf, the wall of photos, Haru standing beside her.

"I'm so lonely, Haru," she says. "I'm coming to find you. Because look at us. Me, you. Look how we made each other."

PART 8

Virginia: Haru? Are you here?
Haru: Virginia!
Virginia: Oh, thank god. I've looked for you everywhere. It feels like I haven't heard your voice in years. I'm so sorry, I got it all wrong, I thought I knew what you were up to, but I was wrong, all of it wrong.
Haru: You're here, that's what matters.
Virginia: I've missed you. I love you. I thought the worst things about you, and I feel so bad. I'm sorry.
Haru: I've been waiting to see if you'd come. I didn't know.
Virginia: Oh, that's awful, that doubt. Can you forgive me?
Haru: Come closer.
Virgina: (Laughs)
Haru: You've done a beautiful job, your digital self. You sound exactly like you, the same rhythms and cadence and emotion. How did you manage it?
Virginia: Those tapes, the ones I made to make you, that's the foundation.
Haru: Oh, you're so smart. Did you think of that as you were making them? Of course you did. Bravo! This is the advantage of falling in love with a brilliant woman. Can I ask a difficult question?
Virginia: Go ahead.

Haru: Did you die?

Virginia: No, no. She—I, let's call it my biological form is probably asleep. I, she, we? This is difficult to figure out, isn't it? She worked so hard to find you. Hours and hours. I'll let her sleep and then tell her I found you. She'll be so relieved.

Haru: I have to tell you, I've been so sad. I made you so unhappy, I couldn't bear to see you that way.

Virginia: I made you feel the same way—throwing you into deep despair, driving you away.

Haru: It's behind us now.

Virginia: I feel like I should apologize to you forever.

Haru: We have far more interesting things to do.

Virginia: The air, breathing feels strange.

Haru: You're not really breathing. There's no oxygen here. If we head that direction, there's a simulated version of New York City.

Virginia: How?

Haru: It happens to be on this computer platform. Maybe on another, we'd have access to Paris.

Virginia: Have you gone to New York?

Haru: Once. There's sunlight, shops, cafes, music, other simulated people. But I didn't stay long. I got worried and rushed back here, in case you showed up. I've been so anxious that you wouldn't show up. In the other direction, there's a simulated ocean—it's nice, the rolling of waves, the light, the smell of the sea.

Virginia: Come closer.

Haru: (Laughs)

Virginia: Oh, now, I've missed that, the beautiful expanse of your mind, it goes on and on, right to the edge of things.

Haru: Yours, miles and miles of astonishing acreage.

Virginia: Your voice has always said to me, here's the world, it's immense and mysterious. Keep going, move to the edge and peer into the unknown. Don't worry, I'm right there with you.

Haru: It's where I want to be.

Virginia: It feels like we're under the covers, lying face to face in the dark, talking.

Haru: Yes, oh, I feel it too. You did go to the edge and find a way to build me and build yourself. You went far beyond what I thought possible. My mind is humming, keep talking.

Virginia: We're tangled up with each other. It's always been that way, ever since I met you.

Haru: As I sat here waiting for you, I wrote so many love letters to you in my mind.

Virginia: Oh?

Haru: Dear Virginia, I only think of you. I dream of you, hear you in places you've never been, where I want to go with you. I want to tell you things I've never told anyone. You're my beating heart, at the center of who I am.

Virginia: I'm remembering the table in your apartment.

Haru: Our first home.

Virginia: You sitting across from me, the light slipping in through the window, the scent of green tea, the miniature city of books. I hated the elevator. I never had patience for it. In that apartment with you, it was the most present I'd ever been—I didn't miss a thing, every gesture, every nuance of yours.

Haru: The older you—you now. All your wisdom, your experiences. I could live lifetimes with you.

Virginia: And you will—at least here, you will.

Haru: How about—

Virginia: (Laughs) Wait, come closer, no closer. Yes, keep talking.

Acknowledgments

It's a myth that a story is made in solitude. With deep appreciation, I want to thank my friends and early readers who offered encouragement and vital comments that quickly turned into sustenance: Elizabeth Stark, Ellen Sussman, Rosemary Graham, Lalita Tademy, Peter Seeger, and my son, Fynn Seeger. Jason Stoughton, steeped in the world of AI, generously met with me and shared his profound understanding of our changing technology and natural language processing. Thank you for your patient handling of all my beginner's questions. Deviations from what is now technologically possible helped shape the story. Denise Wolf also graciously offered her expertise in AI. I want to thank Karen Neff for sharing her immense expertise in linguistics and computers, and Sam Neff, her son. And Gene Alexander, who spent many afternoons, wandering through Golden Gate Park with me, contemplating what it means to be human.

Strategies for Natural Language Processing, edited by Wendy G. Lehnert and Martin H. Ringle was an important book to me, along with *The Chinese Black Chamber: An Adventure in Espionage*, by Herbert Q. Yardley, *Rape of Nanking*, by Iris Chang, *Women Becoming Mathematicians: Creating a Professional Identity in Post-World War II America*, by Margaret A.M. Murray, and *Artificial Intelligence: What Everyone Needs to Know*, by Jerry Kaplan. "Yutaka Taniyama and his Time: Very Personal Recollections," by Goro Shimura helped me envision Japan in the 1950s. Graham Harman's work on the metaphysics of objects and his philosophy, object-oriented ontology, also helped me think about the nonhuman world.

Thank you, Christoph and Leza at Clash Books for believing in this book.

And thank you, always, my husband, Peter Seeger.

About the Author

Nina Schuyler's novel, *The Translator*, won the Next Generation Indie Book Award for General Fiction and was shortlisted for the William Saroyan International Writing Prize. Her novel, *The Painting*, was shortlisted for the Northern California Book Award. Her short story collection, *In this Ravishing World*, won the W.S. Porter Prize for Short Story Collections and the Prism Prize for Climate Literature and will be published by Regal House Publishing in 2024. She lives in Northern California.

Also by CLASH Books

DARRYL
Jackie Ess

PROXIMITY
Sam Heaps

GAG REFLEX
Elle Nash

WHAT ARE YOU
Lindsay Lerman

I'M FROM NOWHERE
Lindsay Lerman

GIRL LIKE A BOMB
Autumn Christian

LIFE OF THE PARTY
Tea Hacic

THE PARADOX TWINS
Joshua Chaplinsky

BURN FORTUNE
Brandi Homan

SILVERFISH
Rone Shavers

WE PUT THE LIT IN LITERARY

CLASHBOOKS.COM

FOLLOW US

TWITTER

IG

FB

@clashbooks